Rin, Tongue AND DORNER

RICH SHAPERO

Rin,

Tongue AND

DORNER

A NOVEL

HALF MOON BAY, CALIFORNIA

TooFar Media
500 Stone Pine Road, Box 3169
Half Moon Bay, CA 94019

Library of Congress Cataloging-in-Publication Data is available.

ISBN: 978-0-9718801-8-4

Artwork by Eugene Von Bruenchenhein
(for more information, visit VonBruenchenhein.com)
Artwork copyright © 2009 Rich Shapero
Additional graphics: Sky Shapero
Cover design: Adde Russell

21 20 19 18   1 2 3 4 5

Also by Rich Shapero

Arms from the Sea

The Hope We Seek

Too Far

Wild Animus

1

ON THE WINDS OF SLEEP

It seemed to Dorner, asleep and twisting in his sheets, that gusts had descended, bringing a fierce heat. They chafed and smothered him. He turned on his hip, unhunching, raising his hand, feeling for calm, for coolness. His neck was lathered with sweat, his lips trembling.

He heard voices in the winds. Female voices. Singing.

One, breathy and fervent, bloomed like smoke. Another yowled out of the distance, flaring as it approached. A third pierced him, sharp with pain and denial. Voices of wisdom, heavy with age; voices of youth, buoyant, slurring over hard enunciations. Others brassy, throaty, troubled and warbling; or sine-simple, urgent as a crisis siren or sweet as a flute.

They were braided with yearning. They had a desperate need, and they entered his ears, goading, promising, caressing his chest and drubbing his thighs, circling his belly and the hooked organ rising from his groin.

I

Dorner fought his arousal. He covered himself with his hand, but a low blast batted it away. He turned facedown, and a heartsick moan bulged the mattress beneath him. Trills tugged at the bedding. Whispers skipped on his back and fiddled his sides. Then an amorous wail yawned over his ears, consuming his mind, swallowing it whole.

The voices were irresistible. They could stir the stars and make galaxies whirl. They could melt the earth, turn buildings to smoke and men to steam.

Why him? Why tonight— Dorner didn't care.

He threw off the sheets, ready to open himself. *I want you,* he thought.

Shame gripped him. He recanted, hiding his face, praying the voices away.

They objected as one, volleying through space, drafting around him, shaking his frame and filling his ears with vicious complaints. But as close as they seemed—hot against his skin, reading his thoughts—something protected him. His fear, his memories, a web of scars. It was a veil they rippled and bulged but couldn't pierce.

Dorner woke suddenly, lathered with sweat, searching the darkness. He propped himself on an elbow and touched his thighs and genitals. No trace of semen. Relieved, he used the sheet to mop his chest and rose. The room seemed unusually cool. He groaned. His stomach felt like a clenched fist.

First light was leaking through the drapes. He stumbled through the dimness, dizzy and muddled, to his bureau, patting its top with one hand, finding the injector. He twisted its top. When the eye blinked blue, he removed the cap and worked the trigger till liquid appeared in the barrel. Then he jabbed the needle into his bicep. Heat and odors, echoing voices—

He had never had a dream so vivid. So treacherous, so troubling.

He stepped to the window and parted the drapes. Beyond the glass, day was dawning on the crowded heart of Clemency, the colony where he'd spent most of his life. The sight calmed him. His focus retreated to the glass itself, seeing his reflection—the steep cheeks and high brow, the snarled hair and hawk nose. And the eyes, with their unexpected ferocity, lit by a private fire.

He made his way to the bathroom, reached into the shower stall and turned on the cold tap. A breath to steel himself, and he stepped into the stall. The icy spray struck his chest. His heart shrank, and he began to shiver. A moment later, his erection was gone.

When he was dry, he put on an undershirt, faced the mirror and combed the black hair back from his brow. Then he raised his shaver and ran its crystal head over his cheek, removing the stubble. He drew it close to his ear, shaving hair from around the flesh-colored nipple of his signaler. The shaver's hum calmed him. As it smoothed his cheek, the sound became a soothing whisper, a caring safeguard against whatever trials the new day might present.

Dorner paused to depress the yellow mole on his wrist. His signaler turned on, and as he returned to shaving, Joinspace spiraled open in the outside corner of his right eye. In a translucent circle, alerts were posted.

Dorner focused on the Joinspace rim, pulled it to the center of his visual field and expanded it. His first call was to Maisy.

Joinspace flickered and Maisy spoke. "Busy day. The Homestead burn starts at ten. In chambers, we have seven hearings. Four of them are appeals."

"I'm not seeing you."

"I'm dressing," she said.

"Sorry." Dorner adjusted the Joinspace to glass-clear and switched his shaver off, regarding his face in the mirror.

Maisy appeared, smiling through her freckles, lifting her ginger locks. Trying to decide whether to wear them loose or piled, he guessed. "There's some sort of situation brewing at the Ibarra," she said. "Is something wrong?" She cocked her head.

"I didn't get much sleep." He smiled. "See you downtown."

He relaxed his focus and her image vanished.

Dorner shifted to the snowflake, checking his personal temp. His libido was moderate, within normal limits, but his mood was far from cool. Maisy had sensed his upset. He pulled the Joinspace back to its corner and switched on the shaver.

As it smoothed his chin, he recalled the voices he'd heard in his sleep. Distant, then closer—insistent, imploring. Ancient and childish, threatening, pleading.

They were more than vestiges of an unruly dream. They

4

took him back to longings he'd buried. Longings he feared. Longings that had marked him for life.

Some things take hold of you. Invade you. Own you. You want to be free of them, but you never will be.

Dorner felt his cheeks. He set the shaver down and looked at his reflection. His face was innocent, his blue eyes sensitive. And there was nothing to see on his chest. His undershirt covered it, and he had a towel around his waist. But the scar on his left arm was clearly visible. It was long and scaled like a snake, coiling around his bicep and down his forearm, its bulbed head seeking. Dorner turned his left hand over and gazed at his palm. An oval scar obscured the lifelines. It was swirled and pimpled where the flesh had melted.

Minole, the super's wife, was short and round, and her hair was draggled. She'd responded to his knock in seconds, her face glowing with affection. She wore an apron, and baking scents billowed around her.

"Squid," she said, handing him a sandwich wrapped in white paper.

Dorner slid it into the pocket of his midnight blue morning coat.

"There's something else," Minole said, turning to the shelving beside her. When she turned back, she held a small box, black with gold filigree. "Miss Bez came by last night."

5

"Bez?"

Minole handed the box to him. "She wants to see you."

Dorner put the box in his pocket with the sandwich.

"You didn't reply to the note she left."

"No, I didn't."

Minole put her hand on his arm. "Don't hurt her."

Dorner nodded. "I won't." Her advice touched him. She cared for Bez, but she made allowances for him, without prying.

"There's no one like her," Minole said.

"No one," he agreed.

On the stoop, the old vet Franklin was parked in his wheelchair. He reached for Dorner's hand. "I hear we're burning the Homestead woodland."

"This morning," Dorner said.

Franklin wore the brown sash that had identified Planning officers in decades past. Dorner untwisted the old man's lapel. His wife had died the previous winter, and his eyesight was failing.

"Controlled burns are dangerous." Franklin's tone was confidential. "We burned Homestead when I was your age. She got away from us."

"I'd like to hear about that."

"You're in a hurry," the old man said, respect in his eyes.

Dorner squeezed his shoulder.

Franklin gave him a proud salute.

As he descended the stair, Dorner grasped the rail to steady himself. His chest ached. He felt a hollow in the pit of his trunk. Lust forgone. *Longing*, he thought. His dream had revived it, and the need made him weak.

He drew a breath and raised his head, scanning the dome. The air exchangers were doing their job. No fog, no condensation. The sweep of transparent glass above him was crystal clear, and the skies beyond were cloudless, pink and purple, taking color from the sun rising in the east. To the north, rains descended from conduits in the spars of the dome, watering the orchards and farms below.

Dorner reached the bottom of the stair and scanned the thruway. People seemed in good spirits, hastening to work, talking to each other or conversing with family or co-workers over Joinspace. He straightened himself and stepped forward. As he merged with the foot traffic, the morning howl of the gibbons began. Of the creatures selected to inhabit the Clemency dome, the apes were the colony's most striking success. They were part of the tribe, sharing humanity's triumphs and setbacks. Seated on tree branches and the dome's lower spars, hundreds of them were whooping to greet the dawn.

On either side of the thruway, shops were opening. Dorner skirted a kiosk and a small group beside it. A little boy smiled at him, and he smiled back. Heads turned, eyes followed. His morning coat marked him as a Planning head, and people knew his face. No one could see behind the mask. The thought reassured him.

The role he played— It was an honor to play it. The colony depended on him. And in dawn's gentle light, they both looked their best.

Clemency's structures were sheathed in white polycrete that was soft when applied. The polycrete could be molded, which had allowed a guild of sculptors to fashion a forest of fantasy towers, cornered with minarets and spires, hollowed by alcoves and grottoes, ornamented with arches, cupolas and rosette windows. The molded curves sparkled like snow when the morning sun hit them.

Here, where the tightly packed buildings cut off views of the glaciers, structures had been raised to the limit—forty stories. All that remained was an eighty-foot airflow gap between the rooftops and the curving glass.

As Dorner turned into the arcade that led to the tube train depot, a young woman pointed at him. An older one stood behind her, following him with her eyes while she drank from a cup. She was short, with gray hair and puckered lips. As he watched, she lowered her cup and her gaze shifted. Then it returned, brazen, unflinching.

There was recognition in her eyes, but it wasn't the face on the news she saw. And there wasn't a hint of curiosity or respect.

She saw things that were hidden. Her eyes burned with naked desire.

I'm imagining things, Dorner thought.

The arcade fed into a courtyard. A group of Kiribati refugees were standing by the fountain, singing a hymn from their native home. Despite the passage of years, the emotions were so rich, a few who had stopped to listen were crying. The Kiribati men were wearing their white bandannas, and their thickset bodies and swarthy features set them apart. One hurried toward him.

"Dorner—" The man clapped his back. "Sing with us."

"I know that one," Dorner nodded.

"My cousin," the man gestured toward the fountain. "He has to meet you."

"I'm in a rush. You understand." Dorner waved at the crowd around the fountain. Two dozen arms waved back.

On the far side of the courtyard, the depot came into view, a retro roundhouse with a bell tower and archway. To the left, the southbound tube train was rising from its tunnel, torpedo nose flashing, chrome car capsules hissing behind.

A woman barged into him, turning, lips parted, eyes bluer than his. Dorner reached out, but before he could grab her, she fell to her knees, dropping a bouquet of scarlet freesias.

"My fault," he said, kneeling beside her. "I wasn't looking."

He retrieved the bouquet and extended his hand to help her up. The woman's eyes flooded with fear. She shook her head, as if he'd suggested something obscene. Then her barbed look relented. Her eyes burned with deep feeling, lids narrowing.

You're aroused, Dorner's signaler warned, using his voice.

He rose slowly, helping the woman up.

Caution, his signaler warned. A crimson temp alert blotted his Joinspace.

The woman eyed his hand. It was gripping her arm.

"Alright," she whispered. "Where should we go?" She touched the yellow mole on her wrist to turn her signaler off.

Caution, caution, caution, Dorner's guidance looped.

9

Something's wrong with her, he thought. A mental case—

"Forgive me," he said, releasing his grip.

"No," the woman shook her head, eyes wide now, face pale. "Forgive *me*."

She had come to her senses.

"You're alright?" Dorner asked.

She ignored the question, grasped the bouquet and hurried away.

Dorner turned and strode toward the depot.

A crackup, he thought. Some personal crisis. Everyone has a breaking point. Dorner touched his pant pocket, relieved to feel the injector.

As he joined the passengers filing beneath the polycrete arch, the *caution* loop stopped, and the temp alert winked out. *Arousal clear*, his signaler said.

Dorner sighed. In addition to their other functions, signalers monitored personal temp during waking hours, watching for emotional swings and libidinal spikes. Adherence to signaler guidance was voluntary, and the signaler could be switched off. But the advice was important, and few chose to ignore it. Least of all, Dorner.

What had begun as an effort to keep the dome's atmosphere within narrow temperature limits had evolved into a belief in emotional restraint. By managing temperature and temperament they could control their fate. In addition to asking citizens to shun open fires, an array of other behaviors were discouraged, including violent arguments, feverish athleticism and extravagant sex. Like everyone, Dorner had been taught the strictures as a child, along with the history of the early Planners who had fathered this wisdom.

He'd been a renegade. He'd learned the hard way. But he championed the strictures now and was determined to follow them. Optimal Temp meant harmony. Rising Temp endangered them all. Around the equator, Clemency was known for its culture of caring. Disputes were few. Optimal Temp was their hope, their future. From a Planning perspective, curbing sexual excess put a damper on reproduction. Keeping the population static was critical to their survival.

Inside the depot, Dorner made his way to the boarding platform for downtown commuters. Repair work was underway, and the grills over the track switchers had been taken up. A tube train approached from the west, hissed around a hillock, slid beside the platform and halted.

He crossed a cordoned catwalk and boarded a car. There were bench seats on either side. The weight of the incoming passengers rocked the car on its airbed. When all were seated, the doors closed. Heads turned, eyes met his. A man with white hair raised his cane to him. A woman pointed him out to her child. The impellers hissed, and the train lunged, leaving the platform and the depot behind.

They entered a tube, and the windows dimmed. Dorner closed his eyes.

The *whish* of the train on its airbed reached him. And the shrilling, as it took the bends at high speed. There was a low note too, a resonance. He'd heard the sounds all his life, but he'd never listened so closely.

An enormous *boom* filled the car, and Dorner jackknifed forward. He opened his eyes. The earth was shaking beneath them. He turned and looked out the window. The train was still moving. They had risen from the tube and were approaching the Hub. Above the speeding car, the dome was shivering.

The passengers were wide-eyed, shaking with the transmitted motion, gripping the stanchions or clutching their seats.

We're out of level, Dorner thought, wondering if the others could sense that.

As he stood, the train's brakes screamed.

Using the overhead bins to brace himself, he maneuvered around the lurching car, peering through windows. To the south, he spotted a plume of ice dust fronting the Ibarra Glacier. An aerial ice-cutter was circling the plume. Dorner expanded his Joinspace and called Maisy.

As the train slowed, two men rose. A woman yammered. The car pitched and grunted, and the brakes screamed again. Then it shivered to a halt. Half of the passengers were on their feet now. Maisy wasn't answering.

Dorner faced the riders. "No cause for alarm," he said.

Through the forward windows, the causeway circling the Hub was visible. Crowds were ganging, frightened, clamoring. The Patrol was nowhere in sight.

"A berg hit us," a bearded man guessed.

Dorner shook his head. "There's been a collapse."

"Where?" a mother asked, cradling her infant.

Others nodded. Where was the danger? They wanted to know.

"The Ibarra Glacier," Dorner told them. "Everything's under control."

"We're tipping," a boy said.

"Nonsense," a man in overalls replied.

"I can feel it," the boy said.

"Look at those buildings," a woman pointed through the window, "and the trees."

Heads turned, groans sounded. The bearded man raised his glasses.

"We've had our eye on the Ibarra," Dorner assured them. "Response teams are in motion. We've handled a lot of collapses just like this. You can all remember."

A score of fearful faces stared at him.

"Calm," Dorner said. "Calm is everything."

The man with white hair raised his cane again and smiled at him.

A young woman bowed her head, lips moving in silent meditation. The mother drew her infant beneath her shawl, and as the babe began to suckle, she closed her eyes. The bearded man put a pill on his tongue. Dorner focused on his Joinspace and called the Crisis Center. The circuits were busy.

"Honest, Mister Dorner," the boy said softly. "We're crooked."

"I know," he nodded.

"We're sinking," the bearded man said.

A woman sobbed. She fell to her knees on the car floor.

Dorner closed the distance and knelt beside her. "Stay with us. Hang on." He clasped the woman's hand and turned her

13

face toward his. "We'll get through this together. Please—help me," he enjoined the others.

The bearded man knelt and stroked the woman's forearm. The nursing mother stooped to touch her cheek.

"Quiet your heart," Dorner said, circling the woman's back with his arm. "Calm your fears. We're all here with you."

"Calm," the man in overalls echoed. "Be calm." And the magic word spread. "Calm, be calm. That's right. Don't forget— We're in control. We know what to do."

Faith in Optimal Temp flowed like a balm between them, commending restraint to the frightened woman and to each other.

"Can you hear us?" Dorner said.

The woman gazed at him through her tears, seeing his devotion and the concern in the circle of faces. She sobbed again and embraced him.

Dorner felt Clemency's truth shining through.

"I don't know you by name," he said, scanning the passengers. "But I care about you. Every one of you. I won't let you down."

The last phrase was part of their catechism. They echoed it back, embracing and patting each other. "I won't let you down, won't let you down—"

"Dorner—" Maisy's voice crackled in his ear. "A helihopper's on the way."

14

The ice dust was thick, and the rotors of the descending hopper churned it. Inside, through the convex glass, Dorner could see others parked at the landing site.

A Planning van met him. In the van, he removed his morning coat and put on an arctic parka, leggings and a pair of spiked boots. While he laced the boots, he watched a clip of the collapse in his Joinspace. From the Ibarra's turquoise face, a sheer panel of ice keeled out, unpuzzling into jagged blocks as it fell. Some went into the sea. Others crashed onto the dome's lip at the bottom of the frame. The van halted. Dorner closed the clip and focused on a live feed as he stepped out of the van.

The feed's camera was underwater, panning across drowned cropland and farms. The collapsing ice had cracked the dome's seal, and the ocean had rushed in. The homes were submerged. The hull of a hatchery skiff appeared. Men were throwing lines to those struggling in the water, hauling them in like fish.

Dorner hurried toward the southern portal. Reporters were gathered there, and the cameras were rolling. He shouldered through them, shaking his head. The portal guards recognized him and opened the airlock.

A moment of warmth and quiet, then he clambered from the chamber's exit onto the weatherworn skirt of Clemency's tilting raft.

He clung to the brace rails, planting his feet on the deck. The freezing cold bit his face. Before him, the sheer blue of the Ibarra towered into the sky, its crest bristling with spikes. The great arc of the dome rose on his left. The declension was serious, worse than he'd expected. Waves were lapping two stories over the colony's rim. Giant blocks were piled on the glass, and a flotilla of bergs bobbed beside it. High above, jagged flukes creaked and groaned on the glacier's brow, threatening to come down.

Aerial cutters swooped before the turquoise cliffs, firing artillery to pulverize the loose fins. As the shots landed, hanging blocks burst or calved and flashed, plunging into the sea.

The dome was moored to the ocean's bottom in a lane of water. There were four sublevels below waterline, and in the lowest, massive furnaces generated the colony's heat. Furnace exhaust was vented around the dome's rim to keep the lane open. But Dorner could see: something was wrong. The water in the lane was boiling, and from the boils, plumes of ash and smoke whirled, rising up the Ibarra's front.

Heat, he thought. Loosening, prying, dividing— Heat made the ice crackle and hiss.

"The charges are set," a male voice said.

The blasting crew's captain was standing before him.

"What's going on?" Dorner motioned at the boils.

"I thought you might know," the captain said. He pointed at the blocks piled on the dome, explaining how many charges there were and where they'd been set. It was a terrible responsibility, and Dorner was there to share it. If the charges were too large or they weren't placed properly, a blast could shatter the dome.

The captain raised his hand. "Excuse me." He turned,

answering a call coming through on his signaler. When he turned back, his face was pale.

"A man's still in there," the captain said.

Dorner could imagine the blaster crawling among the giant blocks, hearing them grind as he wired the charges, wondering if he'd escape with his life. Dorner knew what that was like.

A deafening crack filled the air, followed by an unearthly rasping. The captain shouted, and his men dove for cover. Dorner threw himself to the deck and hooked the brace rail with both arms. Above, a jagged mass broke away from the Ibarra's heights, smoking and turning as it fell. The ice struck the dome, crashing onto the earlier collapse, jolting the colony and rocking its raft.

Amid a blizzard of ice dust, Dorner sprang to his feet. The captain was huddled nearby.

"What's his name?" Dorner asked.

"Kenton," the captain replied.

Dorner unclipped the captain's ax belt, fastened it around his waist and headed into the flurry. He slid the ax from its holster, climbing the crusted glass, picking his way among the piled blocks.

"Kenton," he shouted. Below him, through the settling dust, the rim of the dome was sinking deeper in the turbulent waters.

"Kenton. Where are you?"

The blocks groaned and creaked, tipping and grinding as Dorner scrambled between them. "Kenton—"

A croak rose from a nearby pit.

Dorner dropped into it and peered through a crack. "Speak to me."

"I'm caught," the man gasped.

"Can you see the sky?"

"No," the man said. "My boots are on glass."

"Is your signaler live? I'm Dorner. Send me your position."

A moment later, Dorner's signaler bleeped. He expanded his Joinspace and a diagram appeared. Edging around an icy shelf, he stepped onto a slab that was fluted with rime. His spiked boots held, and he crossed it slowly. The diagram led him into a trough. The powder squeaked beneath his feet. At the trough's end, two blocks were balanced together, meshed like gears. He knelt and belly-crawled between them. When he rose, he was in a chamber, shadowed and icy purple.

"Can you hear me?" he shouted. His breath fogged the air.

"You've faded," Kenton sighed.

Dorner shook his head. He checked his bearing, faced a gleaming panel of ice and swung the ax. Chips flew, the panel cracked and fell to pieces. Through the broken window, Kenton was visible. He was on his belly, covered with shards, with a giant cake wedged over him.

"Crawl to me," Dorner said.

"I can't." Kenton struggled to free himself.

The giant cake groaned and shifted.

"It's got your parka," Dorner said. "Open it. Slide out."

The blaster did as he said. With his arms at his sides, he squirmed through the crush like a larva shedding its skin. He was shuddering and drenched, but there was nerve in his eyes. His blue lips smiled, parting around a cracked incisor. Dorner helped him to stand and hurried him into the purple chamber. Shrieks sounded behind them. The wedged cake spidered with cracks.

"Are your charges wired?"

Kenton nodded.

"Let's get out of here," Dorner said.

He took the lead, belly-crawling back between the geared blocks. They padded through the trough and crossed the fluted slab. As they rounded the icy shelf, the pit appeared.

"My ax," Kenton groaned. He'd left it behind. The walls of the pit were too steep to ascend without it.

"We'll find a way," Dorner said.

"There's no time." Kenton's jaw quivered.

"Grab my belt," Dorner ordered.

Kenton shook his head. "Clemency needs you."

"Grab," Dorner raged, hurling himself at the wall of the pit, sinking the ax blade and driving his spiked boots in.

Kenton grabbed and hung, while Dorner chopped and spiked his way up, hauling the blaster with him. As the wall curled back, Kenton dangled. Dorner turned, grappled the man's trunk with both hands and pulled him over.

As they descended to the raft, the charges fired. The large blocks shattered and slumped from the rim into the sea. As the dome righted itself, scrubbers on leash cables scrambled across the glass to remove the crusts and loose debris.

The captain and his team surrounded Kenton. Dorner

dropped the ax, unclipped the belt, pulled off his parka and handed it to the shivering blaster. Then he continued to the airlock and passed through it. He was making his way through the clutch of news people, when a voice tinged with irony caught his ear.

"Our hero," the woman said.

He'd forgotten her name, but he remembered her face.

"You never called," she said, bringing a microphone forward. Behind her, a man aimed a camera over her shoulder. "Mister Dorner, why didn't the cutters trim those hangers before they fell?"

He headed for the van, but the woman and the camera were on his heels.

"Mister Dorner. Why is the water boiling?"

A roar followed her question. One of the aerial cutters hit a cornice of hanging ice. As it crashed into the water, a cheer went up.

~~~~

Downtown, at Clemency's center, was a green round called Hub Park. Large public buildings circled it—the Archives, the Academy, the Museum of Memorable Creatures, Clemency Hospital and others. Each had forty floors, as did the apartment towers nearby, with connecting bridges on multiple levels. Chief among them was Planning headquarters.

The Planning roof was crowded with radio towers. Its polycrete flanks were graceful concaves, and with its weft of bridges, antiquarians likened the building to an hourglass hung with webs. On the ground floor, above the entrance, was the Planning insignia—a three-pointed star.

Dorner crossed the lobby. When he reached the lifts, he swiped his wrist over the green sensor. Copper doors facing west depicted events from the past: the dark cloud that cloaked the earth, the expanding ice packs, the hurried design of equatorial colonies, the construction of the Clemency dome. Dorner preferred riding in the lifts facing east. Their doors portrayed a future to come: the great melting, the return migration, the earth's resettlement. The last door showed a beaming family before a one-story home.

A door slid heavenward and Dorner boarded the lift.

As it rose, the park appeared through the glassed-in shaft, then the Jubilee Icefield and the Felosia Canal beyond the dome. He watched the numbers mount on the light panel, feeling the floors stacking beneath him. At forty, the lift stopped.

Rivelle was in his office, barking orders through his intercom. He loomed over the circular desk, an imposing figure with his silver brushcut and blue morning coat. Behind him, through a large window, the western sweep of the dome was visible: a giant terrarium floating on a wind-stippled waterway, with glaciers and icefields on either side. Rivelle slapped off the intercom.

"We undercut the ice," he said, glaring. "The exhaust regulator for the southern sector gave out." He struck the desk with his fist. "That furnace is a curse."

"Any drownings?"

"None reported. They're still fishing them out. We had to dam the break, so those in the drink don't get washed out to sea."

"A lot of ice fell."

"I was watching from here." Rivelle glanced at the Ibarra. "The second shake knocked me down." He smirked. "Dorner to the rescue."

"What do you expect, with all those reporters." Dorner laughed while he gauged Rivelle's temp. The boss was very fearful. "Can they fix the regulator?"

"That's the plan," Rivelle said. "We closed the ducts a few minutes ago. Cruisers with blast teams are patrolling the southern rim. They'll clear bergs and trim the shelves until we can get the exhaust system working."

"Those blocks came down a hundred yards from the fuel bunkers."

Rivelle sighed. "Tell me something I don't know."

Dorner regarded Planning's chief and the view behind him. From the 40th floor, the colony looked like the work of an unhinged eccentric—intricate and labyrinthine, crowded beneath a bell jar surrounded by ice. The transparent canopy swept from its circular base to an apex five hundred feet above the sea. The high point was Zenith. Dorner could see the Zenith waitstaff setting tables on the outdoor deck. A track spiraled up the underside of the dome, and the little black tram cars were ascending, carrying the lunch crowd.

Clemency was engineered to last a hundred millennia, on the assumption that the ice would have retreated by then.

But many of the inventions hadn't proved out. The dome's glass, for example, was designed with nanopores that opened and closed to regulate temp and humidity. When the pores clogged, Clemency was plagued by fungi and mold, and a network of air exchangers had to be added. And now the furnace system was failing.

"It's time," Dorner said.

"That's a longer discussion."

"The governors are frightened."

"And you aren't?" Rivelle said.

A new furnace system had been designed five years before. In secret, under the tightest security, components had been fabricated. The fabrications met spec, and the subassemblies were complete. But the system was so complex that only parts of it could be tested. The installation team spoke with confidence, but every time the governors considered it, the date was put off.

"We still don't know if the fuel cranes will work," Rivelle said. "Or the igniters. Or the ducting robots."

"I spoke with the crane team last week—"

"Once they start to make changes," Rivelle said, "we'll never get the old system back." He motioned at the icy landscape behind him. "When I think about replacing that furnace, you know what I imagine? I'm opening a deep freeze, escorting my kids in and closing the door."

Of the glaciers surrounding them, some were sheer and posed the risk of collapse. Others were gently sloped, providing a speed ramp for gales. Blizzards were common year-round. Outside their bubble, conditions were arctic.

"I don't think we have a choice," Dorner said.

"Four hundred thousand people," Rivelle whisked his brushcut with his palm. He stiffened abruptly. His signaler wanted him to calm himself. Dorner watched the boss press the yellow mole on his wrist, muting his guidance.

"I didn't create this world," Dorner said. "I just live here."

"We have a responsibility," the boss replied. "To all of them."

"We're out of time. A reporter at the collapse asked me why the water was boiling."

Rivelle stared at him.

"The four hundred thousand are going to find out," Dorner said. "When they do, we'll lose their trust. That's my opinion. They'll be frightened. They'll know they're not safe. And then the furnace will burp, and we'll have a panic. Just like Mammoth."

Mammoth was a seaborne settlement in the region that had once been Borneo. It was heated by a hydrothermal vent. The colony, then the largest on earth, was destroyed when an earthquake shifted the vent beneath it. Not because the damage couldn't be repaired, but because of the ensuing disorder. There were protests at first, then riots as public confidence eroded. Some buildings were heated and some were not, and in the second week of the freeze, violence broke out. There were warring factions, battles in the streets. The authorities were still trying to restore the heat when the public buildings were overrun. Thirty days later, everyone in the colony had perished from the cold.

"This isn't Mammoth," the boss said. "Our people—"

"Our people were terrified an hour ago. Have a look at the videos of the crowds in the Hub. If there's a spark of fear, the press will fan it."

"No one cares less about the strictures," Rivelle conceded.

"If it were up to me," Dorner said, "the message would be simple: 'We saw this coming. The new furnaces are built. They're flawless, and we're going to install them. We'll have a few days of cold. Expect a chill and bundle up.'"

Rivelle lifted his chin, eyes edged with doubt.

"They don't need our fear," Dorner said. "They need us to drive fear out. Inspire confidence. Deny the possibility of failure. They need courage. Hope. Unflinching resolve. 'Clemency is going to survive this.'"

Despite himself, Rivelle laughed. "That's why they love you."

Dorner laughed with him.

"You're an oddity here," the boss said fondly.

"We are what we are."

"I'll talk to the governors." Rivelle regarded him. "I'm going to have a hard time sleeping until this is behind us. You don't have a family, Dorner. It's different for you."

The object in the filigreed box glittered in the sun. It was a pin, with the letters G and D carved out of polycrete. "Guardian of the Dome." It honored four decades of service managing Clemency's blast teams. Dorner closed the lid and handed the box back to Bez. "I can't accept this."

"He would have wanted you to have it."

Dorner had suggested they meet in Hub Park, on a knoll they both knew. A stream bordered its base, watering trees and reeds, making a home for thrush and dragonflies. When he arrived, she was seated on the bench, in an amber blouse and a green skirt, with sprays of trellised bougainvillea arcing over her.

"His kindness changed everything," Dorner said.

"Dad loved you." Bez set the box between them.

Mardy had sponsored his promotion to Planning. The relationship with Bez had been on and off as Dorner's star was rising.

"You're news again," Bez said.

"The press is treating me well?"

"Don't play that game with me." Her eyes were as bright as ever. "You know how important you are. How much trust they put in you."

"It was a job on the train, getting the commuters to calm down."

"When their home tips, they lose their minds." Her gaze narrowed. "The broadcast I heard— They were asking a lot of questions."

He didn't reply.

"Do you know what caused the collapse?"

"Yes, we know."

Her gaze returned to the box on the bench. A moment of

silence, then she opened it, removed the pin and reached for Dorner's shirt collar.

"No, Bez."

"Stop moving. Damn."

Despite his protestations, she attached the pin. When she drew back, there was a spot of blood on her finger.

"Sorry," he said. "It means a lot to me."

A breeze rustled the bougainvillea, and the shadows of blooms flitted like butterflies across her blouse.

He took the box. "I'll never forget him. Or you."

"Oh Dorner—"

"Please. Don't. No more messages, Bez. No gifts. No invitations."

"I only—"

"You're the perfect woman. But not for me."

Silence.

"I miss you," she said.

"You don't know who I am."

"How can you say that? We've been as close as a man and a woman can be."

"I value the memories. Let's not spoil them."

Bez looked down the knoll. Then her gaze drew in and she stood.

Dorner rose with her.

She took a breath, seemed to settle herself and faced him. "I like the pin on you. Goodbye, Dorner." She turned and descended.

He stood there, feeling the weight of his solitude.

The view corridor to the east caught his eye. Beyond the sweep of the dome, the icy cliffs of Patience Palisades were visible. Admiring them was something people did in the park. Or they could follow the gibbons as they crossed the concave glass. He was like the apes, Dorner thought. An unlikely member of the Clemency family. His success, like theirs, was a lucky accident.

The Clemency founders were latter-day Noahs. They selected plants and animals from around the globe with little attention to how they would interrelate, like a wardrobe purchased at a closeout sale. A few gibbons were included, a choice that seemed odd until a bright Planner got the idea that they could clean the dome. He bred them for the task, and they excelled at it, nesting in the orchards at the dome's perimeter and using the transparent struts to climb and cross it. At any moment, you could look up and see dark asterisks shifting over the glass like hydra in a drop of water.

A gibbon knew what his job was, Dorner thought, starting across the park.

He returned to Planning headquarters and rode the lift up to his area on the 29th floor. As the doors opened, the sound of a party reached his ears. There was a birthday celebration in progress for Nidlers, his chief engineer. Colored streamers hung from the ceiling-mount video screens, and his team turned to hail him as he joined them, blowing whistles and waving paper fans.

Nidlers seemed distracted. He stood by the cake, trying to

look merry, eyes shifting, his bald head and spectacles glancing light.

Dorner stepped beside him and clapped his back.

"I'm facing a tribunal on the furnace valves," Nidlers said under his breath. "In ten minutes."

"Who else knows?" Dorner asked.

"No one. Yet." Nidlers smiled and raised a knife to the crowd. He hunched over the cake, angled the blade, plotting his radii. Then his wiry frame twitched and the knife descended. He handed Dorner the first piece.

"Perfect." Dorner held the plate out and turned to share the exacting cut with the rest of the room.

The broadcast news was running clips of the morning emergency. There was footage of the blocks piled on the dome and a sequence showing the blast.

As the pieces of cake were handed around, Maisy swung a ginger braid over her shoulder and slid beside Dorner, her broad face beaming. A model Clemencian, even-tempered and self-possessed.

"The Homestead burn was delayed, but it's underway now. I switched the fire chief's feed to your office." She consulted a docket on her Joinspace. "Justus attended two hearings, so you have five now. They're all floor additions."

At the time of Clemency's creation, property was deeded to resident groups and partnerships. Additions were overseen by Planning. The need for new work and living space was urgent, but there was nowhere to build.

"Every one of them violates code," Maisy said.

"Ask Justus to attend them. I'm spending the afternoon on something else."

She nodded slowly. "Can you tell me?"

Dorner's face appeared on the overhead screens. All heads in the department turned to watch. He was approaching the blasting team, with Kenton shivering beside him. Dorner removed his ice-crusted parka and handed it over.

Nidlers whistled and a round of applause filled the room. Dorner raised his arms, making a show of accepting the acclaim.

"You've got frosting on your nose," Maisy said.

He let her wipe it away, then he turned and stepped into his office. She followed him. He set the cake on his desk and settled behind it. The video screen on the wall opposite showed a reporter interviewing Kenton. The blaster's hair was matted, and he was shaky from his narrow escape. But he kept his poise and showed some humor, smiling through his broken tooth.

"Call Consent," Dorner said. "I want the summary Install Plan for 'Vapos.'"

"Here?" she eyed the video screen.

"No, here," he tapped his right temple. "And let's scratch our café chat after work."

"I invited Noreen," Maisy muttered.

"Please—"

"It was going to be a surprise," she sighed.

Maisy turned, skirted the folding cot and closed the door behind her.

Dorner expanded his Joinspace and set it to glass-clear.

While he waited for the Install Plan, he switched the video channel to the Homestead burn. In the foreground, men in blue heat suits were lined before the moving front of fire. On the ridge above, the flames were scarlet. They ribboned and snapped, turning amber as the wind pulsed.

Beneath the video screen, a statuette stood on his credenza—a golden man, naked and trim, arms raising a golden disk. The Invincible Sun, the colony's highest honor, given six years before to a junior Planner.

Thousands of miles separated Clemency from Kiribati, but when the sudden advance of a glacier cracked the Kiribati dome, Dorner felt it. It wasn't just empathy for the many who were threatened. It was anger that the other colonies turned their backs. In Clemency, everyone went about their business as if nothing had happened, while the killing cold invaded the Kiribati home. The pundits of Optimal Temp preached dispassion. The Equatorial League rejected the alternatives and the Kiribati perished. Dorner was appalled.

He drafted a plan and fought to be heard, speaking on walkways, on trains and in the park, to whoever would listen. He had little support at first. Then a news crew covered him, and people took notice. Because he was a Planner he got an audience at headquarters. The colonies were overcrowded. Resources were strained to the limit. But he fired their sympathies and melted their hearts, pleading on behalf of those the world had chosen to abandon. At the last hour, his desperate speech in the Round Room with the cameras rolling shamed them into it.

There were six helijets on earth, used to move fuel and raw materials between the colonies. For the airlift, he was able to get all six. Kiribati were loaded, eight hundred at a time, and flown to Clemency with a fuel stop midway.

His detractors were right. Resettlement was a nightmare. The refugees created a crisis in the food supply. There weren't jobs, and there wasn't enough space. Aged parents and children without offspring were asked to rejoin their relatives. Emergency construction pushed the limits of Clemency airspace, shelters were erected in marginal places. And residents were provided new guidance on reproduction and libidinal control.

His memories of the airlift were vivid. At the time, the news focused on the rescuers' heroism and the gratitude of those who were saved. But Dorner rode in the transports, and every time the belly bays closed, there were hundreds still on the ice, scrambling for cover. They saved forty thousand, but more than twice that number were left behind.

With all that, the rescue was as the broadcasters portrayed it and as people remembered it—frantic and joyous. A helijet circled the foundering settlement, spotting a place to land. The roar of the blades was drowned by the wind as the transport set down amid the remains of a city square. The earth was heaving. Ridges of ice rose on either side. A Kiribati emerged from the rubble, a woman with blood on her dress. As she raced toward the transport, others followed. Ragged gangs, families and stragglers— Dorner made his way to the transport's belly.

The hatch motors rumbled, and the giant doors opened.

The wind blasted his face and froze his lids. He reached for the woman, caught her arm and helped her aboard. She was cold and grimy. Others poured past him. A man in tears, another limping. A teenage girl and a boy half her size, his crushed arm in a sling. A man was shouting, a woman wailed— He couldn't understand what anyone was saying. He was gripping them, shirts and shoulders, arms and waists, pulling them aboard, overwhelmed by their smells, their shuddering bodies and the rags they wore, crusted with ice and blood. And by the disbelieving faces, wet with tears. The Kiribati were sobbing and the rescuers too, and Dorner sobbed with them, overcome by the proof that there was someone who cared.

The flutes of a pipe organ appeared in Dorner's Joinspace. He focused on the flutes, and the Install Plan for the new furnace system unpacked, a crowd of documents filling his view.

By the time Dorner had set aside Vapos, the other Planners had left. He rode the tube train back to the eastside and walked to his neighborhood haunt, a place that had once been "Lizzie's." It was "Soledad's" now and the menu had changed, but his seat had not. They kept a table at the back for him.

"Welcome," the waitress said.

Dorner looked up from the menu on his Joinspace. "Who are you?"

"Zuna," she replied. "Annette got married. You're Dorner."
Zuna was tall and olive-skinned. She put her finger through a
coil of hair and twirled it.

"I'll bet you know," she said.

"Know?"

"Why the ice fell this morning." Zuna leaned toward him.
"We've been wondering. Me and my friends."

Her cheek put him on guard.

She leaned farther, giving him a view of her cleavage. Her
lips were snaky, and she had smoky eyes.

"You're flirting with me," he said.

She smiled and nodded. Then the smile dissolved and her
eyes grew hard.

Dorner felt his gut hollow. Zuna's pupils bored into him.

"I want you," she whispered.

Dorner's signaler bleeped. *You're aroused,* his guidance
told him.

"I'm being warned," he muttered, looking at the menu.

"There's a special tonight." Zuna put her hand on his.
"For you."

"What is this?" He faced her. "Why are you acting this
way?"

She stiffened, her eyes still brazen. "I'm a bad girl," she
said. "And I can smell a bad boy." Her words came slowly, as if
she was in some kind of a trance.

Dorner shook his head. Zuna's stare was unflinching.

"I'll have the broiled sea duck," he said.

Without a word, Zuna turned and stepped away.

Smell? he thought. He remembered the strange signals he'd gotten earlier that day. The gray-haired lady peering over her cup. The woman with blue eyes and scarlet freesias. Was there something they could smell? Something they sensed?

He *was* a bad boy, and he'd been visited by voices. When he returned to his apartment, would the voices be waiting? Would they invade his sleep again, pricking his longing? The old cravings were stirring to life, like the heat that had undercut the Ibarra. They threatened him, just as the exhaust threatened the dome.

Dorner peered around the room, checking faces, profiles and the backs of heads. A young man's misdeeds haunted him. A naive young man who imagined he could flout the strictures without any consequence. A young man with a secret.

When he'd finished his meal, Zuna returned. She seemed a different person. The brazen stare had vanished. Her manner was casual, the overtures forgotten.

"Do me a favor," Dorner said. "Go to the door and stick your head out. See if there's a woman waiting outside. An older woman with curly hair. On the walkway, under a lamp, beside the building."

Zuna raised her brows.

"An old acquaintance," he said. "You understand."

Zuna did as he asked. She returned, shaking her head.

Despite her assurance, his exit was cautious. He opened the door slowly, scouted the walkway and started forward with slow steps.

The algal lamps were on, gracing streets and footbridges with their blue-green glow. He wondered again if the voices would reach him once he'd crossed over the threshold of sleep. Could he resist them? His memories of the wretchedness into which his libido had led him were vivid. But the stifled impulses were crying for release. He touched the pin Bez had attached to his collar, praying for the strength to deny himself.

The thruway that fronted his apartment block was empty, and so was the lobby. He rode up in the lift, paused before the entrance to his two-room single, and inserted the passkey. Then he crossed the threshold and closed the door on the rest of the world.

2

LET ME THROUGH

The next morning, after a lengthy deliberation, the governors voted to proceed with the new furnace system. Using the Install Plan milestones, dates were set. A public announcement was scheduled, and Dorner was chosen to make it. He freed Nidlers to work with the implementation team and asked the rest of his staff to cover, so he could give the speech his full attention. He had four days.

He was seated at his desk now, staring at a blank page on his Joinspace.

Confidence. If the colony was going to get through this, that's what mattered. People needed confidence and resolve. He began to dictate, moving his lips silently, watching words appear on the page. He had another thought, jumped to it, then paused and filled in the gap, humming to himself.

A phrase of song had lodged in his mind.

A long build-up would be a mistake, Dorner thought. People would be worried about the cold. He had to answer their fear, quickly. "What will happen to us when the old furnace shuts down?"

The song was still playing in his head. He had heard it in his sleep the night before. A ghostly voice. It echoed as he listened. Then the echoes grew louder. Other voices swelled around the first like a practiced choir. The strange dream had returned, and its rapturous voices had provoked him for hours. They had printed themselves in his mind and were replaying their summons. Or his need was so acute, he was replaying them himself.

As he stood naked by the bed, he'd flirted with the idea of leaving himself unprotected. He'd stifled the impulse, faced the blinking blue eye, squeezed the injector trigger and jabbed his thigh.

Dorner leaned back in his chair, imagining what might have happened if he hadn't injected himself. The limbo of sleep, dark and secret— Drowning in the sea of voices. Not waking, not fighting. Letting them storm him without resisting.

An hour later, he was still leaning back, lids barely slitted, the Joinspace just a ringlet at the corner of his eye. He imagined the voices were insistent. Shrill and bass, nubile and earnest, familiar and sage— The longing he felt, they wanted to know. He opened himself. He spoke from his heart. And they understood.

He urged them to come again that evening. If they did, he promised, they would find no obstacles in their way.

When Dorner left the building at the end of the day, he was angry. Baffled by his fugue. Upset that he'd wasted so much time. He'd written next to nothing. He skipped his dinner at Soledad's, returned to his apartment and placed his injector on the bedstand, vowing to resist the allure of the voices. Then he stayed up half the night working on his speech. He opened with the defects of the old system, highlighted the strengths of the new one, and addressed the dangers of the cutover. Satisfied he'd made a decent start, he rolled into bed. In his exhaustion, he forgot to inject himself.

Within minutes of falling asleep, the choir reached him. It was braided, but as it drew closer, the voices unwound, fervent and trilling, deep and resounding, whistling and mewling enticements.

His vow forgotten, the sleeping man welcomed them, shuttering his past, forgetting the dome and everyone in it. Where had they come from? Were they spirits of his own creation? Was his smothered desire rising up to consume him? Or were they a gift from some other realm. He couldn't see them. But he could hear them clearly, and he could feel their desire as if it were his own. Frenzied, feverish, timeworn, testy and reckless—

Could he give himself over without anyone knowing?

"I'm yours," they sang, "only for you."

Dorner jerked upright. He was aroused and quivering, about to climax. He grasped his erection, then tore his hand away. Where was his injector?

He rose, dizzy and trembling, stumbling through the darkness while the hot winds circled and the voices raved. *I'm awake,* he thought. What kind of dream was this? He bumped into his dresser, found the injector and stuck the needle in his arm, rocking as the cold wave washed through him. Then he found the second drawer, pulled it open and felt beneath the clothing. There was a photo he'd kept as a reminder. He couldn't see it, but the feel of it and the memory of the scarred creature it depicted was enough to wither what remained of his lust.

The singing grew dimmer. And dimmer. The drug, like a pliable membrane, isolated him from the urgent voices. When the membrane was thick around him, he lay back down.

Dorner woke the next morning leaden with shame. He refused himself breakfast. He kept the curtains closed while he dressed, denying himself light. He buttoned his shirt, retrieved the Guardian pin, attached it to his collar and assessed himself in the mirror. Then he removed the pin and put it back in the box.

At headquarters, he shut himself in his office and dove into the draft. Three hours later, it was complete. He reached Rivelle, and after a hurried lunch they reviewed it.

"Your original idea was better," the boss said. "'Expect a chill and bundle up.'" He stepped from behind his desk, scanning Dorner's text in his Joinspace. "There's too much here about risk."

"We need to brace them," Dorner said.

"This bit about potential ignition problems—" Rivelle tapped the air before him with an accusing finger. "Let's not get into that."

"It's the most likely reason for failure."

Rivelle regarded him. "A peculiar sentiment, coming from you."

Back in his office, Dorner reread the words he'd written. Rivelle was right. They were riddled with doubt. The voices had shaken his confidence.

He deleted everything and attacked the speech with fresh determination, toughening his tone. His outlook was bold and hopeful, and the words came quickly. With a strong delivery, the message was one they would all believe.

On the evening train, he lectured himself. Whatever was happening to him at night— He couldn't think about that. He needed his rest. He had to be sharp. Again he missed dinner.

Back in his apartment, his preparation for sleep was thought out and precise. He injected himself twice and jogged in place to get the drug into his system. He looped a collection of Kiribati hymns through his signaler, so they'd play while he slept. Then he stood naked before the full-length mirror.

Remember, he thought. The lamp on the bedstand lit his front. An attractive chest, muscular, with well-defined pectorals and a tapered waist. But you had to look past the scars. And he wasn't looking past them. The webbed mass that erased his nipple and fringed his stomach. The waffle on his hip, sectored like alligator skin.

What twisted sweetheart would smile on this? he thought.

That quashed his desire and shriveled him up.

You're a monster, he thought. Dorner switched off the lamp and lay down.

41

But his precautions did nothing to ward off the voices. As soon as sleep found him, the seduction began. The winds approached, unbraiding, weaving around him, circling the membranous envelope. They clamored and shook it, offering, pleading. "Open your ear," they sang. "Open your heart."

The choir mounted as new voices arrived, thronging, lapping against his shelter. The Kiribati hymns faded beneath them. "Open," they moaned. "Open, open—" As they multiplied, they seemed to blur into each other. For the first time, Dorner could hear a common cadence, a rhythm the voices shared. As if they were the expression of varying moods, time-shifted but sprung from the same throat.

"Don't resist me," they sang. "Don't turn away."

They knew him, knew him well. In some lost past, in some previous life, had he heard them before? Louder and louder, and more united.

"Open your nerves," the choir demanded.

The membrane held, but the winds were punching and battering it.

Dorner curled, trying to hide himself.

"Open your nerves and let me through."

Dorner quaked and gasped and covered his groin.

With a roar, the harem cohered, driving against the flexing shield. The membrane split, a sere blast tore his shelter open—

"Tongue," a voice stormed, "do you hear?"

Winds, voices— One complex nature. A woman of vast proportion, frenzied, frantic for recognition.

"Tongue," she stormed, "Tongue, Tongue—"

An awful heat rushed upon him. The rasp of the wind had claws and teeth, and from the blasts thrusting and thrashing around him, rage emerged. He felt her fury, his body huddled now, taking the punishment on his back and sides. The promise of unfulfilled pleasure turned to pain. She swarmed over him, clawing his ribs, burning his face, plucking his nerves until he thought they would snap. Her voice shrieked and chanted around him, like a demon stirring a sinister sabbath, some leftover madness from the dark ages of man.

Dorner woke feverish, knotted in his bedding, stunned and gasping. He staggered into the kitchen. Through the window, beyond the dome's glass, stars were winking. The sky was starting to pale.

His back felt raw. His thighs were stinging and his shoulders ached. His side was striped red where the claws had dragged. Who was Tongue? Where had she come from? What was happening to him?

He sat naked at the kitchen table, dictating an account to his Joinspace, recording what he had heard and felt.

Dorner stood before the super's door in his midnight blue morning coat, with his jet hair combed straight back.

Minole answered his knock and handed him a sandwich wrapped in white paper. "Squid again," she said with a regretful smile. He traded salutes with the old vet, Franklin, and headed for the tube train depot.

On the thruway, eyes followed, but Dorner ignored them. His mind was on Tongue. His hands slid into his pockets. *There are worse things than squid*, he thought.

He rode the train to the downtown depot, but when he debarked, instead of heading for Planning, he followed the walkway that verged Hub Park. He passed an open-air bakery where cakes were cooking. An aproned woman beat dough in a tub. "Tongue," Dorner heard when her spoon struck the tub. "Tongue, Tongue." Ten feet ahead, a boy pushed a barrow, and at each seam in the paving, the barrow said "Tongue." A man lowered an awning over his food stall, and every turn of the crank was "Tongue, Tongue."

The Academy appeared on his left. Then the Archives, where information about the colony's tech was stored. Records of mankind's achievements were housed there, along with genetic samples of vanished lifeforms. Perhaps Tongue was like them, a lost creature from another dimension, looking for lodging in a disordered mind.

Beyond the Archives, the giant white drums of Clemency Hospital rose. Polycrete angels looked down from the roof, cowled seraphs with spreading wings. The angels gave Dorner no comfort. The sight of the hospital filled him with dread.

In the rush to establish the equatorial settlements, much of science had been left behind. Travel in space was forgotten, along with the know-how to split the atom. In medicine, however, little was lost, and in some domains, knowledge had advanced. The striking progress in neuroscience was spurred by necessity. The people of Clemency were a case study in stress. Mental breakdowns were common.

Dorner had managed to keep clear of doctors who tinkered with minds. But he'd lived with the fear that, some day, he might have to face them.

He left the walkway and mounted the steps. The hospital lobby was like a submarine grotto, rippling with disinfecting blue light. Behind the reception desk, a holographic whale appeared, jaws wide, humming and sweeping the space with its combs.

Dorner passed through the sweep and boarded a lift. His signaler bleeped, confirming his arrival, and the lift started up. He watched the floor count, feeling the stories stacking. The lift stopped at the 19th floor, his Joinspace flashed "Neuro" and directed him down the hall.

The floor was spongy, sighing beneath him, removing microbes from his shoes. Small robot sleds skimmed the walls, casting blue light down the corridors. Dorner halted before an unmarked door, opened it and stepped through.

A nurse was seated at the receiving station. As he approached she raised her head, but before she could speak, sobs sounded from the archway behind her. A woman stood bent, with her face in her hands, and a little girl was crying, shaking with fear. The child held a stuffed animal to her cheek, a dolphin with blue button eyes.

A doctor in a white coat was on her knees, facing the child. The doctor was short, with black hair to her collar. Like most

45

in the colony, her racial mix was obscure, but there was an Asian flatness to her cheeks and brow.

"Is Dolphy hungry?" The doctor touched the child's nose.

The little girl nodded and wiped her cheeks.

The doctor rose and faced the woman. "Your husband's going to be fine." She nodded at the nurse. "Take them to the cafeteria."

The nurse stood and escorted the pair past him. The doctor turned, her eyes brightening.

"Mister Dorner," she said. "I'm Doctor Rin. You're right on time."

Her smile was efficient, her eyes dark and impenetrable.

Dorner shook her hand. *No frills*, he thought. Beneath her white lab coat was a gray shirt and black pants. She was without makeup or jewelry.

"My office is down the hall," Rin said. And then, as if the thought had just occurred to her, "May I show you my lab?"

She was proud of her procedure, he thought. Or she was looking for funding. "I'd like that," he said.

He followed her through the archway into an open area with cabinets, gurneys and carts of equipment. On both sides were doors, most of them closed. One was ajar, and through the gap Dorner saw a small windowless room.

She was leading him toward the rear. Her lab coat swiveled, lacking curves to cling to. "You've seen our device?" she asked over her shoulder.

"On the news," he said.

"We've made some important changes."

46

They entered a well-lit workroom, the shelving crammed with bins and parts. On the counter were bundles of surgical instruments—clamps and scalpels, and a gadget with a black nozzle and a trigger grip. On a red pedestal, inside a glass box, was the object Dorner had seen in the broadcasts.

A shiver scaled his neck. It looked like a silver spider, six inches wide. Its legs were flexed, and antennae protruded from its bulbous head.

Rin lifted the glass, grabbed the spider and set it on her palm. "The future of straddling," she said, fingering its back. "More precise. Much more sensitive."

"It's as intimidating as the original," Dorner said.

"Would you like to hold him?" Rin's eyes laughed.

Dorner held out his hand.

He expected the feet to prick him, but their bottoms were soft.

"We've strengthened the grippers," Rin flexed one of the spider's legs.

She took a loop of cable from a peg, plugged one end into the spider's rear and the other into the console beside her, and depressed a switch. Orange lights flickered across the console's face. "The critical logic is here," she said, "but contact with the patient's nervous system will make or break a session."

She faced him, grasped the spider and turned it on its back. She rotated a dial on the console and a hum sounded. A silver needle emerged from the spider's belly.

"Feel the tip," Rin said.

Dorner pinched it with his thumb and forefinger.

47

"Hundreds of threads, each tapered so finely, it's microscopic at the end."

"How dangerous is the procedure?" he asked.

Rin retracted the needle, switched the console off and put the spider back on its pedestal. "For the patient, not at all." She gave him a curious look.

She's guessing why I've come, he thought.

"For the therapist," she said, "there's potential risk, depending on the patient's condition. If he or she is hallucinating or psychotic, it's possible for the therapist to lose track of reality."

"That could be unpleasant," Dorner said.

Rin nodded slowly. She was waiting for him to declare himself.

"Being inside someone else's head," he added.

"We use filters," Rin said, "to reduce the danger. They give the therapist enough distance to make observation safe."

"Filters?"

"Elements of unreality. Physical locations are reduced to two dimensions. People's faces are blurred. Jitter is added to their movements. Voices are frequency-adjusted to make them less present. In the latest version, we've added a white halo to anything moving in the patient's frame. Would you like to see?"

"Is that possible?"

Rin motioned him to follow.

They exited the workroom, passed a half-dozen chambers and stopped before a closed door.

"She's asleep," Rin said softly. "No talking, not even a whisper. She's not a patient. She's a student volunteer. Once you're seated, I'll connect you." Rin pointed at his signaler nipple. "Open your Joinspace all the way and go black." She smiled. "You're new at this, so I'm going to turn up the filters."

Rin opened the door and Dorner followed.

The chamber was small, just large enough for a padded table and a chair, and it was lit by a single red bulb. A young woman lay on the table in a tunic and pants. She was on her side, with straps around her. A silver spider was perched on her neck, its needle deep in her signaler. A man in a lab coat sat in the chair, staring. A cable descended from his signaler nipple. Its far end was connected to the straddle console on a stand beside him.

Rin touched the man's shoulder. He pulled the cable's end from his neck, rose and passed the cable to her. She motioned and Dorner sat in the chair.

He felt her fingers below his ear. A pressure on his neck, and then the pin of the cable connector entered his signaler nipple. Dorner shuddered, took a breath, expanded his Joinspace and blacked his vision.

He heard a shriek and laughter. Colored images shifted before him, but they were hard to make out. He saw a half-dozen naked boys, their backs to him, seated in a row with their hands on their knees. Before them was the cut-out of a tree. Something was swinging in the tree. *A gibbon*, he thought. The ape chittered, then it talked, face blurred, its black body outlined in white. It scolded the boys in a pedagogue's voice, then it held up a tube train schedule and began to read stops and times aloud.

Something touched his shoulder. A crackle in his ears, a pinching in his neck, and the sights vanished. Disoriented, Dorner shrank his Joinspace and rose, back in the chamber. Rin nodded and they tiptoed out.

"Could she tell I was watching?" he wondered.

"That depends on the intensity of her thoughts," Rin replied. "She might have noticed, or she might not."

She led him through the open area. An orderly was escorting a young woman to a straddle chamber. Both her wrists were bandaged.

"This must be hard for you," Dorner said.

"A doctor faces affliction. You can't turn away from it."

They passed the receiving station, exited the lab and started down the hall.

"We aren't often visited by senior Planners," Rin said.

"No, I suppose not. I'm curious— How can you tell when a patient is having mental problems?"

"Patterns reveal themselves," she said. "Waking thoughts are like badly told stories. They're confusing. Dreams, especially so. The mind uses metaphors that require interpretation. What we learn through straddling is piecemeal and progressive. We can perceive what the patient perceives. We can feel what the patient is feeling. We can't see the psyche all at once, but over time, we can build a picture of what's going on in a patient's mind."

"Is there anything hidden? Can you hear and see everything the person experiences?"

"Almost," Rin said. "Every mind has a few things that are closely held."

A blonde physician approached, holding a rack of test tubes. She beamed and nodded to Rin, her eyes darting at Dorner.

"This started with overgrown signaler shoots," he said, half amazed.

"Yes, it did. I was trying to get a girl through Joinage."

Nerve shoots were germinated in vitro and transplanted into every newborn's head. The shoot sprouted during infancy, and the ganglia became part of the youth's brain. At Joinage, a rite of passage for seven-year-olds, a signaler nipple was surgically connected to the shoot, and the Joinspace was loaded through it.

"My dream—" Rin spoke quietly.

Dorner met her gaze.

"—is to link two spiders. To make the experience bi-directional."

"So disturbed people can share their troubles?"

Rin smiled. "If I could be in your heart and head, and you could be in mine, it would give us a new kind of intimacy."

She held up her hand. "Sorry." A call was coming through on her signaler.

"Mom," Rin shook her head. "I'm in the middle of something. I know it's drafty. We'll file a complaint. I promise. Run a hot bath and warm Tad up."

As the call ended, Rin halted before a door, opened it and ushered him into her office. She motioned him toward a chair and sat behind her desk.

"Well," she said. "Are you going to tell me why you're here?"

He took a breath. There was a photo on the wall beside her. An elderly woman was flanked by Rin and another about her age. There was a gibbon in Rin's arms.

"Someone," he said, "is invading my mind."

"You mean—"

"A voice. I hear her when I'm sleeping. It was pleasurable at first. But now— She's attacking me. I don't know what she wants."

"And you've come to me because—"

Rin's brows were thin as pencil strokes, her lips full and straight. In the harsh light of the lab, her face had looked planar. But in the glow from her desk lamp, it had a graceful dimensionality. It was a sensitive face, and her expression was caring.

"There's this brilliant doctor," he said. "She has a way of listening in. If she hears this voice, she'll know what it is. And she'll know how to treat it."

"When you say she's attacking you—"

"Last night, she lashed me," Dorner said. "I can show you—" He touched his loin, then sighed. "Maybe they were self-inflicted. But— I could feel her claws and teeth. Her voice was so loud— I lost myself. There was nothing, nothing but Tongue."

"Tongue?"

"That's her name."

Rin blinked.

"She's not real," he said, feeling like a fool. "She can't be. I know that."

"Is she with you when you're awake? Are you hearing her now?"

Dorner shook his head. "Only when I'm asleep. But— I can't get the sounds out of my head. They keep replaying."

"When you're sleeping, is the voice always there?"

"No," he said. "She comes and goes."

"I can imagine how distressing that would be."

Dorner bowed his head. Now someone else knew.

"Does Tongue remind you of anyone?"

"No."

"Is she cautioning you? Urging you to take any action?"

Dorner laughed. "She keeps trying to make me spill my semen."

"She's seductive."

"She can be," he said.

"Has she caused you to ejaculate?"

Dorner shifted in his chair. "No. I've resisted her."

"How often do you have intercourse?"

"I don't."

"Are you masturbating?"

He looked away. "No."

"Any spontaneous emissions?"

"No. I took a vow two years ago," he said.

"A vow?"

"Of abstinence."

"As a Planner," Rin guessed, "you want to be a model of responsible behavior."

Dorner didn't reply.

"Are you using an anti-libidinal?" she asked.

He drew the injector from his pocket.

Rin nodded when she saw it. "That's as good as castration, for as long as it lasts."

She folded her hands together. "You're a discerning man, and self-possessed. So I'm going to speak frankly. Tongue may be a product of sexual frustration. I'm inclined to regard her as a recurrent dream fueled by wish fulfillment."

"I can't see her. She's a voice in the darkness."

"A dream woman can take many forms. All she needs is trauma to feed her."

"It doesn't feel like a dream—"

"The strictures of Optimal Temp are trying," Rin said. "For many of us."

"If you straddle me—"

Rin shook her head. "We work with difficult cases, where diagnosis is a problem. There are a lot of talented people who treat repression effects." She slid a notepad toward her and drew a pen from her pocket.

"If you knew how hard it was to come here—"

"I can appreciate that," she said, scribbling on the pad.

"No you can't."

She raised her hand to calm him. "You're going to be okay. He's wonderful." She removed the note from her pad.

54

Dorner stared at her.

She waved the note under his nose.

"Something bad is going to happen," he said. "She's going to break me. I'm going to violate my abstinence."

"Under the circumstances," Rin said, "that might be a good thing."

Dorner stood. He gazed at the note, took it from her and put it in his pocket, trying to keep his poise. "Thanks for your time."

He stepped into the hall, closing the door behind him. When he turned, he was struck in the chest by a man in a straitjacket who was struggling to free himself from the two officers accompanying him. The four fell to the floor. The struggling man kneed and kicked, crying in outrage.

Dorner got up.

The officers pulled the man to his feet. His eyes rolled at Dorner and he gnashed his teeth.

Dorner strode down the hall, swatting the dust from his coat. When he reached the lift, he fished in his pocket, retrieved the referral Rin had given him and dropped it in the refuse can.

/^7

"You're wearing Mardy's Guardian pin," Rivelle said.

The noise from the crowded Round Room made it hard to be heard.

"Bez wanted me to have it," Dorner replied.

"It's a lot to live up to."

They were standing in the wings, behind the curtains, waiting for the preliminaries to end. They'd spent the past two days tuning the speech, arguing over message and wording. Between Dorner's fears about the announcement's impact and his dread of Tongue, he'd gone without sleep, and when he entered the Round Room, he was dizzy on his feet.

With all that, as the moment approached, Dorner felt relieved. The speech was clean. Rivelle was optimistic. The governors had read it and blessed it.

"That's my cue," the boss said, straightening his coat. He left Dorner's side, headed for the thicket of mics at stage center.

The walls of the Round Room were hung with midnight blue drapes, and the front seats had been cleared to make room for the press. Reporters and photographers were standing, seated or kneeling, and the live cameras were rolling. While Rivelle introduced him, Dorner expanded his Joinspace and went glass-clear, reviewing the text he would read. At the rear of the Room, the boss's head filled a giant monitor.

Rivelle finished and looked his way. Dorner buttoned his coat, combed his hair back with both hands and stepped onto the stage.

He drew close to the mics and acknowledged Rivelle. The size of his voice startled him. He drew back a few inches, greeted the colony and thanked the press.

"The furnace system that provides our heat and protects us from the withering cold," he told them, "hasn't lived up to its designers' expectations. Because of its failings, we have endured the damp, morning fogs, damage to our crops, breathing disorders and collapses of ice like the one the Ibarra so recently let loose. I am proud to tell you, and happy as well, that we saw the problems and faced them. Five years ago, we began designing a new furnace system. And while I regret having to announce that the old system is unseasonably infirm and approaching the end of its life, I'm pleased to announce that the new furnaces have already been cast and tested and are ready to install."

The surprise and regard in the Round Room was palpable. On the monitor at the rear of the Room, Dorner's smile was ten feet wide.

"These furnaces are marvels of engineering. Their heating capacity far exceeds the aging units, and their service life should be measured in thousands of years."

Dorner felt a breeze at his back. A warm wind raised the hair on his neck.

"Unlike the old system, each of the new furnaces will be linked to its partners with a Nidlers Valve, giving us a failsafe array. New igniters, new output regulators. And the new components will integrate seamlessly with our fuel conveyers and robotic ducts."

A whisper from his night visitor hissed in his head. Dorner ignored it, fixing on the text before him.

"The new system is being staged as I speak. The cutover will be brief. We'll have a few days of cold—"

A blast from nowhere wuffed around him. Groans and sighs grew thick in his ears. "Let them freeze," Tongue sang, "let them drown. Do you think I care?"

Dorner raised his hand, breath caught in his throat. Spotlights glared above the throng of faces. A female reporter stepped toward the stage, eyes fixed on him, brazen with desire. *I'm imagining this,* Dorner thought. But the storm was mounting. Tongue's voices shrilled and moaned, louder and louder. Not echoes, not vestiges— Somehow she had crossed the boundary of sleep.

"Expect a chill, as I said. Our plan for the cutover—" He touched his temple to quiet the chorus.

"Plan, plan," Tongue squalled. "Did you plan for this? I'm strangling. I'm starving. Do you hear me, Dorner?"

"We will install the new furnaces—"

The winds were fierce. He was shouting to make himself heard. "A week, it may take a week—"

Rivelle was in the wings, his expression severe. He was motioning, mouthing.

Dorner lurched. The blast struck his back and hooked his chest. Groans, screaming. Cries swooped at his face, clawing and pecking. The mad woman was unleashing another howling walpurgisnacht.

"Choke them, skewer them. Eunuchs and spinsters, the shriveled and maimed—"

"There may be a week," Dorner said. "A week without heat."

The press corps looked shocked. Guards hurried toward

the stage. The hair on every head was flying, every coat flapped while the storm blew through the Round Room, chanting obscenities.

"Prick your nipples, milk your glans— Tear your sphincters and chop off your fingers!"

Through the tumult, Dorner saw himself on the screen at the back of the Room. No wind, no storm. The drapes behind him were perfectly still. His shoulders shifted, his lips were twitching. His head bobbed on his neck like a marionette.

"The furnace system that provides our heat," he started over, "and protects us from the withering cold—"

The words made no sense. Tongue's heedless emotions were churning inside him. *Why am I here?* he thought.

"Helpless," he bellowed. "We're helpless—"

A hundred heads faced him, lights beamed and cameras zoomed in, but no one could hear a thing he was saying.

"Nothing will save us. We are outside the Viable Band," he raved. "Everyone, all of you: this is the end.

"This time of—" He raised his fists and shook them. "Affliction! Rabid fantasy. Uncontrolled Temp. Boiling, frantic—"

Tongue's madness consumed him. "Your home, your dome— A mountain of bodies, convulsing, seething— Scrabbling, clawing, seeking the zenith, blind to those smothered and broken beneath."

The house lights went out. Rivelle was beside him, waving his arms. Dorner felt a crush of bodies around him. Hands laid hold and he was dragged from the stage.

59

Rivelle put his hand on Dorner's knee. "I've always comforted myself that if anything happened, you could take my place." His words were reassuring, but his tone was resigned. "I've asked Bayliss to make a fresh announcement. He's going to manage the furnace cutover. Your team will report to him for now."

They were in the private lounge on the 36th floor. Through the window, Dorner could see the morning sun over the boss's shoulder. He was trying to concentrate on what Rivelle was saying, but the words seemed to reach him from a distance. The winds were gone. Tongue's raving no longer tyrannized his mind. But her presence had numbed his senses.

It had been a terrible night. Tongue had remained with him till the early hours. When she finally left off, he was in a ward room. A place he'd never seen before. The lighting was low, and the nurses wore flowing gowns. Maisy was seated beside him. When he was able to talk, she listened and responded, helping him to reconnect. When he felt strong enough, she escorted him to a helihopper and accompanied him back to his apartment so he could shower and dress.

"The message from Planning," Rivelle said, "is that you're having some personal problems. I'm sorry, but— There was no other way."

Dorner nodded. He remembered the cameras and his contorted face on the giant screen. "The broadcast—"

Rivelle looked down. "It's hard to watch. We tried to

persuade them to hold it back." He shook his head. "You know how they are. It ran all last night, and they're hard at it again this morning."

Dorner straightened himself. "How bad is it?"

Rivelle searched his face, as if unsure how much he should share. "By nine, every signaler in Clemency was on high alert. We sent a nitrous sedative through the air exchangers at ten. And we spiked the oxygen just before dawn."

"Bayliss will get them back on track."

Rivelle didn't reply.

He'd betrayed them all. His boss and the governors. His team, the Planners who respected and trusted him. And the sea of believing faces for whom he was a cipher of confidence.

"I'm through," Dorner said. "I quit. Tell them the truth."

"What truth?"

"'Dorner was weak.'"

Rivelle threw up his hands. "Don't be ridiculous. You've got a meeting with Bayliss in twenty minutes to discuss his speech. You're going to do everything in your power to make him successful. After that, there's a manpower review for the cutover tasks."

The boss rose. He extended his hand, but Dorner stood without his help.

"What we do—" Rivelle's tenor was private. "It's an impossible job."

A gnawing look surfaced in the boss's eyes.

"I'm sure I bear some of the blame," Rivelle said. "Lean on Maisy. She can help with your personal affairs. We'll scout around, find someone you trust. This needs attention, and you deserve the best."

Another new day, and the old vet was parked on the stoop. Dorner didn't want to see or talk to him.

He was stepping past, when Franklin grabbed his arm.

"I had a few moments like that," Franklin said. "They thought I'd flamed out."

Dorner laughed and patted the old man's shoulder.

"They were wrong," Franklin said, "weren't they."

On his way to the depot, and in the train car, Dorner mustered his arguments.

At the lab on the 19th floor, the nurse said Doctor Rin was in her office. Dorner rehearsed his appeal one last time as he strode down the hall. Rin answered his knock.

"Yes?"

She had her back to him. She looked over her shoulder as he opened the door.

"I'm not crazy," Dorner said. "Tongue isn't—"

She held her hand up to stop him.

"No," he insisted. "You're going to listen—"

"I saw the broadcast," Rin said, stepping around her desk. She glanced through the doorway. "Let's see what we can find out."

Dorner stood in a straddle chamber, wearing the tunic and loose pants he'd been given. He was barefoot and the tile floor was cold. He seated himself on the padded table, looking at the bare walls, the chair and the stand beside it.

A nurse entered and closed the door. She wore rubber sandals.

"Mm," she admired his togs. "Very handsome. I'm Firooka."

"I'm Dorner," he said.

Firooka was big-chested with mock black lashes and too much lipstick.

"You don't look very cheerful," she said.

He eyed the vent in the crotch of his pants. "There aren't any buttons on this thing."

"So?"

"I may get excited."

Firooka smiled. "We see that all the time. Now. In addition to straddling you, we're going to have a look at your sleep waves."

She set a basket on the table, retrieved a tube and wire, and applied some gel from the tube to an electrode at the wire's end.

"This goes right here." She parted his hair and affixed the electrode to his crown.

Firooka continued attaching electrodes until there was a bundle of wires descending from his scalp. Then she grasped his chin and rotated his head, checking her work.

"Alright," Firooka said, "let's stretch you out. On your left side."

Dorner raised his legs onto the table, feeling her cradling his head in her hands. His cheek touched the pillow.

"Gently," she said. "Let's protect the sensors. That's the way."

He could hear her shifting the cables, felt them pull at his scalp.

"Flex your legs for me," she said. "Perfect. I'm going to put these straps on you. Shoulders. Hips. And your thighs. So you won't roll around."

The straps were thick. Firooka cinched them tight.

"You can move your arms if you like. Is your Joinspace fully expanded?"

"Yes."

"When I say 'bedtime,' I want you to go black."

Dorner shivered. The prospect of trying to sleep in that room, strapped to the table with a spider on his neck, was unnerving.

"Where's the doctor?"

"Here she comes. She's got your spider in her hand. Are you ticklish?" Firooka chuckled and patted his arm. "You'll be fine."

The chamber door opened and Rin entered. She held a console under one arm. Firooka took it and mounted it on the stand. Rin's other hand held a glass box with a spider in it. She set the box down on the table by Dorner's feet.

"How's he doing?"

"Dandy," Firooka replied.

"Comfortable?" Rin asked him.

64

"Sure."

"I have a brand new spider."

Dorner heard her open the case. He caught a glimpse of the creature's bulbous head and its wiry antennae, then he could see Firooka attaching a cable to its tail. The nurse turned and plugged the spider's tether into the console.

"You'll feel his feet shifting," Rin said. "I'm getting him seated."

Dorner fought the idea that the spider was alive, crawling on his neck.

"There," Rin said. "We're in position."

He allowed himself a breath. The creature was still.

"I'm going to lower the probe now," Rin told him. "You'll feel a twinge."

He saw her turn to the console. The thing on his neck began to hum. Dorner imagined the needle descending from the spider's belly, entering his nipple.

"The probe is touching your neural shoot," Rin said.

It was painless. He couldn't feel it. And then he could.

An icy rill, sharp and cold. As it drove deeper, the rill branched and the branches became an icy web.

"We've got him," Rin said.

Dorner heard the snap of a switch and darkness swallowed the room. Another snap, and a small red bulb by the console lit up.

"Bedtime," Firooka said.

Dorner blacked his Joinspace.

"I'll be back," Rin told him, "once you're asleep."

Dorner was motionless. His mouth was slack. One arm dangled over the table.

Rin stepped into the chamber and closed the door behind her. She sat in the chair, unlooped the cable in her hand and plugged one end into the console. The other she fitted into her signaler nipple.

She scanned the readouts, put her finger to the console screen and engaged the straddle. She was expanding her Joinspace to fill her field of view, when something stopped her.

A noise.

A faint whine. Like a fly.

Faint, and then gone. Rin wasn't sure she had heard it. She blacked her Joinspace. The whine returned.

She watched and waited. The straddle was active. But all she could hear was the whine, and there was nothing to see. Nothing but darkness.

The whine divided. It ebbed and swelled. Like listening to a group talking in the distance— Rin could hear what sounded like words.

Were Dorner's lips moving?

She switched her Joinspace to glass-clear, stood and drew close to the table. His lower lip trembled. A thin stream of air was passing over it. The sound from his chest was labored, wheezing.

She held her fingers an inch from his mouth. She could

feel his wind, but it had no rhythm. It was broken, erratic—
As if there were vocables emerging.

Rin raised her hand, eyeing the unconscious man in the scarlet light. All at once, the talkers seemed closer, louder. There were many more voices than she had thought. Dorner's chest was heaving. She lowered her hand again, feeling his staccato breath. His frame jerked against the straps.

An unearthly sound, half drone, half shriek, rose from the throng. Rin recoiled, cupping her ears as if to protect them. She caught herself, took a step back and sat in the chair, turning to the console to switch the sound off.

She straightened herself, took a breath and looked again. His sleep was restless and his wind was erratic. But the chamber was silent. He was just a fitful sleeper, dreaming on the table. She turned the straddle back on.

Voices, loud voices, circled her like a violent storm. Rin tried to listen, but within a few seconds she had lost her bearing. The cyclone of voices sucked at her senses, she felt herself vanishing into it.

Rin switched the straddle off and faced the console, checking the settings, making sure the safeguards were active. Groom filters, frequency fences— She adjusted presence to the lowest setting, then faced Dorner again. In the crimson glow, his shoulders were twitching, and his arms too. His fingers curled as she watched.

With trepidation, she turned the straddle on.

It was madness Rin heard. An inhuman frenzy of fierce

emotion. Was this Tongue? The gyre of voices had a female core. She was pleading, sorrowful, ravenous, unforgiving— Rin felt the fury in the cellar of her gut. And Dorner— He was feeling it too. He was hunching and writhing against his straps, menaced but aroused, straining for contact.

Rin's signaler bleeped, her temp alert flashed. Her hand went to the mole on her wrist and turned the guidance off. Tongue, it was Tongue— What was she saying? Words swam in the flood of emotion. "Starving," she shrilled. "Gaping, crawling— You vain thing."

Tongue's fury choked Rin's throat, squeezing her lungs. Cries she shouldn't set free, pangs she couldn't bear—

The brutal voice overpowered the filters. Despite all the straddle's safeguards, Tongue was running wild. "You," she raved, "Litters of flesh. Never, not ever!"

Rin's higher mind was swamped, but a nether self recognized the outpouring. It was as if she had known nothing of mirrors, and now she was peering into one. For the first time, Rin saw who she really was. Naked. Raw. She didn't have any skin. The mad furor was blood, her blood, thick and scarlet, and it was gushing out of her.

Rin grabbed at the console, pushing sliders, smacking switches, swinging her arm to fend Tongue off. She cut the volume in half, but the voice didn't subside. It grew louder, slyer, more insistent. Tongue was the probing nose of a serpent gliding out of Dorner, into her ear. Tongue was inside her mind, angling, wriggling, out of control, coiling around her brainstem and down her spine.

Rin stood.

Shrieks travelled her nerves, moans rattled her bones. Tongue slid between her lungs and ensnarled her heart, clenching it, wringing it, battering her kidneys and roping her liver. Rin clutched her middle, feeling Tongue in her bowels, distending her belly. A dark expectancy churned in Rin's groin. Tongue's jaws yawned at the head of the canal, her scaly length tangling in the tubes and trees.

Madness a hidden Rin craved, a bright oblivion, was about to be hers. But when she gave herself over, she found herself in the cold. There was heat in Tongue's fangs and rapture in her venom. But it was all for Dorner.

Dorner sat on the padded table while Firooka removed the electrodes from his scalp. Six hours had passed since he'd fallen asleep. "Did she—"

"Talk to *her*," Firooka said.

Had he done something wrong? The nurse seemed upset.

Rin entered the chamber, turned her back to close the door and removed a brimless cap from her head. "Sorry," she said. "I came directly from surgery."

"You're a surgeon?" Dorner said.

"That was my training," Rin muttered. She avoided his gaze, consulting her Joinspace, distracted by other business. "Tired?" she asked.

"Exhausted. Did you hear her?"

"I'm not surprised," Rin said. "Your sleep was anything but restful."

Firooka removed the last electrode. She put her hand on Dorner's crown, as if to smooth his hair back into place. But the hand just sat there while the nurse and doctor gazed at each other in the space above his head.

"She was with me most of the night," Dorner said. "Did the straddle work? Were you able to—"

"Yes," Rin said, "the straddle worked." She turned to Firooka. "Thanks."

The nurse gathered up the electrodes and left the chamber.

"So you heard her," Dorner said. "Tongue."

"I heard a female voice," Rin said. "Vaguely. At a distance."

Dorner laughed. It was a nervous sound, infused with relief. "You were with me. I thought it might be you. I felt like a kid, hiding in the closet with a friend. You were warm. I could smell you. And then—" He peered at her. "You were gone."

"I was called away," Rin said. "I had to cut the session short."

"But you were listening. Could you tell— You've heard voices like that before?"

"Suppressed desire is a possible cause," Rin replied. "There may be a mutiny aboard the good ship Dorner. Or Tongue might be a phantom from the past. Something unresolved, returning to shame you. To wound you."

Dorner's lips parted, then he shook his head and gave her a mystified look.

"You were right about one thing," Rin said. "She isn't a

70

dream. You weren't in REM when Tongue was with you."
She touched her brow. "You were in non-REM, stage three.
Technically, your captivation by Tongue is a parasomnia, like
sleepwalking or night terrors. But—" Rin closed her eyes and
took a breath.

"But what?"

"I'm sorry," she muttered. "It's been a double shift. I'm a
little light-headed."

Dorner stood and reached for her arm. "Should I get
someone?"

"No. I'm alright. It will pass." She removed his hand from
her arm. "I spent last night in the lab. I was on my way home
when you showed up this morning."

Dorner checked his Joinspace. "It's dark outside."

"Tomorrow—" Rin straightened, using her finger to move
the black drape of hair from her eye. "I'll be here at eight. Let's
see if we can make more sense of Tongue then."

"I'm sorry," Dorner said. "I didn't realize—"

Rin waved his concern away.

"I really appreciate—"

"Of course." Rin pointed. "Your clothes are in the far
cupboard."

And she turned to exit the chamber.

As Dorner opened the cupboard, he caught Rin's last
glance. It was the look of a schoolgirl in the Museum of
Memorable Creatures, seeing a monster from the Mesozoic
for the first time.

"You've never been married," Rin said, "according to your medical records."

"No."

"Prior to your abstinence, you were intimate with women?"

"Yes."

"You've adhered to your 'vow' strictly? For two years?"

Dorner nodded. "The esteem of the colony has been enough. It's faceless, but it's been a kind of love for me."

"Going back to the period preceding your abstinence, can you describe your relations with women?"

"I'm not sure that's important."

"If you'd rather discuss this with a—"

"No, no—" Dorner sighed. "I was with a professor at the Academy for almost a year. A smart woman, with a radiant spirit. She was good to me. It didn't work out."

"Can you tell me why?"

"I wasn't—"

The doctor waited.

"I couldn't keep my impulses within bounds."

"The strictures are difficult," Rin said.

"I violated them."

Rin pursed her lips. "You're not alone, you know."

Dorner didn't reply.

"Was this a repeated pattern? Did you go through this with other women?"

He nodded. "Many."

Rin frowned. Something about his answer rankled her. "You felt these 'impulses' were unseemly for a Planner?"

Her harshness surprised him.

"I'm sorry," Rin said. Her look softened. "I want to understand. Your violations— What did you do that felt so wrong? And your partners. How did they react?"

"We're on dangerous ground," he said quietly.

"Fertile ground for Tongue," she suggested.

"Tongue is my guilt," he said, guessing her diagnosis.

"Maybe. Maybe she's your rage."

He lowered his gaze. "Or maybe she's a kind of punishment."

"For what?"

"I haven't been successful in love." He spoke without looking up.

Silence.

"Things only went well when I wasn't myself," Dorner said.

"Are you sure—"

"With a few, I let them see who I am. That was always the end." Dorner raised his eyes.

Rin was leaning forward, hands cosseting the air, as if to coax an answer from it. "Does Tongue know who you are?"

"She knows how to arouse me."

"But you don't reach a climax."

"I hold myself back," he said.

Rin swallowed, and her head quivered. A shudder, not a denial.

Dorner studied her. "She scared you. Didn't she."

Rin didn't reply.

"You're probably not supposed to admit that to a patient. Be honest with me. What were you feeling, listening to Tongue?"

Rin's black hair fell across her cheek, leaving one eye visible.

"I've done nearly two thousand straddles," she said. "I've seen and heard lots of bizarre characters and creatures. They're always distorted aspects of the patients themselves."

"You think Tongue is a part of me."

"How could it be otherwise," Rin replied. "But—"

"I've been getting some unusual attention lately," Dorner murmured. "It's as if there are women who can see Tongue inside me."

"It's too early—"

"I want to be rid of her," he said. "I don't want to hear her."

"One step at a time. We're going to do another straddle, with a real-time scan. I'd like to know which areas of your brain are active when she's with you." Her gaze narrowed. "Let's not think of Tongue as a stranger you can choose to part ways with. It may not be that simple."

3

TONGUE TAKES CHARGE

"Have you ever spoken to her?" Rin asked.

Dorner shook his head.

"Maybe you should try."

They were in a different chamber of the lab. A console was beside the observer's chair, and a scanner was parked by the padded table, its ivory yoke suspended over the pillow. Dorner sat on the table in tunic and pants, chilled and nervous.

"It would make her more real than I want her to be," he said.

Rin powered up the console and looked back at him.

"You're past that point. Don't you think?"

He searched her eyes. They were dark and emotionless.

"What if she answers?" he said.

"Ask her who she is, what she wants."

Dorner tried to imagine how Tongue would respond.

"Maybe she'll tell you why she's singing," Rin said. "And arousing you."

"I'm here to unload her. I don't want to know her better."

"If you're talking to her, it will make it easier for me to identify the circuits she's using. I'll see that in the scan."

"And then?"

"There might be some clue about who she is and what she's doing."

Rin was eyeing the console. Dorner could sense her trepidation. She was as nervous as he was.

"I know you'd like more than that," Rin said.

"You're the doctor," he sighed.

He lay down, and after Rin had cinched the straps and mounted the spider, she maneuvered the yoke, lowering it to bracket his head. Then the overheads blinked out, the red bulb came on, and she left the room.

Dorner considered her advice. Speak, to Tongue? Would he speak firmly? Politely? Should he be indignant? That's how he felt. The scanner made a pulsing sound. Every time he budged his head, he could feel the yoke, and the spider legs were tickling his neck. How did Rin think he was going to get to sleep?

Tongue reached his ears thinly at first, hesitantly, as if she knew something was afoot. After circling at a distance, she grew bolder. The winds blowing out of her mounted quickly, then all at once she rushed upon him, and the darkness was filled with her voices. They were swooping over him, weaving past, clipping his flanks and yipping in his ear. One puffed in his face, peeved and provoking. Another wowed as it wailed, like a harpy beating her chest. And then the great braid of Tongue's choir was winding around him.

Dorner braced himself.

Can you hear me? he thought.

The voices whipped and streamed, unchanged.

Are you listening? he asked.

If she answered, would he have the nerve to respond?

I'm talking to you, he tried again.

Tongue seemed not to notice.

More forceful, he thought. *Who are you?* Dorner demanded.

His voice joined Tongue's, echoing in the blind abyss of his mind.

All at once, the voices changed. One faltered, one choked, one faded to a whimper. The thick braid was loosening. Then a deep moan rose, drowning the others.

"Forgotten." Tongue's voice filled the void. "Utterly forgotten."

She was troubled, grieving.

Is it true? You're inside me?

"We've been together from the start."

I was born with you inside me?

"No, my precious. I came first. I am your source."

The last was spoken softly, with pain and regret.

Dorner didn't reply. The winds sighed and suffed, raveling around him, expressing a mournful isolation, a solitude much deeper than his own.

"Dashed from your thoughts," she whispered.

In Tongue's breath was a plea, and the plea wrung his heart. A memory, the vestige of a child's loss, denied and ignored. Like the stranded innocent he had once been—

"You're my world," Tongue said.

You're torturing me.

"Torture?" she cried. "Affliction. Is that what I am? You scorn me, starve me—"

The streaming winds stiffened and whipped, binding tighter.

"You're a vile imp," Tongue raved, "a spinster's devil. Me, me— You've done this to me!"

What have I—

But she was drowning him out. Her reweaving braid was a howl of vengeance and a chorus of rage. The moment for answers had ended. She was storming now, shaking him as if she meant to eat him alive.

Tongue was no frightened child, he thought. Look what she'd done to his purpose, his dignity, the little peace he'd found. She'd endangered everyone around him.

You're ruining my life, he said. *There's no one but you now. No one and nothing*, he seethed. *Goading me, thrashing me, flogging me—*

"From the start," she'd said. Maybe it was true. Tongue had been with him all his life—the voice of defeat, potent and inward. He had deafened himself instinctively, knowing she had the power to destroy him.

In the hall outside the observation chamber, Firooka was briefing Rin.

"Shallow for the first twenty minutes," she said. "But he's deep now."

Rin turned to the door. It was time to join Dorner, and Tongue.

"Are you alright?" Firooka asked.

"I'll be fine."

Rin took a breath, opened the door, stepped through and closed it behind her. She peered at the chair in the dim red light, the straddle console on one side and the scanner control on the other. Then she turned to Dorner.

His head was motionless, but his body was restive. His shoulders bulked, and his legs fought the straps. The pulse of the scanner filled the room, but there was another sound with it. A small sound, coming from Dorner's lips. It would be loud and real when she plugged the cable in.

She approached the console and raised the sliders, setting the filter fences at max. Her hand shook. Her lips were trembling. *There's a shield between you*, she thought.

A brushing sound made her jump.

When she turned, she saw Dorner's arm had slid off the table. The sleeve of his tunic was bunched at the elbow, and the red light gleamed on the naked limb. A scar wound around it like a scaled serpent. Rin extended her hand and touched the scar. The serpent's skin was stiff.

She sat in the chair, expanded her Joinspace and blacked it. Reducing the straddle volume, she unlooped the cable, plugged one end into the console and nerved herself. Then she raised the cable's free end and fitted the pin into her signaler nipple.

"I'd rather die," Dorner was raging.

"Deaf, you're deaf," Tongue wailed. "Listen to me—"

The voices assaulted Rin's senses. She could feel the fear beneath Dorner's fury. *He's getting more than he expected*, she thought. The Joinspace was black, as before. There was nothing to see. She pulled it to the corner of her eye.

Gall burned like an acid inside Rin. She was filled with it. Her stomach was twisting, fumes seared her throat. Rage, the rage of betrayal— Was it Dorner's emotion? Had he trusted Tongue? The two seemed so close— No, Rin thought, sorting her turmoil. The gall wasn't his. The rage of betrayal was coming from her.

From him— Rin felt fear. The snarl of guilt, of doubt and weakness. What had he done, she wondered, to call this plague down on himself? One leg was jerking. His shoulders tugged at the straps. *Who is he really?* Rin thought. Tongue was so biting, so bitter. What heartless offense could have—

Suddenly everything changed. Rin felt a yearning, rash and deep. Was it Dorner's? No, he was still resisting. The yearning was Tongue's. Feral, mindless— She was yielding to Dorner. Surrendering.

Rin came forward in her chair.

Tongue's voices were wounded, her song was weeping. And Dorner, so incensed and heedless the moment before, turned slavish and meek. Between the man and the woman inside him, a desperate need bloomed.

Tongue's braided voice turned silky. Dorner softened, accepting her caress. Rin felt it gliding over her, and when she looked at the man on the table, she could see how aroused he'd become. Tongue's tenderness touched her. A beautiful voice, so rich with emotion. Could any woman on earth feel things so deeply, or express them so keenly?

Rin reached for the console, then stopped and drew her hand back. *Reckless*, she admonished herself. *What are you thinking?*

Dorner's neck craned, and his lips parted. The spider winked scarlet light. In Rin's ears, Tongue's song wormed, fervid, ascending. Dorner was swept away.

She checked the scan, studying the screen. What Rin saw confused her. She shook her head, trying to make sense of the image. Then she shuddered, and her heart lost its beat. There was a peculiar object at the edge of the screen, and as Rin zoomed in, the object came alive. It was swelling and shrinking, throbbing in time to Tongue's song.

Tongue's voice was suddenly bigger than life, unmuffled, present. Rin stood, astonished. It was as if Tongue had slid out of Dorner's head and was coiled on the floor before her, singing to them both. The walls of the chamber seemed to quiver and bend. Rin reached to steady herself. The walls were squeezing, like the sides of a bellows, and the red bulb flickered in time. She turned to the console. All the settings had changed. The safeguards were gone.

Tongue was lost in an ardent entreaty. Dorner was quivering on the table. Rin hung breathless between the two. Lovers were feasting on each other, and she was in the room adjacent with her ear to the wall.

Tongue's song pulled her inside out. Longings, hidden and buried, welled to the surface. Aspirations, long flown, returned all at once. Rin imagined the voice was her own. She was finally unleashing the stirrings she felt. She put her hand to the cable, frightened, but she didn't remove it. She couldn't stop listening. Tongue's song had no claim, no thesis, no rational frame. There was nothing but need, blind and unyielding—

Dorner groaned. He lay twisted, half on his back, with his spider glimmering. His face was sweat-glossed and bathed in red. Through the vent in his pants, his erection emerged. Rin took a step toward him, Tongue thick in her ears. *Close the vent*, she thought. She couldn't ignore it. She took another step, and her hip touched the table. She reached her hand out, then drew it back.

Tongue's orison swelled. Rin felt faint, her whole body trembling. A moment of madness. The bowed organ gleamed before her, scarlet in the spectral light, quivering like a serpent about to strike.

She drew a breath, getting control, reaching again to close the vent.

Suddenly Dorner's eyes opened. Wide.

He grabbed her arm, pulling her toward him.

Rin cried out, wrenching free. She yanked the cable out and hurried from the room.

"The speech is this afternoon," Maisy said.

"Bayliss will do it justice. What about staging?"

Dorner was dressed, standing in the straddle chamber, talking to Maisy over his signaler. He was foggy. He put his hand on the padded table to steady himself.

"Manifolds, strikers, pipes and grates have all been moved," Maisy told him.

The plan was to stage the furnace components in a blocked-off thruway.

"How are they treating you?" she asked.

Firooka opened the chamber door.

"I'll call you back." Dorner disconnected. "What happened last night?" he shook his head at the nurse. "I feel like someone vacuumed my brain out."

"We gave you a hypnotic and a memory blocker." She looked troubled. "You needed some sleep."

Firooka led him out of the chamber to a viewing room at the rear of the lab. When he entered, Rin was standing beside a large monitor. "Rested?" she said.

"I suppose."

"Tongue continues to surprise." She turned to the monitor.

Something that looked like a quartered citrus, pink and gold, filled the screen.

"It's a sectional view of your brain," Rin said. "A recording of the left hemisphere taken last night, at 2 a.m."

Dorner stared at the filamentous glitter, uncertain what he was supposed to see.

Rin pointed at the center of the citrus. "When Tongue is singing, this area is lit up. When she's silent, it's not."

"What does that mean?"

Rin zoomed in while she spoke. "Because the singing is intermittent, it seems she comes and goes. But she doesn't." On the screen, an image grew larger and larger: two orbs glowed above an egg-shaped structure; below the egg, three trunks descended like the legs of a stool. "That's her."

The image was four feet across.

"She's an anomaly," Rin said.

Dorner gazed at the image, speechless.

"The ovum-like object," she raised her thumb and forefinger with a small gap between, "is the size of a snap button."

"Anomaly?"

"Something we haven't seen before." Rin's hand moved to his head, touching a spot above his left ear. "Here—"

Dorner's face felt hot. The floor seemed to shift beneath him.

"—between your reasoning brain and your amygdala. I can't tell you if she's a neoplasm—a tumor—or just an unusual bit of brain tissue. And I can't tell you how she got there. But she's a physical reality."

He could see the agitation in her eyes. And amid it, this mooring, this new fact.

Rin zoomed out. Tongue grew smaller and smaller. "She's suspended above this area bordered in black. The old brain mappers called it the Island of Reil, because it's separated from the tissues around it. Sexual impulses are often triggered here."

Dorner stared at the image.

"I'm sorry," she said.

"Can you remove her," he asked, "without damaging my brain?"

"I'm not sure that she needs to be removed. Or should be. And— She's in a difficult place."

"Cancer," he said.

"I've never seen a cancer that looked like that."

Dorner closed his eyes. "I don't want her in my head."

"An operation could change you," Rin said, "in ways we might be sorry about. Look what happens to you when she sings. If Tongue goes, some of the best of you might go with her. Not just your sex drive. Your desire, Dorner. Your passion for life."

"What can you do?"

"Quite a few things. You may be surprised."

He was silent.

"We learned a lot last night," Rin told him. "But this is going to take time."

"You look exhausted."

"A straddle as intense as that one," she replied, "strains the observer."

85

"Do you ever sleep?"

"When I work nights, I often go home in the morning. Sometimes I sleep here. I have a bed upstairs."

"I'm grateful," he said, "for what you're doing. I trust your judgment."

"We're going to find our way through this," she told him.

"It's strange," he said, "that something so small could be so terrifying."

After Dorner departed, Rin exited the viewing room.

Firooka was waiting by the door.

"I'd like to know what's going on." The nurse put her fist in her pocket.

"It was a grueling straddle," Rin said. "I needed a break."

"Again? Why did you ask me to give him a blocker?"

Rin's eyes shifted with taxed patience.

"When I came in," Firooka said, "the console was at full volume and all the filters were off. And his trousers were open."

Rin waved her away. "Everything's under control."

/⁊

It was a neighborhood filled with grand old apartment buildings raised two centuries before. The graceful towers evinced the taste of the architects who'd pioneered the style. Portholes ornamented their heights, and trees fountained from the roof gardens. A buzzer sounded on the 21st floor.

Eudriss stepped toward the door. An older woman, she

was Rin's height, with Rin's rounded nose and planar brow. She wore a sweater and a knit hat.

"Yes?" She peered at the three men standing before her.

"You're having problems with airflow?" Dorner said.

"Finally," Eudriss sighed. She tucked a straggle of gray hair behind her ear. "Come right in."

He crossed the threshold, feeling the air with his hand. "Definitely breezy."

"It never stops blowing," Eudriss said.

He turned to the technicians.

Eudriss' gaze narrowed. "You're Dorner, aren't you?"

Rin entered the front room. "What are you doing here?" she said.

"Repairing your air system," Dorner replied. "We'll need to see the utility closet."

"By all means." The old woman extended her hand to him. "My name is Eudriss."

He shook it. "Yes, I'm Dorner." He motioned to the technicians, and they filed past. He avoided Rin's gaze, eyeing the furniture and wall hangings. They were of mixed vintage. It looked like an apartment that had been held in the same family since the colony's inception. At the room's rear, a gibbon peered suspiciously from behind a potted plant.

"Very thoughtful," Rin said.

Eudriss peered at her daughter. "You know Dorner."

"Yes, Mom. We . . . met on the tube train."

When the repairs were finished, Dorner escorted the technicians to the door.

Eudriss hurried out of the kitchen with her apron on. "Wait—"

He turned.

"I want to thank you." Eudriss took his hand in both of hers.

Rin rose from a wing chair. "I do too."

"Guess what?" Eudriss turned to her daughter, eyes glittering. "Dorner's staying for dinner."

"No, Mom—"

"But you're friends."

"I can't," Dorner said.

Eudriss kept hold of his hand. There was more than gratitude in her eyes. Dorner saw tenderness and care.

"Yes you can," she said.

"You saw the speech this afternoon," Dorner said. "What did you think?"

"He was reassuring," Rin said.

They had finished setting the table. From where Dorner stood, he could see a colony broadcast screen in the front room. "Our Planners thought it went well." He gazed at Eudriss. "It was the speech I was going to give."

Rin was silent. Eudriss looked pained.

"The new furnace— How hard will it be to get it working?" Eudriss asked him.

The buzzer sounded.

"My niece," Eudriss said, moving toward the door.

A taller woman strolled into the apartment, gave Dorner a glance and approached a full-length mirror, adjusting her scarf, regarding him in the reflection. The scent of anise reached him.

"Anja works at Fili," Eudriss explained.

A high-end clothier. Anja was occupied with her lips, her lashes and her hair.

"Dorner's going to join us for dinner," Eudriss told her. "Imagine that."

"Glad to meet you," he greeted Anja.

"Our air's back to normal. Can you feel it?" Eudriss said. "Dorner saved us. No more sweaters and caps."

"Sweaters are foul." Anja turned to face him. Her dark hair was coiled to one side. There was a yellow bird, a cloisonné canary, nested in the coil. "You'll see more flesh this winter. Low necklines and thighs. Does that appeal to you, Mister Dorner?"

The question surprised him.

"Not all of us favor revealing garments," Anja said, looking at Rin, who was wearing a knit pullover.

"There's more to a woman than her clothing," he replied.

Anja nodded. "How do you know Rinnie?"

A shriek sounded from the apartment's rear. The gibbon

89

leaped into the front room, snarled at Dorner and hugged Rin's knees.

"Tad—" Rin spoke the ape's name to comfort him.

Tad's face was dark, and the ring of white fur around it gave him a bottled look. He whimpered.

"Don't be jealous," Rin said.

Tad climbed into her arms.

"All that blowing was hard on him," Eudriss told Dorner. "His ancestors lived in the jungle, you know."

When they were seated in the dining room, Eudriss brought out a large steaming bowl. Tad carried a smaller one. Gibbons were common pets. Their intelligence enabled sensitive interactions, and the tidiness bred into them for glass cleaning made them well-suited for household chores. After placing the bowl on the table, Tad took an elevated chair between Rin and Anja. As the food was being passed around, Eudriss spoke.

"This dinner is our 'thank-you' to Dorner. He's helped so many, and today he's helped us."

"You're very kind," he said.

"Saving the Kiribati was a gift to the human family." Eudriss looked at Dorner as if she knew who he was. "An example of compassion none of us will forget."

"Too bad about the crack-up," Anja said.

Rin pursed her lips.

Eudriss pretended she hadn't heard. "They met on the tube train," she said, passing a vegetable platter to Anja.

"Really." Anja's eyes were as dark as Rin's, but they had a cynical glint.

A silence fell over the table. They continued serving themselves. On the wall opposite, Dorner saw framed diplomas, certificates and children's drawings.

"He got his start as a blaster," Rin said.

"We all know that, dear," Eudriss nodded.

"Actually," Dorner said, "I dreamed of being a Planner when I was a kid. Before public access was banned, I visited the furnace level on a school excursion."

"Use your fork," Anja scowled at Tad. "Look at this." She picked gibbon hair from her thigh.

Tad sniffed and chewed on a cube of squash.

"Anja has a date tonight," Eudriss explained. "Do you travel a lot?"

"I was in Eden last spring," Dorner answered, "to negotiate our fuel contract."

Eden was moored in the vicinity of oceanic methane deposits, and they did a good business providing fuel to the other colonies.

"Rin and I talk about getting away," Eudriss said, "but it never happens."

Inter-colony air shuttles had been terminated, but limited seating was available on helijet transports.

"She's busy at the hospital," Eudriss went on, "and I have my volunteer work. And of course there's the question of where to go. Too much crime in Penguin. They say Avalon's on the brink of civil war."

Ten minutes later, Anja's date arrived. Rufus was a floor manager at the Hall of Builders. He had a black velvet coat and long orange locks. Anja stood and faced him, opening her arms with a huff. "Look at this. I'm covered with hair."

Rufus led her to the mirror and picked the hairs from her dress while she reapplied her makeup. When Anja was satisfied, they returned to the table to say goodnight.

"All better," Rufus assured them. He gave Anja an open-hand tribute. "Isn't she gorgeous?"

Anja turned and stepped toward the door. "Good luck with Rinnie," she said, glancing at Dorner.

He stared back, stone-faced.

"Dorner might enjoy hearing some of our history," Eudriss suggested as they cleared the table. She retrieved a box of old photos and a candelabra with three flame-shaped bulbs, and led the way into the front room. She set the candelabra on the low table. Rin switched off the overheads, and they sat on the well-worn sofa together. Tad curled in Rin's lap.

Eudriss pulled photos from the box and shared memories of years past. There was a picture of Rin with baby Tad, Rin receiving her university laurel, and earlier pictures from excursions and birthdays. As the years rolled back, a man appeared in the photos, tall and jet-haired like Dorner, but with a playfulness Dorner had never known. He made faces to amuse his daughter.

In one, Rin stood on a garden wall in a heroine costume, while her father watched from below.

"She thought she could fly," Eudriss said. "She was a brave little girl." Eudriss raised another. "And the famous picture—"

Rin smiled at Dorner. "Famous to us."

Dorner recognized Tropica Bay, home to Clemency's automated beach. The man was waist-deep in the water, holding Rin in both hands, sailing her over the waves. There was joy on both their faces.

Eudriss turned to him. "He was tall, like you, with blue eyes. And your jaw is like his. Strong. Manly."

"Mother," Rin said.

Eudriss waved the objection away. "Dorner knows he's handsome. Here— Before I was married." Eudriss raised another photo. She was waggish in this one, attractive, with a sportive gaze and a smart figure. She camped between two other women, touching her necklace and biting her lip. "During the epidemic," Eudriss said. "We brought meals to the sick."

Eudriss showed him photos from her childhood. On the Homestead Trail, watching the quetzals fly to and from their nests in the mango trees. Building a snowman on the Jubilee Icefield. In a tram car, halfway to Zenith. As she relived the ride, her vernal spirit filled the room. Rin laughed and made opportune comments. She'd heard the stories many times before. Tad examined the photos with them. When the talk was thoughtful, he made a circle with his lips. When there was laughter, he rocked and shook his head.

Eudriss sighed and leaned back in the sofa. "When I'm troubled and I can't get to sleep," she told Dorner, "you know what I think about? I picture us all together. All of us clinging to life, and all of those who had to let go. I imagine the ice has melted, and the earth is once again a home for us all."

The hope in her eye jumped the distance between them. Dorner bowed his head.

Her recollection of the past had reminded her of a past they'd all lost. He felt the loss too, in a different way. The photos, with their unskilled composition and blatant poses, were windows on a world he had never known. A place where moderation wasn't forced. A place where real clemency was alive and well.

"The past few days have been difficult for me," he said.

"I'm sorry," Eudriss murmured.

"Your daughter's trying to help me."

"I wondered about that."

"I'd be sunk without her," he said.

"I'm sure she's doing the best she can."

He was a stranger to Eudriss, Dorner thought. But she'd shared so much with him.

"I'm still full-time at Planning," he said. "Out of public view."

"You're important to all of us," Eudriss nodded.

Her warmth was softening something inside him.

"The people I work with know I'm in trouble, but—" Dorner paused. "Only Rin knows about Tongue."

"Tongue?" Eudriss said.

Rin shook her head. "That's confidential."

"I want to tell her."

"I'm listening," Eudriss assured him.

He looked into her eyes. "There's a woman," he said, "inside me."

Eudriss didn't recoil. Her expression was thoughtful.

"She says she was there when I was born."

"She talks to you?"

He nodded. "And she sings. She has a powerful voice."

"We all have memories," Eudriss said.

"She's more than that."

Eudriss looked to Rin for help.

"Tongue is a part of Dorner," Rin said, "he never knew was there."

Eudriss took Rin's hand. "We haven't been troubled by anything like that. Have we?"

"No, Mom. We haven't."

"I'm afraid this is beyond me." Eudriss seemed to be asking his forgiveness. "You're a good man. I know that."

"We get closer to an answer," Rin said, "every time we're together."

Eudriss rose. "I'm going to say goodnight."

He stood.

"No, no," Eudriss waved him down. "Thank you again for fixing our problem." Then to her daughter, "Don't let Dorner miss the last train."

Eudriss turned, clasped Tad's hand, and they disappeared down the hallway.

Rin gathered the photos and put them back in the box.

"Be honest," she said. "Was this all terribly boring?"

"No. It was kind of your mother to include me."

He was sincere, and he could see his sincerity touched her. She drew back the black drape of hair. They sat there in silence, reading each other in the soft light.

I'm falling, he thought. Her command. Her intelligence. Her boldness in braving the perils inside him. Her warmth and deep feeling. And the allure of her cryptic eyes. He remembered what it was like to have sex with a woman. And he wondered what it would be like to have sex with Rin. To experience that intensity together.

Dorner looked away. He'd turned off his signaler earlier. He took a breath and reached into his pant pocket for his injector. Rin shifted toward him and put her hand over it.

"You don't need to do that for me," she said.

He regarded her, then he put the injector back in his pocket.

"I'll walk you to the door." Rin rose. "It's warm in here, isn't it." She raised her arms and removed her pullover. Beneath was a black chemise.

Rin was silent as they crossed the front room. When they reached the threshold, she turned to him. "Tongue is a riddle," she said. "But there's something I want to try."

"During a straddle?"

She nodded. "I want to see if I can turn on your sight. I've done this before, a few times, with paranoid psychosis. When a patient hears voices but the straddles are dark."

"You think I'm psychotic?"

"No," she said, "but sight might help. For psychotic patients, adding vision can make their voices disappear. We don't know why. Maybe sight undermines the aural delusions.

Even when the delusions persist, eyesight may help. If the patient can see the threat, he can face it directly. Understand what it is."

"How do you—"

"By stimulating your ocular pathways during the straddle. I use chemical injections and electric probes. It's all non-invasive. The chemicals are encapsulated. I can trigger their release without touching you. The only risk is—"

She paused. Dorner noticed a flame-shaped birthmark on the curve of her breast.

"—the sights themselves," Rin said. "Sometimes they're more than the patient can handle."

She leaned her head, as if to evade an unwanted thought.

"Is this safe for you?" he asked.

"Turning on your sight is—"

"I mean the straddles." Dorner caught her drape of hair with his finger and drew it aside. "Look at me. You said an observer could be consumed by a patient."

Her eyes were suddenly limpid and frail.

"Listening," she said, "has been hard for me. The first straddle— This hasn't happened before."

"What hasn't happened?"

"What goes on, between you and Tongue— The way I'm reacting—"

"I've been worried about that," he said.

Rin's hand curled against her sternum. "It's crazy. It's not what I—"

"You're in danger," he said.

"So are you." Her eyes searched his.

Dorner touched her cheek.

She put her palm on his chest.

His arm circled her waist, and she pressed against him.

Their lips crept closer, then Dorner drew away.

Silence.

"You're an unusual man," she whispered.

"If things were different—"

"Different?"

"Well," he said. "I'm with someone."

Rin laughed and opened the door.

Freight transports began hauling the new furnace components to the combustion arena. Dorner spent the day on the furnace level with the engineers, laying conveyance track for the new pipes and igniters. That night, he was back in the scanning chamber, strapped on the table with the ivory yoke bracketing his head.

While Firooka prepared the injections, Rin stood with a metal tray at her elbow, arranging instruments.

"Tongue knows what we're doing," Dorner said.

Firooka raised her brows.

"I suspect she does," Rin replied. "Where are the spare probes I asked for?" She turned to Firooka.

"We're waiting on the shop."

"You tell those slugs, if I don't have them before noon tomorrow, they'll be herding bergs in a longboat this Christmas."

"Yes ma'am." The nurse turned and spoke into her signaler.

Rin glanced at Dorner. "I'm a dragon in surgery."

She raised one of her probes so Dorner could see it. The thin rod had a copper pommel and a rickrack head. "You won't feel a thing."

Dorner closed his eyes.

He could hear Firooka's carping, the *clink* of instruments and the pulse of the scanner. Then he felt the spider settle on his neck.

He blacked his Joinspace and tried to relax.

A descending whine filled the void, like an emergency van approaching. He was in darkness again, blind and helpless, hearing the braid of Tongue's voices winding toward him. Longing, pain, wrath and supplication— The emotional storm drew closer and closer, an onslaught that meant to rule and consume him.

Then, strangely, the darkness rippled like a window being splashed.

The murk below eddied and dissevered. An image appeared, shifting, confused. He could make no sense of it. And then—

I'm in the sky, Dorner thought.

99

He was looking down. Through the murk, he could see the transparent lens of the dome, and the hive of buildings crowded within. It was night, and the tiny windows were lit. There was Hub Park, Planning headquarters and Clemency Hospital with the angels on its roof. The radiating thruways were marked by the blue-green dots of algal lamps.

Tongue's voices were loud now. She was drawing close.

He shifted his gaze. He could see, he could really see—

Above him, ribbons of color were swimming through the slurry, scarlet and amber. The ribbons moved with Tongue's sounds, alive with her voices, kinking and streaming with cadence and feeling.

She sang in hot colors, painting the darkness, her long moans and harrowing cries rippled and scalloped like fingerprint trails. Closer and closer—

A silver nodule was floating in space, and the ribbons parted around it, like the fibers of a stream flowing around a rock. As he watched, the silver mass grew, bulging and lobing. Its curved sides gleamed, its top frothed with silver bubbles. And then— It began to throb.

A heart, he thought. His heart.

He could feel its rhythm, the pulse jarring his senses, brightening his thoughts. A silver halo surrounded the heart now, and with every chug, the halo expanded.

My chest, Dorner thought. He could feel his chest swelling, with the silver heart throbbing inside.

From the borders of his chest, chrome limbs pushed

out; arms at the sides, thighs below. Around his thoughts, a chromed head was growing.

He was a physical creature, a silver man, suspended in space, skin sheening as Tongue's singing winds streamed past.

You've done it, he thought, hoping Rin could hear.

In the hospital chamber, Rin stood by his slumbering body, Joinspace wide, cable hanging from her neck, her rickrack probe raised like a magic wand. She smiled, hearing what he heard, seeing what he saw, as if his sleek figure belonged to her.

The straddle's filters were off and its fences were down. Rin floated with him, the night sky above her, glittering with stars. Her head and heart had silvered like his, and the hot colors of Tongue were ribboning around her.

Rin felt a rush of warmth, a surge of gladness. *Dorner's feelings*, she thought. Or were they her own? A welling of gratitude for the gift of sight, or for the care she had shown him. The gladness mounted, crowding her insides— If these were Dorner's feelings, she had opened more than his eyes.

There's no one like you, he said.

Was he speaking to Tongue, or to her? Or were these her words, spoken to him?

Rin set down the probe and closed her eyes. His sleek arms reached. She could see them extending from her own body, as if she might touch him. His silvered heart beat, and it was her heart too, beating for him.

Can you hear me, Rin?

Rin nodded. She choked, and a tear slid down her cheek.

"Dorner," Tongue cried, "Dorner, Dorner—"

The winds drubbed his back and chafed his sides, jolting his senses, ending the tender moment with Rin, shaking them apart. Into the gap, Tongue's craving poured. Her strands coiled thickly around him, orange and red, ropy and scaly.

"She's given you eyes," Tongue exulted.

His sight hadn't banished her. Tongue was more real than ever. Her ribbons glittered in the distance, streaming toward him through the inky night.

"You think you can reach me?" Tongue whispered.

Could he? Dorner wondered. How far was she? In what dark cavity of his mind had she lodged? What was waiting at the end of those ribbons?

Peace or terror. Sense or madness—

"Is that what you want?" she asked.

Yes. That's what I want.

To understand Tongue. To meet his seductress, his raving tormentor, face to face. Rin would be with him, seeing what he saw, hearing what he heard, feeling what he felt. Rin was listening, he thought, hoping he would accept Tongue's challenge.

And it was much like he imagined. Rin stood in the chamber, gazing at her Joinspace, praying the invitation from Tongue would be a path to self-knowledge, and that Dorner would have the courage to follow it. *I'm with you,* she thought.

Dorner looked at his body. It was flawless, gleaming. He could feel the strength in his chest and his arms. He twisted his trunk, and the chromed flesh flexed, not soft, not fragile.

Impervious to burns or bleeding. A body Rin had given him to discover himself. Could he control it?

He pressed his arms to his sides.

Stretch, he thought. And his torso stretched, legs spindling behind.

Forward, he thought. His body inched forward.

What was he doing? Who was Tongue really?

Her clamor ceased, and the braided chorus converged on a single high note. It pierced him, thrumming every nerve with unfulfilled longing.

"Come to me," Tongue whispered.

Fly, Dorner told himself. And he shot through the night like a rocket.

Around him, Tongue's choir swelled. The orange whips fluttered, the red ribbons curled, the golden streams twisted, lighting the trail.

Taper, he thought. His torso thinned, his legs tapered behind. Twenty feet, thirty feet— *Wings*, he thought. His arms turned into blades, long and flat, cambered like airfoils. *Hawk-headed*, he thought, and speed flattened his lips and stretched his eyes. His brow receded, his beak cut the night.

"My one," Tongue said.

Her sigh quickened his pulse. Her whine pricked his ears. He shot through a billow of dust and her breath filled his head with heaves and smoke. Ahead, scarves of purple gas drifted on either side, and Tongue's braided trail ran between, glowing through the darkness like the line of a fisherman reeling him in.

His heart was full, his pulse in his ears. His chrome body quivered with ardor and speed. But the idea remained: a woman on earth—a woman he loved—was somehow along.

Are you near? he thought.

"Nearer," she sang, "nearer—"

He remembered the image he'd seen on the screen. Bizarre. Inhuman.

"Imagine," Tongue said. "Can you, can you?"

Stars sprinkled and thistled every reach of the sky. He recalled the first night he'd heard her, how irresistible she'd been. On his left: a transparent orb, blown by a star at its center, like a child's soap bubble. On the right: a trail of green gas, riffled like a mermaid's wake. He curdled the air as he passed, leaving a knotted white tail.

"Deeper," Tongue sang, "deeper, deeper."

Ahead, a glittering nebula bobbed from the darkness, wrinkled and rolled around its natal sun like a golden cabbage. The braid of Tongue's voices ran beside it—fuller now, woven thickly, oily and gleaming, dripping with stars.

He was far from the earth. And the woman—was she still with him? Rin was her name. A moment of clarity: he was disappearing into Tongue's realm. *I can't turn back*, he thought, aiming the message behind him.

Beyond the cabbage, a great wormhole appeared, flaring like a tube train tunnel; and through it, at its end, a red light was pulsing.

"Deeper," Tongue sang.

He shot past the cabbage. The Wormhole gaped, the red

light grew bigger and brighter. Tongue— He'd see her, he'd know— Every atom of his being trembled with anticipation. How easy: to let everything go, every thought, every memory—

"Deeper," Tongue sang, "deeper, deeper . . ."

A *click* sounded in Dorner's head, and his vision shook.

He was in the Wormhole now, and Tongue owned his mind.

In the hospital chamber, Rin's Joinspace went dark. She shrank it, turned to the console and checked the settings. In her ears, there was only silence.

"Firooka," she barked. "I've lost him."

The nurse lifted the scanner yoke and swung it aside. Dorner's body was stiff and straight.

"Give him a jolt," Rin said, eyes wide.

Firooka pressed a metal waffle to Dorner's forehead. His body jumped on the table, but he didn't wake.

"Don't do this—" Rin's voice was threatening. She reached for the instrument tray, raising a syringe with a long needle and a barrel full of copper liquid.

Dorner was in the Wormhole, flying beside Tongue's deafening braid. Desire screamed inside him. The fleeced walls were flowing, and the pulsing red egress filled his sight.

Something spiked his right wing. When he looked, he could see the ghost of a human arm. Without warning, his long silver body collapsed like a spyglass, and his momentum reversed. An invisible force sucked him back through the Wormhole.

He hurtled from its entrance, past the Golden Cabbage and the Mermaid's Wake, metallic no more. He was frail and fleshy, splayed and flailing, tumbling through the dust and purple smoke. The stars winked out. There was only darkness. And then below him, a white snowball some child had formed.

He was plunging toward a frozen planet.

Rin tried to nap in the chair by the console, but her eyes wouldn't close. For five hours she stared through the scarlet gloom at the man asleep on the table. She rose when Dorner lifted his head.

He squinted at her. "You brought me back."

Rin exhaled. She unfastened his straps.

Dorner sat up slowly. "You saw?" he asked her. "The braid, the Wormhole—"

"Until you entered it."

"And then—"

"Nothing. The straddle couldn't follow you in. Your mind is guarding the opening."

Dorner remembered hurtling through the Wormhole, crazed, engulfed by the pulsing light, Tongue's chorus roaring around him.

"Did you see her?" Rin asked.

He shook his head.

"I don't like losing my connection," she said.

"I understand." Dorner peered at her. For a time, he'd

forgotten Rin. She must have felt that through the straddle. As a doctor, she'd worried about his return. As a woman— "I'm going to ride back with you on the train," he said.

The car was empty. Neither had spoken on the way to the depot or while they were boarding. They sat together, and as the train took a curve they leaned as one. Dorner put his hand on hers.

Rin didn't remove it. She pinched his sleeve and hiked it, looking at his wrist. "That's a burn scar," she said.

"A memento from Kiribati. We were evacuating the last refugees. A fuel station exploded."

The tube train righted, accelerating on its airbed.

"Last night, when you gave me eyes—" He peered at her.

Rin was silent.

"You heard my thoughts?"

She nodded.

"That's how I feel," he said.

Her head turned. The drape of black hair hid her face.

The train hissed on its bed. It was slowing.

"I feel the same about you," Rin said.

Dorner rose. "We're getting off here."

"It's not my stop."

"No," Dorner said. "It's mine."

Rin stepped inside Dorner's apartment, halted by the sofa and looked around. It was tidy, but the lamps needed polishing and the curtains were worn. On the wall above the desk was the Planning insignia, a three-pointed star with each leg labeled: Temp, Conscience and Perpetuity.

"It's not much," he said. "You can see the Cayambe Cliffs from the roof."

"How long have you been here?"

"Two years." Dorner took her coat.

"You have it to yourself," Rin said. "Mom and I are always in each other's way."

Dorner stepped toward her and circled her with his arms.

"Are we going to do this?" she murmured, leaning against him.

"I don't know. Are we?"

Her presence filled the modest space. He wondered if the bleakness would return when she left.

"Moderation, yes. But abstinence—" Rin looked at him. "It's not healthy."

"I'm going to close the drapes."

He moved around the room, sealing the windows, and when he returned the apartment was dim.

"You're not afraid of me," he said.

"A little. I am. I'm not very experienced." She touched her brow. "I've watched a lot of patients in the lab, but—"

Her voice seemed to belong to a stranger, someone he'd never met.

"I've never seen anyone . . . act like that." Rin was barely audible. "The second straddle— I had to leave." She put her arm across her middle, as if to protect herself.

Dorner put his hands on her hips. The doctor had vanished. The woman before him cared nothing about spiders and scans. She sighed and then she pressed against him. Her breath grazed his neck. He put his lips to hers.

Rin's mouth was warm, and her tongue sought his. In the darkness, his heart spoke. And in the quiet, hers answered.

He felt her palm on his chest.

"My guidance is unhappy," she said.

Dorner found her wrist and depressed the mole. "I turned mine off on the train."

"Will you undress me?" she asked.

He kissed her again and unbuttoned her blouse. Her skin was poreless, smooth as porcelain. When her breasts were free, she stared at him, trying to be bold. Dorner caressed her shoulders and removed her skirt. Her body was simple, lithe and trim.

Rin's lips trembled. Was she trying to speak?

She's been nursing a fantasy, Dorner thought. He took her in his arms and lifted her onto the sofa. Rin hid her face.

"Relax," he said softly. "Close your eyes."

He touched her lids to seal them. Then he spoke again.

"Tell me what you've imagined Dorner might do."

After a long silence, she began to whisper. It was a rambling list, innocent and predictable. He put his finger over her lips.

"I'd like to try the first," he said. "Would that be alright?"

109

"Yes," Rin said.

Twenty minutes later, when her spasms were abating, Dorner held her.

Rin began to cry.

"What is it?"

She shook her head. "You were so selfless. I've never been treated that way." She put her hand on his shirt shoulder. He was still fully clothed.

Rin raised herself from the sofa and drew Dorner up. Holding his hand, she crossed the floor and entered his bedroom. Dorner closed the door. The darkness was thick.

She crawled onto the mattress, folded her legs and motioned him to sit opposite.

"I want to know who you are," she whispered. "Really."

Dorner sat across from her. *What did you expect?* he asked himself. There was no way to avoid this.

Rin touched his knee. "Your love life. Tell me."

"How far back—"

"The one who understood you best," she said. "Start with her."

He could see her silhouette, but her eyes were lost in the darkness.

"It's not something I'm proud of," Dorner said.

"Please."

"I was a virgin. She was the mother of one of my classmates."

"How old were you?"

"Twelve, when it started."

"Did anyone—"

"No. Nobody knew. At first, I thought I had what every boy wants. An experienced guide. I felt lucky. But— It was wrong. All wrong."

"She took advantage of you."

Dorner shook his head. "It wasn't that."

Stray sensations surfaced from memory. Her scent filled his head. Her curls were a cave. His shoulder blade prickled, and he squeezed her waist.

"I had some strange ideas," he said. "I was reckless. And she—"

Rin waited.

"I followed my imagination," he said. "It led me to a sorry place."

"What was it you did?"

Dorner took a breath. "This is hard to think about."

She shifted closer, touching her folded leg to his. "Is there a picture I can see?"

"She was tall," he said. "My height. Cinnamon curls and blue eyes, and skin that was perfectly pink."

"She was beautiful," Rin said.

He nodded. "I couldn't let go of her. Even after I began seeing girls my own age. I moved to Libreville, thinking the distance would finish us. But my affairs with women at college made me miserable. I expected furnace doors to open, to be consumed by the heat and the roar. I thought they would all be like YoEllis."

"YoEllis." Rin spoke her name.

"When I returned to Clemency, I went back to her."

"And when you joined Planning—"

"I couldn't do without her. I was friendly with other women. I treated them the way I thought they wanted to be treated."

"And?"

"Some responded. It didn't matter. There was nothing for me." He looked away. "With a few, I took off the mask."

"You mean—"

"I acted like I would have with her."

"What happened?"

He didn't reply.

"Tell me," Rin said.

"They were frightened. Repulsed."

The pain in his voice hung in the space between them.

Rin touched his thigh.

"When I took the vow—" Dorner exhaled. "I had to."

The silence closed over his words.

"I'm sorry," he said. "Some other time."

"No," Rin insisted. "Now."

Dorner eyed his palm, rubbing its scar with his thumb. "It was terrible." His voice was hushed. "She had already lost her husband and her looks. She started doing things to . . . hurt herself. To make a show of her own destruction. She didn't care." He took a breath. "Finally, I ended it. And then—"

"Then?"

"She tried to kill herself. She thought it would bring me back."

Rin sighed in the quiet.

"That night— I wish I could forget it," he said. "Getting the call. Stepping into the room. Seeing what she'd done to herself. Watching her open her ruined arms, smiling, expecting everything would be forgiven."

It's happening again, Dorner thought. His past was poisoning his future.

"You called Tongue a punishment," Rin said. "You were thinking of YoEllis."

He nodded. "I've earned my haunting."

"And you're afraid the same thing might occur with other women. That's why you were so generous with me on the sofa."

Dorner didn't reply.

"What was it about her?" Rin said.

He rubbed his palm with his thumb.

"Why couldn't you stop?" Her voice was soft and dark.

"She understood me," Dorner said, choosing his words. "She loved me. Loved who I was. There were no hesitations, no regrets. The things I felt with YoEllis, I've never felt with anyone else."

His candor put a wall between them. *I'm sorry*, he thought.

"I want to see you with your mask off," Rin said.

Her words alarmed him, and so did her brusqueness.

She leaned toward him to open his shirt. "It won't be like it was with the others."

He grabbed her wrist. "That's not what you want."

"Don't tell me what I want."

He rose onto his knees. Rin rose with him.

She reached and pulled his shirt tails out. "Be the man I felt through the straddle." Rin slid her hands up his back. "Understand *me*. Love who *I* am."

Insistence curled her fingers. He could feel her nails digging into his back.

"Take your clothes off," Rin said.

He knew he shouldn't. But her command and her naked body overruled his judgment. Dorner wiped his brow, edged off the mattress and stepped into a dark corner to remove his clothing.

Rin pulled back the bedding. "Can we have a little light?"

He turned on a lamp in the bathroom, leaving the door barely cracked.

They stretched out together.

"Don't be too quick to indulge me," he cautioned.

She kissed his ear.

"Stop me if things get out of hand," he said.

"Dorner," she whispered. "Do whatever you like."

The memories were stored in his nerves. The licks returned quickly. From a grave dug with denial, his libido rose. The first prongs of pleasure were like flames struggling up, and with them came a likeness of YoEllis. Her smoky fragrance, her scarlet lips. He buried his face in the cinnamon curls. *Rin*, he thought. Dorner forced himself to replace his ideal with the black-haired stranger, slighter, smaller, but eager and close.

He inhaled her scent. He clasped her waist, he kneaded her thighs, feeling her flesh and the bones beneath. His flames twisted, and as the heat rose, he made her groan and cry out.

Rin was flush with new sensations, aswarm in gasps and thrusts, clutches and muffled entreaties. She kissed his face, her legs tensed and relented. Her hands wandered his neck and back. The skin was smooth and then rough. Pitted and pocked. A band of tatted flesh ran from his shoulder to the knobs of his spine. Her fingertips followed it. Her other hand felt a patch on his loin, a swirling thing, where the flesh had been stirred. And another below it, rigid and sectored. *Scars*, she thought, like the one on his arm. Were they all burns? How many were there?

Dorner paused. He said nothing, but her discovery echoed between them. He'd foreseen a moment like this. Rin felt his dread, and it chilled them both. Then her courage returned, and her heart along with it. Forty thousand lives were saved. These were a deliverer's wounds. Who was she to call them defects? She closed her arms around him and kissed his lips.

Dorner returned to the fire he'd been nursing. In the depths of his mind, fresh flames rose with a billow of smoke. He saw oiled skin, and as embers fell, the skin blistered and popped. His limbs grew hotter, crooking and cramping, sinews taut. From his throat came brute rasps, and from the kettle of his bowels, a rumble as his churning vitals reached full boil.

He felt Rin responding. She came weakly through the ferment, vanished completely, then surfaced again, louder now, as if she'd found something matching inside her.

This was no Bez, he thought. Rin was unpracticed, but inside, she was like YoEllis. Impulsive, feral. Teeth pierced his shoulder and her claws dragged. He saw flames dancing around them. The heat was intense. Their skin was gummy, and their bones were creaking. "Rin," he whispered. Her face bloomed in his mind like a portrait in a shrine, dripping with sweat and tattooed with blood. Behind it, a fan of scalpels spread like a rising sun. "Rin, Rin—" The scald of antisepsis. Scarlet incisions. In blood to her elbows without losing her nerve. YoEllis leached from his mind and Rin took her place. His imagined fire raced over her, blackening her skin, dripping from her hair.

"I'm here," she answered, pressing against him.

An angry gust chafed his back.

Dorner slowed, trembling. The wind mounted abruptly. Its throbs beat the earth, shaking the building.

Tongue? he thought.

A thick braid of song blared in his ear, and then his mind was lit by Tongue's streams. Red and gold, they were flashing around him.

"This is my time," Tongue said.

Dorner hugged Rin's body, keeping her close. Tongue's ribbons whipped and chorused, prying, insistent. "Mine," they sang, "mine, mine."

Could Rin hear? he wondered. No, not without her spider. Her ardor persisted. He felt her caresses as if nothing had happened. But Tongue's fury was mounting, her lashes biting, her choir snapping, honed and spiteful—

Dorner spoke fond words in Rin's ear, keeping the pace, trying to mask his alarm. Tongue clouted his hips and clawed his back while the bright ribbons shrilled. What were they saying?

"Blood," Tongue moaned, "our blood."

Dorner felt her inside him. In his heart, in its throb, in the sensations he felt. Her breath drove his thrust, her yearning was his, the fire in his loins belonged to her.

"Fuel," Tongue sang, "your fuel—"

Her flashing streams, all crimson and gold, were the long tongues of flame snaking inside him, licking Rin's body. His nerves crackled, his head clotted with smoke. Rin and Tongue—he could feel them both.

"Burn—" Tongue's fury burst like an overdriven heart, and the flames went wild, winding around Rin, hissing as one. "Burn, burn—"

For a moment, there was nothing but Tongue. Then Rin's groan pierced the tumult. He felt her legs clinch him, and her fingers dug in. "Dorner," she gasped. But the flames tore them apart. Tongue's lashes, Tongue's forbidding cries— He tried to outshout them. "I'm here, here—"

Did Rin hear him?

His hope dimmed. Tongue had consumed her like a log on a grate.

Dorner searched with his hands. Mud or putty, soft and wet. What was he touching? Leaking innards, hair and goose-flesh slicked with sweat—

"You've left her behind," the choir sang.

Tongue had taken charge. Her thundering lows, her ominous cries—

"Other paths, other nights, other flames—" She mined the past. "You saw me then," Tongue grieved. "You didn't hear what I was asking."

Asking?

"Listen," Tongue implored. "Hear me, hear me—"

He tried to resist, he tried to fight free.

"All I am asking—"

Something grabbed his hair and shook his head.

"Look at me," Rin screamed.

Dorner opened his eyes. Rin's pierced his mind, tearing through the blaze. The inferno exploded, sending crimson spatters and a crowning groan far into space.

In a heartbeat, his two-year debt was paid. The storm of Tongue's fury beat helpless around him. Then Dorner was pitching, falling headlong into a cold abyss. The keening and droning faded quickly.

4
PYRONAUT

Rin slept with Dorner's arms around her and his breath in her ear. But when she woke the next morning, he wasn't beside her. He was standing by the window, wearing a robe, gazing through a part in the curtains.

She rose and stepped beside him.

"Finally," he said. "Peaceful sleep."

"Tongue didn't bother you?"

Dorner shook his head.

"You were all used up," Rin smiled. "She was with us, when we were closest. Wasn't she."

He hesitated. "Could you hear her?"

"No. But the sounds you were making, and the way you moved—" She slid her hand beneath the lapel of his robe. "It was a thrill, to feel her frenzy."

"She wanted my attention," he said. "You stopped her. You said, 'Look at me,' and I did."

Her eyes met his. "Yes, you did."

"Do you think I'm cured?"

"We'll see," she said.

"She shrank to nothing. *Whoosh.*" Dorner swept his hand to the side. "I could hear her retreating. Howling with pain."

Rin was silent.

"I can hope," he said.

"And I'll hope with you. But this isn't a fairy tale. There's no magic kiss." Her eyes softened. "Even from me. We may not be through with her."

"I'm not going to think about that," he said.

Rin drew away from him, put her hands on the curtains and moved them apart. "Will you take off your robe?"

He didn't reply.

"I could feel them," she said.

He bowed his head.

"Let me see," she said gently.

She took the robe in her hands and slid it over his shoulders. It fell to the floor.

With the morning light on their naked bodies, Rin stepped around him, inspecting his scars. The band on his back was two inches wide, pink and pocked where the flesh had bubbled. The swirl on his loin was a puddled depression. Below, on his buttock and hip, was an ugly hatching, sectored like alligator skin. Both his calves were fluted. She lifted his forearm, seeing the scar coiled down it, then she came around his front, running her hand over the top of his thigh. It felt like a rake had been dragged across it. She halted, with her eyes on his chest. The left pectoral was webbed with scars and the nipple had melted away. The flesh had been, for a terrible moment, elastic.

It was worse, much worse, than she had imagined. Rin could see he was braced for repulsion. And she was repulsed. Then she sighed and pressed her body to his. "The wages of mercy," she said, kissing his chest.

Dorner looked in her eyes.

"What kind of woman," she said, "would refuse you because of this?"

He found his voice. "I would never have expected—"

Silence.

"Say it," she said.

"You played her part."

"YoEllis," Rin said.

Dorner nodded.

There was blood on his clavicle. And teeth marks. She touched them.

"I've never been like that with a man," Rin said.

"You didn't seem frightened."

"Science tells us," she eyed him coyly, "when the amygdala shrinks, it cedes power to the reptilian brain."

"You were a glorious reptile," Dorner said.

⁁

Dorner spent the morning on the furnace level, setting up sleeping and eating quarters for engineers. During the outage, while Clemency was without heat, they would work round the clock in twelve-hour shifts. At noon he was back at headquarters, with the Agro swat team. Crops were being harvested and stored; fields had been covered and trees wrapped. Livestock would be corralled on sublevel two.

Then a meeting to finalize the water plan. Twenty hours before cutoff, pipes and ducts would be emptied to prevent bursting, and local supplies would be jugged and dispersed. After that, it was Operation Igloo, Planning's boldest move. Blasting teams would mount the dome and spray it with desalinated seawater. The frozen shell would provide insulation. But there was a risk the dome couldn't support the additional weight, and if the igloo cracked and slid into the sea, it could swamp the colony or sink it.

He had an hour for dinner. Rin brought food to the Museum of Memorable Creatures, and they fed each other while they wandered by mammals and sea beasts. She paused to laugh at a whimsical pet bred for centuries in Europe called a "poodle." They ended in the wing filled with scaled creatures—dinosaurs, pterosaurs and prehistoric snakes. In a dark alcove across from a diorama of a two-thousand-pound boa, they kissed and fondled each other.

"I've been such a lily," Rin whispered. "There were three men before you. Only three."

Dorner unhooked the hair from behind her ear.

"The last was like a pelvic exam," she said. "A doctor."

"And the first?"

"It was nothing like you and YoEllis," Rin said. "I was

twenty-three. We were in his room. It hurt, and I began to cry. He put his hand over my mouth. He was worried his family would hear."

Her candor pierced him.

Dorner thought about his secrets and lies, and the events that had led to his abstinence. What a cold hell he had made for himself.

"Don't wait up." He handed her his apartment passkey, and they found their way back through the halls. Rin called Eudriss to explain she'd be spending another night with Dorner. As they exited the museum, Dorner slowed, scouting the steps and the walkway around Hub Park.

"What is it?" Rin asked.

"Nothing."

"Tell me."

Dorner faced her. "Sometimes she follows me."

"YoEllis."

He nodded. "She'll be across the street. Or on the tube train, at the other end of the car. Or checking her Joinspace outside the Planning entrance."

"Why?"

"She thinks my resolve will crack."

"Is this the young man?" Rawji, an elderly lady who lived upstairs, was having tea with Eudriss. She turned as Rin led Dorner in.

"You're spilling your drink," Eudriss said.

"Oh my," Rawji set down her cup. A tremor busied her head and hands, and her eyes bulged behind thick glasses. "He's tall." Rawji looked at Rin.

Dorner laughed. Rin kissed his cheek.

"This is my daughter," Rawji said. "And my joy in life— she was five last week."

Dorner smiled at the child and the young woman seated beside her. The woman was lifting a breast from her bodice. The child stared at Dorner, stepped between her mother's thighs and attached herself. Like most preschoolers, she was unweaned. Breast-feeding kept children calm and reduced the fertility rate.

"Sit down," Rawji urged Dorner. "I want you to tell me about this new furnace." She wagged her finger at him. "Don't scare me."

"He can't stay long," Rin said.

As Dorner sat, Rin motioned to her mother and started down the hall. Eudriss followed. Rin went to the closet and took towels from a shelf. "Dorner's staying the night."

"I'll make up the sofa."

"In my bedroom," Rin said.

Eudriss was silent.

"We're serious about each other," Rin said.

"This is rushing things, isn't it?"

"Mother—"

"Word will get out," Eudriss warned. "People will talk."

124

"Let them talk."

"Sweetheart—"

"We're going to sleep together," Rin said. "And you're going to need earplugs." She handed the towels over. "Put those in the bathroom, please. I'm going to package up some food for him."

Dorner woke to find Rin beside him with her hand on his groin. "Anyone visit your sleep?" she asked.

Dorner shook his head. "What about you?"

She laughed, rose on her elbow and kissed him.

They entered the dining room together. Eudriss was making breakfast. When Dorner greeted her, she smiled politely and turned away.

Tad had a more violent reaction. He leaped from his elevated chair, chattered at Dorner and bared his teeth. When Dorner ignored the threat, Tad rushed him, hooked his hand around Dorner's calf and bit in, drawing blood. Eudriss shrieked.

Rin hurried to pull Tad off. She escorted Dorner to the bathroom and washed his wounds. "He'll get used to you," she said, daubing the punctures with ointment. "He's an affectionate little guy. He's never like that."

She bandaged his leg and stood. "Do you have time to eat?"

He glanced at his Joinspace and shook his head.

"If you get a free minute—"

"I'll call you," he said.

Clemency's sublevels were off limits to all but Planners and the workers employed there. The uppermost sublevel was a helium-filled matrix that kept the colony afloat; the one below it was reserved for power systems, aqueducts and waste management. The third sublevel was an aquaponic farm where vegetables were grown. The maze of dripping trellises with pastel lights beaming through—turquoise, peach, banana and mint—each tuned for a crop, was a fantasy world. With one eye watching for pickers and pruners, Dorner held Rin in a bower of hissing cress, feeling the spray and licking her neck. He pulled the top of her dress down and kissed the flame-shaped birthmark on her breast.

"You wouldn't dare," Rin murmured.

He wondered himself. He pressed against her, and before he could stop them, the words came out.

"I want to marry you," he said.

Rin didn't reply.

"I don't want this to end," he tried to explain.

"Neither do I." She bowed her head. "But I want my marriage to be like Mom and Dad's."

"Without desperation."

She nodded and took his hand.

Dorner remembered the man in the photos. "He was lucky."

"My protector," Rin said. "My inspiration. But— Not lucky."

"What happened?"

"He had an aneurysm." She touched her forehead. "No one knew."

"Is that why—"

Rin nodded. "Brain science seemed very important."

"How old were you?"

"Nine," she said. "They had a ritual. 'Private time,' Mom called it. She tucked me in. 'Go right to sleep,' she would say. I could hear their bed squealing and the sounds they made. That night Mom's screaming woke me. She called the hospital, and a van came."

They regarded each other in silence. Dorner raised her hand and kissed it.

Then he winced. "Your pet has sharp teeth. What am I going to do about him?"

Eudriss was on the sofa reading. Tad was on the floor, propped on one knee, polishing the side table with a rag. Rin had just returned from the hospital and was standing behind her mother, her eye on the entry.

The buzzer sounded. "I'll get it," Rin said.

She crossed the carpet and opened the door. Dorner stepped into the front room with a gibbon in his arms. Like Tad, the animal had white hands and feet, and a white ring around its face. The bow of a red ribbon adorned its crown.

"Lizabet," Dorner introduced her. He whispered into the gibbon's ear and let her down.

"Adorable," Eudriss said. "Is she yours?"

"No," Dorner replied. "She's Maisy's. My assistant."

Tad was transfixed. His rag fell to the floor.

Lizabet clutched Dorner's leg with one hand. She raised the other, put it over her face and peered at Tad through her fingers.

Tad whimpered and took a step toward her, arms curled high.

Eudriss laughed.

Tad got to within six feet and halted. He looked up, growled at Dorner, then he slapped the floor, shrieking and wagging his head.

Dorner knelt, pulled a small tomato from his pocket and held it between the two apes. Lizabet sniffed. Tad stared. He turned to Dorner again, took the tomato and rolled it in his hand. Then he sidled toward Lizabet and presented it to her.

Dorner stood. Eudriss faced him, brow furrowed, as if she was watching from a distance and had caught sight of something familiar. Her eyes were soft.

There was a park and garden on the rooftop. While Rin prepared dinner, Dorner took Tad and Lizabet to the roof to swing in the trees.

Eudriss escorted them to the door. "Can you eat with us?"

"I'm sorry," Dorner said. "I wish I could." And then, "I'm in love with your daughter."

Signs of the pending crisis were visible on the rooftop. The fields were hidden by white tarps and the trees looked like mummies. Through the shell of ice that covered the dome, the declining sun was a dim smear, and the light that reached them was eerie and leaden.

Tad was hanging from a bough, making small talk with Lizabet, when Dorner's signaler bleeped. As he expanded his Joinspace, Rivelle's face appeared.

"Trouble," the boss said. "They were disconnecting the midtown ductwork, and the splitter nave fell to pieces. Rotted clean through. There are still untested igniters, but we don't have any choice. I'm announcing the cutoff in forty minutes."

"I'll be there in ten," Dorner said.

The broadcast was short. When it ended, Clemency watched the clock. Fear swallowed the colony like a cold wave. Some were able to sleep, some were not. The furnace system was powered down, but there wasn't a noticeable change in temp until four in the morning. After that, it dropped quickly.

When Rin woke, the apartment was frigid. She retrieved

Tad from the pantry and huddled him in her arms. Eudriss, draped in blankets, made soup for the neighbors. At the hospital, back-up generators kept a handful of wards warm for emergency patients. But the rest of the hospital staff, Rin included, shivered in their parkas and fogged the air while they treated patients.

Dorner and the other senior Planners met on the furnace level to review the early reports. They were encouraging. People were rational, following directions. Conservation tutorials had been posted on Joinspace, along with exercises to reduce metabolic function through muscle stasis and breathwork. The new alert guidance was "Save your ergs." Dorner couldn't disclose what was going on, but when they spoke by signaler, Rin could hear the frenzy of machines and people as the subsystems were tractored into position. Dorner didn't return that night. He slept with the engineers in the combustion arena.

On day two, the temp continued to drop. The air was gauzy and humid. The people of Clemency had heard the low thrum of the furnace all their lives. Its absence was strange. Except for Patrols, the streets were empty. On the furnace level, the sounds were thunderous. Dorner worked with a team that was dismantling old furnace pipes. In the afternoon, he checked the feeds from the barges. They were circling the dome, trying to keep the sea ice from closing in. Temp readouts crawled across a large monitor attached to a fuel crane, posting data from every sector. Clemency was cooling fast.

By day three, the old system had been dismembered and

the new components were being assembled. That evening the temp was subzero at most locations.

Rumors began on day four. The igniters were faulty. The Nidlers Valves hadn't worked out. When a furnace pipe failed, coverage would be spotty. Some would get heat, and some would not. Rin saw the fear in others' eyes, and she felt it herself. When they spoke, she shared what she'd heard with Dorner.

In fact, the assembly was going well. Pipes and igniters were in-line, the new ductwork was nearly complete, and the first of the cranes were loading the grates. The problems were outside. The barges were icebound, and open water was no longer visible. There was nothing but a flat white ring reaching from Clemency's hull to the glacier walls. And the igloo had cracked. From Zenith, halfway down the south side, the shell of ice was loose, threatening to fall and take the dome with it. They had little time left.

On the morning of day five, the first deaths were reported. Dorner was with Rivelle when he got the call. Infants and elderly, the head of Patrol explained. And a man who had lost his wits. Residents of the towers near Hub Park saw him racing over the frozen ponds, naked and howling. Dorner helped the boss draft a secret alert to the Equatorial League, apprising them of the danger. An hour later, he received an empathetic but divorced response. There was no chance of help, and no refuge for survivors if Clemency failed.

"We'll do it in the Round Room," Rivelle said through his muffler.

He and Dorner stood at the edge of the combustion arena. The concrete beneath them was covered with frost.

Dorner shook his head. "Do it here, beside a striker. And broadcast it live. Show them ignition. Before your speech is over, they'll be feeling heat from their vents."

"And if the cutover fails?"

The engineers were saying they needed another three days.

"If it fails, they'll be part of the failure," Dorner said. "They'll see there's no deception. If the glaciers don't crush us and the igloo stays put, we'll get another chance."

Rivelle closed his eyes. "I'm not the right person to do this. You're on the mend. If we're going to play to the crowd—"

"I won't be there," Dorner said.

"What?"

"No one's forgotten," he sighed. "I would cast a dark shadow. This has to be a moment of hope."

The door buzzer sounded.

Dorner, with coat and leggings on, crossed the front room. Tad leaped ahead of him in a thick sweater and cap.

It was Anja, alone. Beneath her parka, the neckline of a sequined top was visible. She pulled back her hood. Her hair was parted in the center, with cascading curls on either side. The canary was behind her ear.

132

"How are you," Dorner said.

"Sick." Anja moved past him.

She removed a handkerchief from her purse and blew her nose. Then she settled in the wing chair. He took the blanket from the sofa and draped it over her shoulders. Anja was always bad-tempered, but she was worse than usual.

"Dorner," Eudriss called.

"Coming."

With blankets and a shawl wrapped around her, Eudriss stooped over the cooking niche. Food was warmed through conductive glass, flame-free but useless as a hearth. "Will you help me?"

Dorner removed a trio of baked hens on a bright copper pan and set them on the counter. The door buzzer sounded again. "I'll get it," he said.

When he opened the door, an attractive blonde smiled at him.

"You're Leese."

"And you're Dorner." She clasped his hand.

"My husband," Leese turned. The man behind her was older. He had a shock of white hair and grave features.

"Severans," he introduced himself. "Chief of Pulmonology." He lifted his chin, regarding Dorner through his glasses. "You're in Planning, as I recall."

Leese entered the front room beside Dorner. "Can you tell?" She glanced at her parka front. The midriff was bulging. "We'll survive this," she said with a gloomy smile. And then, spotting Rin, "She'd be a marvelous mother, wouldn't she?"

Dorner returned to Anja.

"Are you comfortable?" he asked.

She shook her head.

"I'll get a pillow for your back."

"Stop pampering me."

The door buzzer sounded again. It was Rawji and her clan.

"They're starting," Rin told the guests. "Fill your plates."

Without a word to one another, they served themselves from the food on the dining room table and filed into the family room. The colony broadcast screen showed the manifold of a chrome igniter and the base of one of the furnace cylinders. A man in a fur coat was briefing the viewers.

Leese and Severans sat on the couch, making room for Anja. Eudriss settled on an ottoman by the screen with Tad in her lap. Rin stood beside Dorner. It was a grim occasion for a dinner party, knowing—as they all did—how close to ruin the colony might be.

Rivelle approached the camera.

"Do you know him?" Rawji asked Dorner.

Dorner nodded.

Rivelle cleared his throat and spoke into the mic.

"We're close," he started. "Very close. We wanted you all to be a part of this first attempt. The furnaces are in place. The valves have been tested. The cranes have put the first blocks of methane on the new grates.

"Planning wants to thank every one of you for your patience and fortitude. This hasn't been easy. As always, Clemency has been a model of calm.

"We're going to try to fire the igniter you see behind me. I'll do the honors. So, without any further dramatics— Let's bring back our heat."

Rivelle turned and stepped toward the igniter. The silver manifold loomed six feet over him.

Rin set down her plate. The room was quiet. They had all stopped eating.

Every eye in Clemency was on him as Rivelle raised the striker's jimmy arm. He stiffened, straightened his shoulders and threw his weight against it. A *snap* sounded from the screen's speakers, and a flash crossed the igniter's glass. Then—nothing.

Dorner glanced at Rin.

The giant furnace was silent and the igniter was dark.

Rivelle stood motionless. He looked at the camera, his face chiseled in stone.

"Again," he said, grabbing the jimmy arm.

Dorner could feel the chief's dread. The crisis was taking its toll on the old warhorse. *Snap.* A flash. And then a rumble sounded in the family room. Rivelle looked up, fixing on the giant cylinders in the combustion arena, out of view of the camera.

The walls and the floor of the apartment began to hum. Leese hugged her husband. Rawji's daughter gasped. Rin clasped Dorner's arm.

Rawji rose, crossed the room and knelt by a vent. They all watched as she cupped her hands over it. In the walls, the ducting bonged and creaked.

"Is it back?" Rivelle asked the colony. "Can you feel it?"

"Well?" Anja grumped.

Rawji turned to Rivelle. "I can," she shrilled. "Yes, yes—"

Dorner laughed. Rin put her head on his shoulder. Severans joined Rawji at the vent. Eudriss rocked Tad. Leese turned to Rawji's daughter and the two embraced.

A cheer went up from the exhausted engineers, and the camera swung toward them. Dorner imagined the flames erupting, rising through the pipes as the whine of expanding metal joined the roar of lit methane. Then Rivelle was back at the mic, reading confirmations from his Joinspace as the reports came in. Across the colony's frozen five acres, a half million vents were emitting heat.

/⁊

The bedroom was warming. As Rin undressed, Dorner stood by the mirror, listening to messages. There was one from Rivelle, expressing relief. The exhaust vents were working. There were gaps in the ring of ice. The lane of seawater was reappearing. One from Bayliss, full of fellowship and thanks. An oddly heartfelt message from Nidlers. And a second from the boss. The threat from the igloo was gone. As blasters were readying to ascend, the shell of ice had slipped from the glass. The last message was from Maisy. It started joyous and ended tearful.

"I'm sorry for you, Dorner. They don't know you—all the people who crawl into bed tonight, safe and warm. And I'm sorry for myself and our group. We give so much to Clemency. We feel forgotten when you're not there."

Maisy's lament pierced him.

"What is it?" Rin drew beside him.

Dorner shook his head.

"You look hurt," she said.

"It was hard. Not being there."

Rin touched the Guardian pin on his collar. "You're needed, Dorner. You know that." She unbuttoned his shirt.

"Severans tried to pretend he didn't recognize me."

"He's always playing status games."

"I can't strike a chord with Anja, no matter what I do."

Rin laughed.

"Leese thinks I'm ready for fatherhood," he said.

She unfastened his pants and knelt to remove them.

In the mirror, he could see the scars on his chest. He touched Rin's crown. How long would this last? *They don't know you,* Maisy had said.

Rin rose. "You're the man in my life, so you're a part of theirs. It's as simple as that."

Was it really? Rin clasped his hand, and his hope resurfaced. Commitment. Constancy. If he tied his future to hers, that would be enough. All his life he had heard and repeated the Planner's pledge to the family of man. Maybe the spirit of Clemency was finally reaching him.

Rin lay down. Dorner switched off the light and stretched beside her. She rolled onto her hip, and he followed, spooning, his front to her back, making a silent oath to trust her instincts. But as sleep descended, it seemed to divide them. Confused and alone, the hope Rin had given him leaked from his heart and dissolved.

That night Tongue returned.

She attacked him, and it was like nothing he'd lived through before. He could see the winds. They descended in a rush, bound tightly and lined together, the ribbon ends waving, like a scarlet snake eagle with its talons bared. "Dorner," Tongue shrieked. "Dorner!"

She grappled his back and turned him over. "Who are you?" Tongue seethed, her long fingers lashed his front. "Who—"

He tried to speak. He opened his throat, but nothing emerged. The golden claws hooked him and rolled him.

"Look at me, Dorner. Look at *me*!"

Whatever protections Rin's love had raised, Tongue had found her way through them. The massed ribbons thrashed, a gleaming beak clacked, the claws stitched his chest and lifted him.

"Your frozen dung ball," Tongue hissed in his ear. "Your blister of glass, with all the sad insects crawling beneath it. Useless! Caponized sires, suckling tykes. And the dams are worst. Dumpy, dreary—"

Tongue hurled him down. "You cringe and grovel— The

one I loathe most," she raved. "Needles and straddles, her frigid heart—"

Her talons lifted. They flashed and shot toward his belly.

With a scream of triumph, Tongue razored him open. Dorner's torso split from his groin to his heart, and everything in between spilled out.

Smoke, fire— His innards were burning. Flames crackled and danced on his glistening parts. He rolled beneath her, agonized, moaning, holding the terrible things in his hands.

When Rin woke the next morning, Dorner lay beside her, eyes wide and vacant. It took her a full minute to bring him around.

Finally his gaze sharpened. He recognized her.

He raised himself slowly and looked at his middle, moving his fingers over the unbroken flesh.

"She's back," he rasped.

When quitting time came, the lift dropped Dorner twenty-nine floors. He hurried through the downtown bustle toward the hospital.

Before he left for Planning that morning, he and Rin had wrestled with the night's events. And they'd talked multiple times that day.

"Tongue was out of our lives," he said. "I opened the door."

"You did your best."

"She was furious," he said. "It was so much worse— I can feel the pain, here and here."

"There's no wound," she assured him.

"She tore me open," Dorner insisted.

"Buzz me when you get to work," Rin said.

An hour later, they spoke by signaler.

"You've turned on my eyes," he said. "And now—"

"What you saw was an invention," Rin replied. "A creation of your mind."

"Hearing her was bad enough. If every night was like that—"

"Let's not get—"

"What am I going to do?"

"I want to straddle you tonight," Rin said. "We're not defenseless. Please, Dorner. Try and calm down. I've got a surgery now. Call me back after ten."

When he called, she suggested a new approach.

"Your vision's persisting," Rin said. "Let's think of that as a good thing. You're going to have eyes in the straddle tonight. You can do things you couldn't before."

"What would I—"

"I stopped you from entering the Wormhole last time. I was being cautious. Now that you can see—"

Dorner was silent, trying to imagine.

"You need to pass through it," Rin told him. "You have to face her."

"'Look at *me*,' she said."

"She's a part of you." Rin spoke gently, sensing his dread.

"I wish you could be with me."

"She's a personal demon," Rin said. "She's not going to answer to anyone else."

At lunch, in the Planning cafeteria, Dorner felt a tap on his shoulder. Behind him stood a woman with a whiskered lip. She was sallow and lanky—an engineer—that much he recalled. He nodded and waited for her to speak.

Her gaze shifted to one side and the other. Then she fixed on him with a brazen stare, unmasking her need. Dorner shuddered and hurried away.

He reached Rin again in the midafternoon.

"What should I say?"

"Don't say a word," Rin told him. "Don't fight her. Don't threaten her. Don't ask her for anything."

"Just look and listen."

"That may be hard," she said. "Tongue frightens you. She frightens me, too. Give yourself the same guidance you'd give the colony. Stay calm. Keep your balance. Let Tongue show you who she is."

"No more wishing she'll just go away," he reproached himself.

"I've been wishing too," Rin said. "Wishing you weren't a patient. Acting as if my life hasn't changed. It's time to face things as they are."

⁀

Once Firooka had strapped him down, Rin mounted the

spider. She stooped over him and kissed his lips. Firooka was watching, but Rin didn't care.

Dorner felt the strength of the kiss inside him.

"We're in this together," Rin said.

The overheads blinked out, and the red light came on. He expanded his Joinspace and blacked it, repeating Rin's counsel. *Don't fight her. Don't threaten her. Don't ask her for anything.* Just look and listen.

The next thing he knew, he was tumbling in space, feeling the vastness, drawing a cool broth of mist through his nose and mouth.

Had any time passed? It seemed none at all.

Tongue, he thought.

Her voices reached him. Faintly, from a distance. He rolled onto his back and opened his eyes. He was nested in a shimmering fog. Above him, a few red ribbons appeared, and behind them, a sky full of stars.

It's a beautiful night, he thought, talking to Rin.

Then he reached his arms toward the stars, and his feet swung down.

Fly, Dorner thought. *Fly, fly*—

His legs spindled back. His torso thinned, his arms turned into blades.

"Fly," the winds echoed. Their tone was plaintive.

He was stretching, twenty, thirty feet long. Then all at once, he was shooting through space, and the placid darkness was full of life. Pulsing flares, gauzy and elastic; blooming gas clouds in nursery pastels; and on every side, pinwheels of stars with raveling tails. His body was sleek and silver, cleaving the night. The braid of Tongue's winds twisted and tightened, leading into the distance.

Rin's with you, he told himself. *Be calm.* But his breath was short, and his silver heart was ringing an alarm. He trimmed his resistance, holding his cambered wings close and tapering his legs.

The Soap Bubble expanded, irised and wobbling around its nuclear star. Warm breezes peeled from the gassy scallops of the Mermaid's Wake. The Golden Cabbage lit up, and then the Wormhole appeared, its rim quivering, flaring to receive him.

Your home, he thought, wondering where the Wormhole would take him.

"Yours too." Tongue's choir softened.

He imagined Rin back on earth, in the dim chamber. Was she seeing what he saw, feeling what he felt? She seemed so distant. He wished he could hear her voice, then he wondered if he would ever hear it again.

The Wormhole's fleeced walls were flowing. He aimed himself at the gape, head narrowing, speed gaunting his face, knowing Rin was about to lose him. A *click* sounded in his head, and his vision shook. Then the blur resolved, and the fleecy walls were racing past.

We're alone now, he thought.

Tongue roared at the pronouncement.

Dorner shot forward like a gnat into a tubular bloom, through webs of stardust and gas, the bright ribbons twisting beside him. The tunnel's suck fined him. His shoulders compressed, his arms fluoresced, the rear of his head ruddered back. In the darkness at the Wormhole's far end, he could see the red glow, alive and pulsing.

"Closer, closer—" Tongue's chorus rose to greet him.

The red glow grew and grew, and then it ballooned.

Fire. There was fire, flames roaring up. Sheets on sheets, spires on spires, a hundred waves, scarlet and gold. The winds were close, frenzied around him. He was free of the Wormhole, soaring over a conflagration. Amid the blazes were stretches of ground, seeping and flowing—folded hills, winding rivers, cobalt lakes. Tongue's song swelled in his ears as the heated winds beat against his chest.

"Fire," she sang, "our fire—"

Dorner's senses were reeling.

The heat and crackling, the roar and the smoke— A lightning bolt pierced the haze, igniting a lake beneath him, and as a fountain of flame erupted, bangling the air, his mind centered. Every guess vanished. And every hope for the future. Every question he could frame for Tongue or anyone else.

You know, Dorner thought.

"I know," she replied.

Dorner was a well of despair, but Tongue seemed oblivious. Another bolt struck, igniting the back of a ridge. The winds swooped, carrying him with them. The voices sizzled with rapture. Below, through a sooty haze, he saw mountains and valleys with clouds of fire blooming above, like storms bursting over a fabled island.

A dark scud drifted aside, and there in the sky before him, Tongue appeared.

She was the living image of the scan he'd seen in the lab. The two orbs were moons, giant eyes, low in the sky. Their edges were bright, the centers swirling with feeling.

"Dorner," she sang, "oh Dorner—"

His heart hammered. *Look and listen*, he thought, trying to quiet his fear. He leveled his wings and let himself glide. Below the twin moons, the curving top of the Ovum was visible, translucent and white. It looked like Tongue's world had been born from an egg and was hooded by the shell from which it had hatched.

"For you," Tongue said. "All for you."

The Ovum looked soft. As he watched, its margins shifted, and its density too. Inside, reddish billows were boiling. Dorner batted his wings. The winds were pushing him down. He could see the Ovum's underside now, curved like its top. A floating bladder—

"Secured," Tongue said, "by love's arteries."

Three giant trunks rose to meet the Ovum like the legs of a stool. They were rooted on the land below.

"Look down," she said. "Your tissues are flowing—"

Below, between scarves of smoke, he saw bloated ridges, sagging bastions, sinuous valleys. The land was gleaming. Every slope was wet, and in every bed, a river or stream was winding.

"Closer—"

A hot wind circled his body, trimming his wings.

"Headfirst," Tongue whispered. A blast from above put him into a dive.

He passed through a swath of smoke, eyes stinging, blinded, inhaling the fumes; then his vision cleared, and the view reopened. A pink and gray land, rising and falling, the hills distended, canyons leaking. A resinous odor filled his head.

"Look," Tongue said. "Look what I do."

The Ovum rumbled and lightning broomed from its belly, striking the land in a dozen places. The seeps flared, fire clouds bloomed, and flames fountained up. The nearby grounds marbled gold and vermilion, and in the valleys nearby, the rivers turned orange, winding and scaled like searching snakes.

"Remember?" Tongue said.

The passion in her voice took him back, back to breathless ignitions and reckless nights. He was still descending, plunging toward a burning lake. On its surface, sheet fire humped and trenched. A giant face rose, sculpted in flame.

"You were in love," Tongue said.

Dorner choked. There was smoke in his throat. His eyes were tearing, and he was aching inside. A chorus of laments swelled around him, singing his grief and feeling his shame. The face that had thrilled the boy and haunted the man. As he watched, YoEllis melted and sank into the lake.

"Closer," Tongue urged him.

The Ovum blanched and shook. Lightning forked from its underside, starting fresh fires beneath him. His face was burning, his chest, his belly. He twisted his trunk, trying to open his wings, but the plunging wind kept them clamped to his sides. The Ovum was above him now. He could see the twin moons shining through it, watching.

"Closer," Tongue said, "closer, closer—"

No. Please—

Dorner understood now.

Tongue was his devil. This was the hell she had made for them both.

I'm close enough, he begged her.

"My one, my one—" Tongue's voice hollowed with feeling. "My pyronaut—"

Rumbling, flashing— A deafening crash, and lightning struck the earth twenty feet below. When the dazzle cleared, Dorner could see the unity of fire and sound.

Fins of flame quivered, and in the haze at their tips, bright flags released, hissing and snapping. Fiery eels twitched and wound into a sink, tangling with groans and glottals. Blazes ripped a hillock, shrieking like saws, raising clouds of sparks. Tongue's voices sprang from the fires themselves.

"Hot and hot and hot and hot—"

Tongue was chanting, lost in her witchcraft.

Stop, he cried. *Enough—*

A brute wind struck him. He crumpled, batting vainly. A dozen feet from the ground, his wings caught a gust. He burst through a hayrick of flame, fire searing his chest and lighting his wings.

"Match-mad," Tongue crackled. "Scaly man— There's no erasing the one to whom you belong."

His front was on fire. His shoulders, his back— All he could see was the strobing of flames and his own bleeding flesh.

From the fuel-soaked ground, snakes of flame rose and stood on their tails.

"Your hunger," Tongue raved, "your craving, your faithless moods— Mine, Dorner, mine. You are mine to use."

The snake heads broke off, glittering and snapping as they wriggled through the smoke. "Burning," she sang, "the treasure you buried."

A sickness, a curse—

"My gift to you."

Rin, please—

"You're not going back," Tongue said.

Dorner stalled.

Rin— He panicked.

The ground slid beneath him in a slow-motion blur. Sparks bit his thighs. Flames licked his chest. The air was sucked out of his nose and throat. Furious heat, heat and cold both—

Please. Rin—

Suddenly his legs were freezing cold. His chest was white as a ghost's.

There was ice in his blood, ice in his heart. The fires sputtered and dimmed. Not just those near him—every fire in sight. And Tongue's choir was fading.

Dorner felt himself jerked through a rain of embers, dragged between drapes of smoke. Whatever had hold of him was tugging fiercely. The air was thick with caustic vapors.

And then he was through them.

"A man in name only," Tongue cried. Her words reached him faintly. And then she was singing, as if to herself. "Life without Tongue is no life at all."

/⁣⌒⁣⁣/

"His pulse is steady," Firooka said to Rin.

They were standing on either side of an elongated vat. Dorner was in it, lying on his back, buried in chipped ice.

His face was red. His lids fluttered and his head shifted.

"Here he comes," Rin said.

As Dorner's eyes opened, an orderly dumped a bucket of ice onto his belly and groin.

Rin stooped over him. "Do you know me?"

A choking sound emerged from Dorner's throat. He reached to grab hold of her.

Firooka put her hand on his shoulder. "Welcome back."

He was breathing hard. He tried to sit up.

Rin nodded to Firooka, and the nurse departed.

Dorner drew his arm from the ice. He grabbed the vat's rim and lifted himself, hair dripping, tunic soaked.

"Drink this." Rin handed him a bottle.

He raised the spout to his lips.

"Slowly," she said.

He was too thirsty to speak. His hand was shaking. Shivers crossed his chest.

"You'll be fine," Rin said, reassuring them both.

Dorner lowered the bottle and looked at the vat. "Why am I here?"

"Your temp soared and your heart rate doubled. You were burning up."

He absorbed her words.

"I was frightened," she admitted.

She circled his shoulders with a towel.

Dorner leaned away, frowning as if he was trying to remember.

"You flew into the Wormhole," Rin said.

He nodded.

"Did you see her?"

Again he nodded. "I can barely talk," he said hoarsely.

Rin refilled the bottle and passed it to him. Dorner closed his eyes while he drank.

"There's a floating world," he said finally. "An asteroid. Tongue's there."

Rin waited. Was he bleary, trying to remember?

"She was like the scan you showed me," Dorner said. "But— Enormous. She has moons for eyes. And the egg-shaped thing, the Ovum—" He raised his hands, as if he was holding it. "It's suspended in the sky." He met her gaze. "The three trunks—I saw them too. They connect the Ovum to the asteroid's surface."

"What happened?"

"She raged at me," Dorner said. "She hates me. She wants to destroy me."

"Why?"

Dorner shook his head.

"Were you aroused by her?"

"No."

"Your heart was racing."

"I panicked," he said.

"Your temp was a hundred and eight."

"The asteroid—"

"What?"

"It's a desert."

"Hot."

He nodded. "Dark. Barren."

He isn't struggling to remember, Rin thought. *He's deciding what to tell me.*

"I failed," he sighed. "I saw her, but—I don't know any more about Tongue than I did this morning."

Rin was silent.

"She said she was going to keep me there."

He looked at Rin.

"Could she do that?" he wondered.

A knock sounded on Rin's office door. The door opened and Firooka stepped forward. Dorner was on the 24th floor, completing a battery of diagnostics.

"You'll like this," Firooka said. "Some woman slipped past the receiving nurse during Dorner's straddle."

Rin rose.

Firooka's eyes flared. "She was outside the chamber while you were with him."

"What did she want?"

"She told the nurse she was Dorner's sister."

"Did they get any—"

"She came and went," Firooka shook her head. "Strange outfit, to hear them describe it. Full-length dress and a long-sleeve bolero. A broad-brimmed hat with a veil. And dark glasses."

"Why won't you tell me what happened with Tongue?" Rin said.

"I told you," Dorner replied.

"You aren't a bad liar. But I wasn't fooled."

They had ridden the tube train together in silence. They were in the lobby of Rin's apartment now, boarding the lift. She swiped her wrist past the sensor, and the lift started up.

Dorner was silent. Rin could see the deceit in his eyes.

"What are you hiding?"

He struck the door with the flat of his hand.

"YoEllis is feeding Tongue," Rin said.

"I've forgotten YoEllis. Why can't you?"

"Forgotten? She's your measure of perfection. She's engraved in your mind. She's the source of Tongue's power."

"That's enough."

"Don't let secrets come between us. Please."

Dorner swung his head.

"There's an answer to the riddle of Tongue," Rin said. "We can find it together. You know all about my past. I know nothing about yours."

"That's not true."

"You're the man I love," Rin said.

"Please," Dorner implored her.

"You're not listening to me—"

"The answer is no."

Dorner faced a worn six-story, with Rin beside him. The ground floor was a dingy shopping complex. They were in a neighborhood to the northeast, near the colony's rim, a place frequented by few but its residents. Afternoon shadows were crossing the walkway.

"We were on four," he pointed. "That pair of windows."

As the dome curved down, building height fell. Apartments facing the rim were terraced and inset, following the glass. Some had views of farms and orchards. Those on the street side looked at the untended structures nearby.

"The three of us," Dorner said. "My grandmother, Zeb and I. She kept pictures of my father on her dresser. She was short and thin. A high brow and white hair."

Rin took his hand.

"I was seven, returning from school. I stood by that lamp-post and watched them load her into a shuttle. Two weeks later, the court turned me over to my foster parents."

"You must have missed her."

"Zeb was heartbroken. They'd been together for years. He was a harvester before his injury. He liked it out here. He'd walk in the orchards."

"He took you with him?"

Dorner shook his head.

"Did you see him, after your grandmother died?"

"No. My foster home is ten minutes from here. Nicer than this."

"You started with YoEllis when you were there."

He nodded.

"Weren't they watching?"

"They had kids of their own, and—" He laughed. "I took some trouble to hide what I was doing."

Rin didn't see the humor.

"Please," Dorner said. "No pity. If I exceeded my prospects, it was because I refused to think of myself as a victim."

"You weren't a victim to YoEllis," Rin guessed.

"No. For her, I was the prize. I didn't know women like that existed. She was a creature of instinct, with me at least."

"She was all you had."

Dorner didn't reply at first. He inclined his head. "When she deserted her family, she had no one but me."

Rin faced him. "During our straddle yesterday, we had a visitor."

Dorner's eyes grew wider and his lips parted.

"She lied her way into the lab," Rin said. "While you were burning up, she was standing by the chamber door."

"I'm sorry," he muttered. "Why didn't you—"

"It was YoEllis," Rin said angrily. "Wasn't it."

"Is that why we're here?"

She grabbed his arm. "Dorner—"

He shook her loose. "I told you, I don't want to talk about her."

"You don't trust me."

Fury rose in Dorner's eyes. He turned away.

"Maybe you never will," Rin said. Her tone was beaten, but she wasn't retreating. She stepped before him. "You still love her."

"No I don't." He sounded disgusted. "I went to the bottom with her."

"Bottom?"

"It was my fault, not hers. I started it."

"At twelve?"

"The power was in my hands. Even then. She lost herself. And I let it happen. No, that's a lie. I *made* it happen. She loved me, and I used her. I made her a slave to my obsession."

"Dorner— You were a child." He wasn't listening.

"I see that clearly now. For the first time."

Rin was looking into his eyes. Dorner was only inches away, but it was as if his words reached her from the far side of the Wormhole.

155

As Rin entered the apartment, Eudriss peered out of the kitchen. She could see how upset her daughter was, and she hurried to embrace her. Rin couldn't speak. She shuddered, and then she was a child again, sobbing in her mother's arms.

"What's the matter," Eudriss said.

"Everything. Dorner is hiding things from me. We're fighting. We've never done that." Rin rocked her head. "I don't know a thing about being close to a man."

"Give yourself time."

"I just want to help him," Rin said.

"Of course you do. What is he hiding?"

"There's a woman. An old affair. It lasted a long time."

"Is he seeing her?"

"No. But she's part of—"

"What?"

"The maze. His past. All these secrets—"

"You love Dorner," Eudriss said.

"I do." Rin wiped her cheeks. "I can't help myself."

Eudriss smiled. "Neither can I. He's a wonderful man. But—" Her voice softened. "I'm not surprised. Someday, when you're a mother, you'll understand. Children have to be protected. If they aren't, the wrong things enter in."

"I know," Rin nodded.

"I see Dorner putting on his face," Eudriss said, "talking to Anja and our friends, doing his best— But it's a struggle for him. Our life is a mystery. Nothing he does in this home comes naturally.

"His childhood wasn't like yours. He was practically an orphan. Where were the people who loved and cared for him when he needed it most?" She drew Rin against her and kissed her temple. "You and Dorner are very different. You grew up in a family. You understand what a family is. Dorner doesn't. He has to learn, and you have to teach him." Her tone was somber. "That won't be easy."

"There are things in the way."

"This old affair?" Eudriss set her hands on Rin's shoulders. "She was beautiful, he says."

"But it's over."

"He has a wound," Rin shook her head, "and it's festering."

"He's either your lover or your patient," Eudriss said. "He can't be both. Oh Rinnie— My heart aches for you. I want you to be happy. But— Don't get fixated on some old romance. If Dorner has things in his past he wants to keep private, let him. If the two of you are together ten years from now, you'll know his secrets. He'll find the time and the place to share them."

Rin closed her eyes. "I'm sure you're right."

As she entered the hospital the next morning, Rin passed the Records office. Despite her intentions, her steps slowed.

She stopped halfway to the lifts and turned, eyeing the clerks behind the counter. Then, her decision made, Rin strode to the counter, picked up a pad of paper and wrote on it.

"Can I help you?" a Records clerk asked.

"I need some contact information," Rin said. She handed the pad to the clerk. "Shouldn't be hard to find. It's an odd name."

The sun was setting over a faded sector, not far from Dorner's foster home. Factories were interspersed with the run-down apartments that wormed their way into the rural zone. The shadows of the buildings were long, with sharp edges, and the tree shadows reached between with elastic limbs.

Rin halted before a dilapidated two-story with a mold stain across its front and checked her Joinspace directions. A weedy path led to a six-foot gate. Her heels tapped as she followed the pavers. She paused before the rusty bars and scanned the second floor windows. The building was quiet. Elsewhere people were returning from work, starting dinner. She opened the gate. Its hinges squealed and its ground bolt dragged.

She continued along the path till she reached the stair. As she mounted the first tread, a cat yowled above. The familiar sound calmed her. When she reached the second floor, she strode past the first apartment, checking her directions. The one she was seeking was at the end of the landing. Her steps were slow, and she made them quietly. Finally the door was before her.

Rin squared herself, took a deep breath and knocked.

There was a window, but the curtains were drawn. Not a sound from inside.

Rin knocked again.

"What do you want?" a low voice said.

Rin started. A woman was standing behind her, taller and older, her eyes all pupil. Her hair was a wasp nest, massed with mud-colored curls. Creases dove from her nostrils, and her lips were cracked. She was holding an orange tabby by its scruff. The cat had a neckband with a heart-shaped tag and a silver bell.

"I'm looking for YoEllis," Rin said.

The woman wore a high-neck sweater with long sleeves. As she put the cat into a frayed bag hanging from her shoulder, Rin saw her fingers. They were pimpled and plashed. Both of her hands had been burnt, and from the look of the wrists emerging from her cuffs, her arms had as well.

"What if you find her?" the woman said.

Rin didn't reply. The side of the woman's face was webbed with scars. Her neck was tattered from collar to jaw. From what was visible, it seemed burn scars covered her entire body. The woman was watching her, reading her mind.

Rin found her voice. "I want to talk about Dorner."

"Dorner—" The woman spoke the name as if it was unfamiliar. "Come with me." She grasped Rin's arm above the elbow.

The woman headed back along the landing. Rin went with her, too stunned to resist. She could see the cat's claws pricking the canvas. It was trying to get out.

"Where are we going?"

"To visit my sister," the woman said. "She's close to Dorner. Closer than I am."

"I don't want to talk to your sister. I want to talk to you."

YoEllis let go of Rin's arm and descended the stair.

Rin kept after her. "How far is it?"

YoEllis didn't answer. At the bottom of the stair she took a path that led around the building. Rin followed.

Something's wrong with her, Rin thought. And her next thought was, *I don't know Dorner. I don't know him at all.*

The path wound through the weeds, away from the dwellings and into the greenbelt. YoEllis was hurrying along it.

"Slow down," Rin called out to her.

"If you're afraid, stay behind."

Rin huffed and hurried to catch up.

The path reached a turn, and another. An orchard appeared. Most of the north rim, where the ceiling was lowest, was given to plantation. Meltwater was pumped from sublevel three, up to the stream heads at the edge of the dome. It flowed through orchards and cropland, and pastures with livestock.

YoEllis stopped in the middle of the orchard and turned her scarred cheek, regarding Rin out of the corner of her eye.

"You can't fix him," YoEllis said, uttering the "fix" with biting contempt.

How long has she been watching us? Rin wondered.

YoEllis continued along the path. The orchard gave way to an onion field.

"No one lives out here," Rin said.

YoEllis ignored her.

Stop, Rin told herself. *This is crazy.* YoEllis was outpacing her. Rin speeded up.

The path turned into a rutted trail that verged a stagnant canal. Fifty feet along it, YoEllis veered right and barged through the leaves. Rin was a half-step behind her.

"Two months in wet rags," YoEllis grumbled. "No sleep, no drugs, no grafts— You don't love him like that." She lifted her chin and the scar tissue stretched. "Do you."

A rotting log lay on the bank of the canal. As they approached, Rin saw an object perched on it, motionless, twice the size of a human head.

A turtle. Rin could see the patterned shell, and the nose peeking from its front. "What are you—"

YoEllis lifted the cat out of her bag. It yowled and twitched its whiskers.

Rin could see the engraving on the heart-shaped tag. "This is some family's pet."

YoEllis lowered the cat toward the turtle's nose. The scaly arm tensed, claws clenching. A corded neck shot out, the turtle's beak gaped, and the hooked jaws engulfed the cat, tearing its body away.

YoEllis turned to Rin and shook what was left—the cat's staring head and a stump of neck—ringing the bell. Then she grabbed Rin's coat pocket and dropped the head in.

Rin recoiled, choking, stumbling onto one knee. YoEllis tipped her head like a puzzled spaniel.

As Rin rose, her jaw yawned, a silent scream filling her chest. Then she turned and fled back along the trail, away from Dorner's old flame, the cat's head jouncing in the pocket of her linen coat.

She struck the path without slowing, splashing through wallows, across the onion field and through the orchard, gasping for breath. Alive, at the center of her mind, the monstrous beak gaped—the pebbled chin, the ropy throat—confused and combined with the burnt woman's fingers, her vicious scowl and her all-pupil eyes.

As Rin approached the two-story, she looked back. YoEllis was nowhere in sight.

She slowed and nerved herself. Then she grasped the furry thing in her pocket and flung it into the weeds. Her hand was streaked with blood. The neckband was still in her pocket. As she hurried down the street, she could hear the silver bell tinkling.

What kind of man, she thought, *could love a woman like that?* Rin remembered how they'd used YoEllis to stir their lust, and the recollection sickened her. When she reached the train depot, she ducked into the lavatory to wash her hands. When they were clean she stared at the bewildered face in the mirror. The hopes she'd had, a life together— The idea of tying her future to Dorner's seemed absurd.

5
YOU WANT ME

Rin's shoes were muddy, and there were blood spots on her coat. Dorner reached for her hand. She ignored the gesture and pushed past him, into his apartment. When he motioned toward the sofa, she ignored that too, planting herself in the center of the room.

She was angry, or frightened. Dorner couldn't tell which.

"I've been with YoEllis," Rin said.

Her words struck him in the face.

"Lies," she said. "Nothing but lies."

"You wouldn't listen to me," Dorner said half to himself. The woman he loved had exhumed the one he had tried to bury. It was as if YoEllis had entered the room.

"Whose blood is that?" He gazed at her coat. "Are you alright?"

"I'm fine."

"Did you hurt her?"

163

Rin erupted, lunging toward him as if she was going to thrash him. "What happened to that woman?"

"She set herself on fire. A neighbor smothered the flames with a blanket."

"Because you left her."

He nodded.

"And you're covered with scars because a fuel bunker exploded."

"Sit down. Please."

She remained standing.

"The scars are my doing," he said.

Her eyes were wary, as if he was someone she had never met.

"I have fire in my past," Dorner said.

He struggled with where to start, feeling his isolation acutely.

"When I was a boy— I collected paper animals. The ones you see at food stands." The words crawled out of his mouth. "My grandmother found me in the alley. I'd stolen some matches. I was burning the animals.

"'What are you doing?' she said." Dorner turned to the curtained window. "I tried to explain. The flames were . . . hungry. I was feeding them.

"Zeb gave me a beating. He was going to call the Patrol, but she stopped him. She was afraid word would get out.

"I left the matches alone and retreated into my fantasies."

Dorner took a breath.

"I imagined I set fire to myself. At a fruit market near the

164

apartment. I stripped and stood on a crate. I poured cooking oil over my body and ignited my leg.

"People gathered. I couldn't hear them—the blaze was too loud. But I could see their excitement. They were admiring me like a tree in fall color. They wished they were naked and burning with me."

Dorner's admissions brought a grim relief.

"I came out of hiding. I started a real fire in the choir room at school. The music teacher— I adored her. The fire was nothing, but I imagined it consumed the building. She was trapped inside. She couldn't get out. She was burning, and I was with her. We were burning together while the choir sang."

He'd avoided Rin's eyes. Now he looked. They were sick with dismay.

"When I met YoEllis, she was a wife and a mother. She knew the mechanics of sex, and that's what she taught me. But the fantasies were mine. I wanted fire, and she went along. Games at first. Things kids would do."

"No kid I know."

Dorner turned his head, accepting the reproof.

"We'd take yarn balls," he said. "Soak them in alcohol. She would light one and roll it around on my chest. She'd make snake bread. Loaves of sugar, baking soda and furnace oil. When you light them, glowing snakes coil out. We put them around her bed," his voice dropped, "and had sex with the snakes crawling over us."

Rin was silent.

"As I got older, things got more serious. We took more

risks. I didn't care about the strictures. Fire was something I couldn't live without. There are other people like that. You might have seen them."

"Once," Rin said, "in a workshop on mental disorders."

Dorner nodded.

"YoEllis took up my obsession. Cherished it as a secret the two of us shared. The first mark," he touched his loin, "was an accident. She was still with her husband. I was a junior Planner. We piled up rocks in a meadow and dug a fire pit behind it. We'd meet there at night. We were . . . beside the pit. She was holding a torch over my back, and the head crumbled. It triggered my climax.

"It was like nothing I'd ever experienced. After the wound healed, we started burning each other on purpose."

"For the pain."

He shook his head. "If fire touches you after the orgasm starts, there's no pain at all. The sensations last forever, and they're a hundred times more intense. The pain comes after the spasms have passed."

"You were storming your nerves," Rin said. "That happens with seizures or massive paresthesias."

"You're being a doctor."

"I *am* a doctor."

She circled her middle with her arm.

"Our bodies were damaged," Dorner said.

"Hers more than yours."

"Hers more than mine. She couldn't say 'stop.'"

"She left her husband and her children."

Dorner nodded.

"She imagined a new life," Rin said. "With you."

He didn't reply.

"You told me she was a beautiful woman."

"She was," Dorner said.

Rin was baffled, unable to join his words to what she'd seen.

"That terrible night— She was fulfilling my fantasy. Giving me what she knew I wanted. When I had sex with YoEllis, I imagined I'd set her on fire."

"And with me?" Rin said.

He bowed his head.

Silence filled the room.

"You have no idea what love is." Her words were bleak and interior.

"Please," Dorner said. "I bared myself. As much as I could. I was trying to put YoEllis behind me. To protect us."

"You were protecting yourself."

"We care so much for each other—"

"No, Dorner."

His voice sank. "If our private minds were made public— everything in them—we'd all be shut away."

But Rin wasn't listening. She was turning, reaching for the door.

Two days passed without a word between them.

On the morning of the third, Dorner was waiting for Rin outside her lab.

"I'm your patient," he raised his hands to avert a protest. "That's why I'm here."

"Another doctor has agreed to take you." She buttoned her lab coat. "I should never have gotten involved with someone I was treating."

"Please—"

"He'll decide whether to continue the straddles."

"Don't abandon me," Dorner said.

She pursed her lips and looked away. When she looked back, her eyes were harder. "I've reviewed your problem with him. And the likely connection between YoEllis and Tongue."

"You don't treat your other patients this way."

"No," she said. "You're special."

Firooka shouldered past them, smiling and batting her lashes at Dorner. As she entered the lab, he returned to his appeal.

"I confided in you. You can't just throw me over. That's not right."

"I don't care if it's right or not. I don't want you as a patient. You're making me late."

"I'm going back through the Wormhole," Dorner said.

"Your new doctor may not approve of that. I explained what happened."

"You were right. I have to face Tongue. Come to terms with her, whatever the cost. She says she's been with me all my life. Maybe that's true. Maybe she knows me better than I know myself. I have to go, and I'm going tonight."

"Talk to him."

"I'm not doing this with a stranger," Dorner said. "If you won't help me, I'll go alone."

There was alarm in Rin's eyes.

"You gave me sight," he said. "I can silver myself. I can fly on my own."

She didn't reply.

"Two nights ago," Dorner told her, "I rose above my bed. I felt the wind and heard the voices. And when I let myself go, I felt myself rising into the sky. The dome was below me. I could see Tongue's ribbons streaming through the darkness.

"Last night, I silvered myself. I went slowly. It took me till dawn to reach the Soap Bubble. The voices guided me like they did in the lab."

"That's crazy," Rin said.

"I can reach the Wormhole without you."

"What if your eyesight fails? What if it happens mid-flight? And the heat— Once you're through the Wormhole, you could cook before you know it."

"That's why I need you," he said.

"I'm not spending another night in your mind, Dorner."

"Just watch over me."

He had vowed not to make a spectacle of himself. But his eyes were swimming, and the sight of Rin standing firm, shaking her head, filled his heart with pain.

"Tongue's taken everything," he said.

Dorner was a javelin in flight, and the braided voices were twisting beside him. The Golden Cabbage vanished at his rear. Ahead, the rim of the Wormhole was stretching, swollen like glacier-baked lips. As he entered it, the *click* sounded and his vision shook. He pictured Rin, seated in her chair, staring at the sudden black of her Joinspace. She'd been distant as she mounted the spider. Was there any love left? He forced her from his thoughts, bracing for Tongue.

The fleecy walls raced past. At the Wormhole's end, the red glow expanded. The voices were inviting, but he remembered his last encounter with Tongue, and he expected the worst. Her moons would glare and her bolts would strike. She'd rage and assault him. He needed all the self-possession he could muster.

As he emerged from the Wormhole, fires filled his view. He descended headfirst as Tongue's choir swelled. The voices were joyous. He wondered how long the welcome would last. Her moons glowed in the sky before him, gurges turning in each. Whirling clouds, caverns of feeling—

Below were ranks of smooth-topped ridges, some gray, some flesh-toned. As Tongue followed his dive, the Ovum rumbled. Then she fired her bolts, and where they landed, flames flared up.

"It's been dark," she said. "I've been quiet. I missed you."

Peaks with slick skirts, glistening swales, slopes drenched and scored by oily runnels— Everywhere lightning struck, flames shrilled and reared, twitching with feeling. She knew his mind. There was nothing to hide.

I confessed to Rin, Dorner thought.

"I heard every word," Tongue replied. "Scorn. Sauce and temerity—"

It was painful, he thought.

"Her spite. And loathing— Your shame made me ill."

Below, the surface was humped with fleshy hills. They rose to a labyrinth of spurs, folded together. A bolt struck, and an explosion billowed from a narrow canyon.

"You called this glory 'a curse,'" Tongue said.

She was hurt.

Above the hills and folded spurs, wet cliffs rose, weighted with swollen buttresses. Thunder, lightning— The cliffs burst into flame. Crimson cascades, spouts of gold, exploding butterpots with flying lobes. Dorner angled his wings to steady himself.

"'A curse,'" she said. "Words stay with me."

I've lost her, he thought, *because of you.*

"I want you to land," Tongue said.

The command shook him. If he set down, could Rin bring him back?

"You think I'm going to hold you here," she said.

You tried, last time.

"You don't understand."

The surface was approaching quickly. Tongue's winds were forcing him down.

"You can land," Tongue said, "on the shore of that pond."

171

A forked bolt tore through the sky, lighting the pond, fires erupting on either side. The wind dashed him between the billowing crowns, embers flying. The air scorched his face, the resinous fumes so thick he feared for his lungs. He couldn't land amid the blazes, and the pond was bubbling. But there on the shore, where the fuel had congealed—

"You'll be safe," Tongue said.

His wings widened as he fanned them, and when he swooped they decurved. His trunk lost its streamline, his hips reappeared. He banked around a glittering fountain, eyeing the crescent of motionless shore, letting his legs swing down.

"Down," Tongue sang, "down, down—"

For a moment, he floated with the smoke, then he stalled and settled. His legs shrank back, his wing blades narrowed, turning to arms. Tongue's eyes fogged, and a great exhalation canted all the flames the same way. The crescent of shore was rising to meet him.

Dorner tried to make himself limber. As his feet struck the ground, the wind moaned; his knees flexed, then he lost his balance, twisted and took the fall on his hip.

All Tongue's voices, her numberless flames, sighed at once.

He rose slowly, naked, blazes around him. He heard ripples and bubbling, saw the cobalt fuel in the pond before him, glimmering with moonlight, scalloped by tides.

"Fuel for fantasy," Tongue whispered.

The resinous odors filled his head. Heat from the fires nearby drew sweat from his skin. *I'm here*, he thought. His next thought was fearful: could he return? What if some mishap or treachery by Tongue marooned him?

"Look into my eyes."

Through the enormous Ovum, Tongue's moons looked down.

"What do you see?"

Tongue's eyes were dazzling. They grew as he watched, and what he saw in their depths was— Love. Not cryptic or fractional. Love summed. All the love he had offered to anyone. All the love that had ever been offered to him.

"Follow the path," Tongue said.

Before him, a crusted track wound through the oily pools. He started forward, skirting the gelatinous blue. Shrub-sized flames bordered the path. As he moved they frizzed, quivering and snapping. On his left, a bog burbled, venting iridescent steam.

"What do you wish?" Tongue said.

Turn the flames off, Dorner thought. *For good.*

"The confinement of ice," she murmured.

Or keep them so low, they won't ruin my life.

"The silence of clay," Tongue said.

As he rounded the bog's margin, a blazing wave rose, twice his height. Its fringe curled over him, he felt its heat and the brazen suggestion in its whispering embers.

"You want me," it sang, "you want me—"

The path turned and a slope rose on the right, folded and seamed, slick with fuel. From a crevice a flame licked out, reaching and splitting, scissoring his body. "Want me," it clashed. Heat seared his back and belly, and the skin looked scorched. But his feet were still moving. Flames like glow-worms crossed the path. "You want me," they tittered, "you want me, want me—"

I don't, Dorner thought. *Not anymore.*

"She knows what you are," Tongue said. "I'm all you have left."

I'm going to change.

"Change," Tongue echoed. "Doubt and remorse. I hear your laments. All the trouble I've caused you. My one— If you only knew what trouble meant. When the caresses you crave can never be felt. When your body belongs to someone else."

Thunder in the Ovum. Lightning beneath—

From a nearby pool's top, scarves of flame peeled off. He felt the heat sear his thigh and rise into his belly. There was a danger— Something about heat he was supposed to remember. Something Rin said.

A jet of blue fire thrust from the soil before him, then others on either side, thrusting and retracting. "You want me," they *whooshed* with a throaty dolor. These weren't like the gas jets on earth. The cones were silky. When the blue swords ran through you, they left wounds of rapture.

Ahead, a giant fire-whirl leapt the hillocks like an un-leashed tornado five stories high. Blood red, spiral-striped gold, the whirl dipped as it twisted, flaring and contracting. As Dorner watched, it convulsed, disgorging from within: a great fiery head with a blazing mane and jaws that dripped flames.

"You want me," it sang. "Want me, you want me—"

The slaver that fell from the monstrous head turned into serpents, winding fires that hissed as they approached. "You want me," they sang.

I don't, Dorner thought. *I don't. What I want is back on earth.*

"What you want," Tongue said, "is right here."

The path made a turn and disappeared into a cloud of smoke.

"Stop," Tongue said.

Dorner halted. The ground beneath him was throbbing, oily fluid bubbling from its pores. A fierce wind rose with a chorus of voices, opening a gap in the cloud of smoke. As the gap grew, a chasm appeared. He was standing on its lip.

"The gorge of Sealacium," Tongue said.

A great declivity yawned below, crowded with flames. They writhed and twisted like the petals of a red chrysanthemum.

"And the Sealacium Trunk," Tongue said.

In the center of the gorge, Dorner saw the translucent roots, and as he watched, the wind cleared the smoke higher up. The tree was enormous. It rose into the sky, its high branches woven into the Ovum's belly.

Tongue moaned and the flames moaned with her.

Flashes crossed the Ovum's translucent expanse. Then lightning fired and bolts drove down, igniting rivers of fuel flowing into the gorge. A new chrysanthemum bloomed as he watched, like a sun being born, filling the chasm.

Down in it, the new flames crowded around the trunk's

gnarled roots, and as Dorner watched, the roots sucked them up. Through the translucent bark, he could see the flames inside the trunk's glassy arteries, ascending the massive column.

"Like blood," Tongue said. "Feel it?"

Yes, Dorner thought. He could. As the rush of flames mounted the trunk, an ache and yearning rose in his chest. The fiery effluvia reached the tree's crown and flowed out of its branches into the Ovum. He could see the flames joining the churn within, staining the bladder's underside red.

"And now," Tongue said. "What do you feel?"

A conquering presence, feverish emotion— Alien sensations consumed his own. His breath caught, his limbs shook. A storm broke inside him, ruthless, heart-rending, beyond his control.

The Ovum's underside glowed like a furnace.

"Return," Tongue sang, "return, return—"

Dorner watched the fiery effluvia descending the trunk, flowing through a different set of arteries, to the gnarled roots. The roots spewed the flames back into the gorge, furious and transformed. They were leaping with Tongue now, crackling her frenzy and hissing her need, singing Tongue's songs. From where he stood, he could feel the heat and the cinder spray like a magnetic field.

"This is love," she said. "For Tongue and for you."

Fire's madness, its daring, its mystical rage and its serpent soul— Those furious emotions that had spellbound and enslaved him— They all came from her. It was Tongue in the fire. It was Tongue he had worshipped for all these years.

"I've kept you alive," Tongue said.

Dorner felt the old craving as never before. *There's no dividing us.*

"No dividing," she said. "That's how it is."

How enduring was her love? Nothing but death could end it, he thought. Her devotion was absolute.

"Not like on earth," Tongue said.

At the mention of earth, Dorner thought of Rin. She was in the chamber, waiting. What was in her heart? Had she given up? Was she still hoping—

"Are you fire or flesh?" Tongue asked.

An ember landed between his feet, and a blue fireball rose. "Dorner," Tongue whispered. In the gorge, the flames were howling. Scarlet tongues thrashed, orange tapers bawled, hissing gold sheets flowed up the walls. "Are you fire or flesh?"

Dorner stretched his arms back.

All the flames watched him, singing, lapping Tongue's question. The cliffs and peaks shook, the smoky sky trembled. "Fire or flesh? Are you fire or flesh?"

Dorner's arms silvered and turned into blades. His chest chromed, his neck locked and his legs spindled.

"Why don't you stay?" Tongue sang.

The flames in the gorge were shaking as one, disbelieving, objecting. "Don't let this end," they implored.

Dorner ascended slowly. Very slowly, as if some new gravity held him down.

"We've waited all this time," Tongue said.

He gazed through the Ovum, into her luminous eyes. *I'm going back.*

As he spoke, his body streaked through the smoke.

In the heat haze, at the fire's horizon, where the peaks of the flames met the caustic air, Dorner looked down. The flames were dimming, foundations retracting, nothing but flags and snake heads, suspended and snapping.

From that dizzying height, with the burners turned down, he could see the design. Like magnetic lines, the fires curved and knotted around the three trunks, channeling their energy into the Ovum above.

He faced the Wormhole and pressed his wings to his sides. In an instant, he was moving at astral speed.

When Dorner woke, he was in the straddle chamber. The red bulb was still on. Rin saw him trying to raise himself, and she moved to unstrap him. The spider was on the counter, back in its box.

"How do you feel?"

He sighed and nodded, exhausted.

"Your temp was within limits." She put her hand on his wrist. "And you returned on your own. I didn't have to inject you."

She was reassuring him. *She still cares*, he thought. Maybe the risk he'd taken had softened her.

He eased his legs off the straddle table. Something pulled at his chest. He touched his tunic, then opened it. Blue squares were stuck to his chest and belly.

"Dermal hydration patches," Rin said.

"Knowing you were here," he spoke softly, "made the difference. I couldn't have done it alone."

Rin didn't reply.

She's wondering, he thought, what it was that he'd done.

"She didn't attack me," he said. "She asked me to stay. I left on my own."

Firooka entered the chamber. Rin passed her the boxed spider. Firooka retrieved the cables, and as she left the room, Rin turned to switch off the console.

He stood and touched her shoulder. "I came back for you."

"Don't," she said.

"Please. Sit down. I want to tell you what happened. I landed."

Her gaze narrowed.

He motioned at the chair, and she complied. He sat back on the straddle table.

"First—" He took a breath. "The story I gave you, after my first time with Tongue, wasn't the truth. Her home isn't a desert. There's fuel everywhere. The lakes are full of it. The hills are swollen. It flows out of the mountains in big rivers."

"Fuel?"

"And fire," he said, "when she ignites it. Tongue lives in a world of flames." He lowered his gaze. "When I saw that, I panicked. I couldn't tell you. I was too ashamed."

"Your ideal of fire."

Dorner touched his temple. "Tongue was already here when I met YoEllis. Maybe I was born with her, or she found her way inside me when I was a child. Maybe what she says is true—that she's my source."

"You're accepting her," Rin said.

"I don't have any choice." Dorner shook his head. "Tongue and I are—one."

He could see the depth in Rin's eyes.

"She's a part of me," he said. "You were right."

Rin sat forward, hooking her hair behind her ear. Feeling her duty as a doctor, he thought. Or remembering how fond they had been of each other.

"Tell me what happened after you landed," she said.

Dorner recounted what he'd seen and heard, describing Tongue and her Ovum, and the way she set fire to the asteroid's fuel. He explained what had happened on the lip of the gorge. Rin questioned him about the trunk, the way it cycled the flames, and the powerful things he'd felt.

"A different world," Dorner said. "A name came to me, while I was on my way back. The code name we used for the new furnace system: 'Vapos.' Heat and smoke."

"Flawless," Nidlers said proudly. "Not a burp."

Dorner turned to Maisy. It had been three weeks since the

furnace cutover, and the only Planning worry was a winter blizzard.

"Advisories have gone out every ten minutes," she said, "since eight last night."

Dorner and his team were seated around an oval table in the meeting room on the 29th floor. The exterior wall had a large window, with views of the Cayambe Cliffs when the weather was clear. But the view was gone. The dome's glass was white.

The door of the meeting room opened, and Rivelle strode through.

He nodded to those seated, stopped behind Dorner and lowered his hand onto Dorner's shoulder. "It's time."

Silence fell over the room. Dorner started to rise.

"Wait," Maisy said. She huffed at herself, then turned to Rivelle. "Just a little while longer." Then to Dorner, "Let Bayliss do it. You have twelve hearings today."

"Dorner's fine," Nidlers sighed.

"Well?" Rivelle asked.

Dorner nodded and stood.

Rivelle looked at Maisy and raised his brows. "He's the voice of Clemency."

The stalks were leaning, and the air was leaden. Eighty feet above the rooftop garden, the dome was covered with snow. The glass trembled and shook as the blizzard raged past. In their heated family room on the 21st floor, Rin and Eudriss sat on the sofa, facing the broadcast screen. Tad stood before it, scratching his wrist. Dorner was taking the stage.

"It's Christmas again," he began. "When the wind settles, kids will be skating on the Jubilee. Till then, we'll stay warm and wait. The storm will pass."

Tad shrieked, waving his arms as if Dorner could see him.

"We've been through this before—"

The camera zoomed in. Dorner's head and shoulders filled the screen.

"A crisis like this is hard on all of us. And every time, a few of us crack." He lowered his head and laughed to himself. "We'll live through it together. We're in control. I'll do what I can to keep you calm. I care about you. Really, I do." He paused and stared into the camera.

Eudriss clasped Rin's hand.

"I won't let you down," Dorner said.

He drew a breath and began to discuss the practical matters.

"If you have seafood in the freezer, enjoy it. If not, you can count on a small ration of meat, along with your normal choice of produce. The damage to our fleet must be repaired before the fishers can return to work.

"Our floating generators are protected now. They'll be ready to go the moment things clear. But the colony batteries are very low. Power will be on for six hours a day. Check Joinspace for your neighborhood's schedule.

"I know you've all been following the upset on the western rim. I'm not going to make light of the problem. The growers who seized the power plant last night are in a stand-off with the local Patrol. We haven't sent reinforcements. We aren't going to attack you," Dorner said, addressing the growers. "We know you'll calm down when the storm is spent. We need you. We care about you. Please— Return the power to us all."

Tad wailed, turned in a circle and slapped the floor. He sidled to the sofa, whimpering, and climbed into Rin's lap. She let him curl there, stroking his crown to console him.

Between two of the giant angels on the hospital's roof was an aviary and greenhouse. Patients with infectious diseases convalesced there without exposing the colony to the risk of contagion. Dorner was standing in the sun by the greenhouse doors when Rin stepped out.

She saw him and halted.

"Dorner," she said, angling her head.

No embrace, he thought. But she wasn't unfriendly.

"Firooka said you were here." He smiled.

Five weeks had passed since their last straddle.

"We saw you on the news," Rin said, "during the blizzard. The accord you struck with the growers was a lesson for us all. Tongue is . . . out of your life?"

"You needed a vacation from me," he said. "I've been handling Tongue on my own."

"Really."

He nodded. "I've been to Vapos four times."

"By yourself."

"Yes. From my bed."

Rin studied him.

"The flights are as fast as they were in the lab, and my vision is better than ever. My relationship with Tongue—"

She looked away.

"—is different now. I see her without feeling fearful or wicked, and I return on my own. I wanted to say hello. And share what's happened."

Rin started forward. The lift door was between the folds of an angel's robe.

"And to get your advice," he said, walking beside her.

Rin was silent.

"When we got our first look at Tongue, you refused to operate. You said I might need her. Well— I know now that I do. And she needs me."

Rin watched him out of the corner of her eye.

"She's less of an enigma," Dorner said. "I'm understanding her better. She's not all bad. I think my challenge—I want your opinion—is to manage her. Control her. Learn how to live with her."

They stopped before the lift door, in the shade of the angel's outstretched wing.

"That sounds like a good plan," Rin said.

He could feel her eyes probing him, searching for the flaw in his composure.

"The problem," he said, "was that I thought I was power-less. But now— I know I'm not."

Rin was silent. Then her eyes turned kindly.

"You can do it," she said. "I'm sure you can."

"She's not going to oppress me."

"I like your resolve," Rin said.

"I've been visiting her at night, staying with her till dawn. She shows me new places. Lighting fires, burning my fuel. She's agreed not to disrupt my work."

"Can you hold her to that?"

"I'm not sure." He swiped his wrist across the green sensor to call for the lift. "To be truthful— I look forward to our nights together. The flames she lights— I can't live without that. My love for you—my desire—comes from her."

Rin turned her head and raised her hands to ward him off.

"I'm sorry," he said.

"You know how I feel."

"Yes," he nodded. "I know how you feel."

The lift door opened.

"I've got five new projects underway." Dorner laughed. "I've even gotten some credit for the furnace success."

At the 19th floor, Rin bid Dorner goodbye. As she started down the hall, her hand dipped into the pocket of her lab coat. When she drew it out, a lock of black hair was between her thumb and forefinger. She raised the lock, held it below her nose and took its scent.

Two days later, Dorner called Rin.

"Planning is having a celebration at Zenith," he told her. "Come with me."

"No," Rin said.

"Two hours. That's all."

"I think you should find someone else."

"I'm winning my standing back," he said.

"That's good news."

"It's just dinner. I need you there."

"I doubt that."

"There are rumors that a woman I've met has changed me."

Rin was silent.

"It would help keep the rumors alive," Dorner said.

Eudriss didn't greet him when she answered the door, but as she led Dorner into the front room, she took his hand. Tad did a backflip and hugged Dorner's knees. When Rin entered, her appearance threw him. She was wearing a sleeveless white dress. Its simplicity took no notice of the festive occasion. As if to counter the effect, she had reddened her lips, and on her head she'd pinned a fascinator, disk-shaped and scarlet, with a spray of golden beads.

"We found it at Fili." Eudriss smiled at Dorner. "An artisan—"

"If I want him to know, I'll tell him," Rin snubbed her mother.

Dorner could feel Rin's joy. She had missed him. The love was still there. But on the tube train ride to the Zenith depot, she was silent. Her thoughts seemed to impound her.

"What is it?" Dorner asked.

She dithered her head. "I had a nightmare."

"About—"

"YoEllis."

"Please," he begged her. "Let's not talk about her."

Zenith was a place for weddings, birthdays and hosted events. Tram cars, hanging from the track that spiraled up the dome's underside, carried visitors. Cars left from the depot at the north rim and made a full circuit before reaching their goal. Small and dark, they were like hansom cabs from the Victorian era, with oval windows and a pair of algal lamps. When they boarded, Dorner took the icy side.

As they rose, the quiet drew out. There was nothing but the hum of the hanger climbing the track. Rin watched the settlement shrink beneath them. Dorner watched the declining sun graze the walls of Patience Palisades. A cutter jet appeared and shot a rocket at one of the faces. On the water below, barges were plucking bergs from the sea with steel claws.

"Thanks for doing this," he muttered.

Just then, a gibbon interrupted its cleaning routine to leap onto the car and hang from the window rail. Rin's startled laugh made the car rock. Her eyes met Dorner's, jet black, framed by the red lips and fascinator.

When the gibbon departed, Dorner clasped her hand. "You're beautiful tonight."

Their car slid into the Zenith portal. Dorner saw Rin compose herself as they debarked. They climbed the stairs, joining the others on the main level. The women had gone all out. Rivelle's wife wore a lemon gown with a conical headdress. Maisy was in a tight, body-length fuchsia tube with a high collar. Nidlers was her escort, and when they spotted Dorner, the two approached.

Dorner introduced Rin.

"The mystery woman," Maisy said.

Rin didn't flinch. "I've heard a lot about you."

Maisy put her hand to her sternum and bowed. "The clueless matchmaker." She smiled. "You must be very special."

The sun set, annealing the distant icefields. A gentle breeze rustled the areca fronds, and Angolan swallows sounded in the dome below. A bell rang, and the guests were directed to a long dinner table with name cards on it. Rin was seated between Rivelle and his wife.

After introductions were made, Rivelle turned to Rin.

"The old Dorner's returned. Because of you—that's how he tells it."

"I'm hopeful," Rin said.

"Your 'signaler straddling' should get more attention." The chief cleared his throat. "He tells me you had a run-in with a snapper."

Rin froze, her drink halfway to her lips.

Rivelle smirked. "You know the story?"

She shook her head.

"The founders wanted a turtle. They were going to make

it the colony's mascot." He waved his hand. "A dome on its back, has a long life— That kind of thing. The docket said box turtles, but some fool warden collected snappers. Dorner's drafted an extermination plan. Awful creatures. We should have gotten rid of them years ago."

When the entrées arrived, Rivelle stood and extended his glass. "Here's to a millennium or two before we have to think about those furnaces again." The planners toasted.

They ate and talked. The long table was like a lifeboat adrift on a darkening sea. Slowly the stars came out. At the end of the meal, two waiters carried the pièce de résistance to the table: a large confection sculpted in the likeness of the furnace system, with pipe organ stoves, serpentine ducts and tiny beet sugar blocks burning on the grates.

"Furnace cake!" Maisy clapped.

"The valves are wrong," Nidlers pointed out.

"By the way," Rivelle looked at Dorner. "The blaster you saved the day the old furnace wheezed— He got himself a promotion."

After the dinner ended, Rin and Dorner stood on the lower deck, waiting for a tram. Their bodies were lit by the portal floods, but their heads were in darkness.

"Do you think about me?" Dorner asked.

"I talk to you."

"What do you say?"

"I tell you I'm afraid."

Silence.

"I had it out with YoEllis," Dorner said finally. "I told her there would never be a second chance. I asked her to leave us alone."

"Will she?"

"I hope so," he said.

An empty tram car pulled into the portal, and the tender blew his whistle. The couple boarded, and the car began its spiral descent. Below, thousands of algal lamps glittered blue-green inside the dome's ambit, like a phosphorescent swarm floating in a submarine crater.

I'm still afraid, Rin thought. The shock, his grisly secrets—Would she ever be able to accept his past?

Dorner shifted on the seat. His knee touched hers.

Was there any way to stop a woman like YoEllis, Rin wondered. Could Dorner keep Tongue in check?

The tram car was halfway down, but it seemed to Rin they were still far from the earth. Dorner was barely visible, but she could see the lit edge of his profile shifting as he turned to face her.

"May I kiss you?" he said.

Rin crossed the threshold of Dorner's apartment slowly. She saw the place where he'd stood when he told her about his obsession. And how he came by his scars. She pushed the images of YoEllis to the back of her mind. If she let them come forward, they would destroy the evening.

Three days had passed since the party at Zenith. They had

talked over Joinspace each afternoon. Finally, she acceded to his appeals and agreed to meet him in the hospital lobby at the end of the day. They had dinner at a crab shack on the Hub, a casual place where the downtown crowd mingled before heading home.

Dorner closed the door, removed his morning coat and folded it over the chair by his desk. Then he faced her, raised her hand and kissed it.

The kiss calmed her. His apartment was different, she saw. He'd moved the furniture. The Planning insignia had been taken from the wall, and in its place was a painting of a couple holding hands on a sunset beach, facing the horizon together. Behind them was the giant triton they lived in.

"That's us," Dorner said.

"It looks like Tropica Bay." She wrapped her arms around one of his.

They stepped into the bedroom together, undressing each other slowly, making light of the new self-consciousness they felt.

Rin sat on the bed. Dorner remained standing. He eyed her with deep regard, as if he had never quite believed her affections would return.

"I'm going to shock you," he said, stepping over to his dresser.

He opened the top drawer and retrieved a small column with a collar at one end. "I removed the light and the wiring," he said. Then he raised a white candle from the drawer and fit it into the collar.

"Where did you get that?" Rin wondered.

"I have my sources." He twisted the wick.

Rin crossed her middle with her arm.

"People used to think they were romantic," he said.

He set the candlestick on the nightstand. Then he turned and reached back into the drawer.

Rin watched his hand emerge. There was a match between his thumb and forefinger.

"You want me to serve your fetish?" she said.

"No," he replied. "I want my fetish to serve you."

He snapped the head with his thumbnail, and a flame popped up.

"Dorner. I don't think—"

"Fire is my gift." He lowered his hand.

The match flame engulfed the candle wick, and a golden taper rose from the wax. An elongated tear with an opal core. He turned and switched off the overhead light.

"Put it out," she said.

Dorner knelt before her. "Don't worry. It's just going to sit there and flicker beside us." He set his palm on her arm. She was holding it over her breasts.

"I need to do this," Dorner said. "I'm giving fire a place in my life. It's not going to be something twisted and fearful. I'm learning to live with it. You understand that. I know you do."

On the bedstand, Rin could see the little flame dancing. It had a delight of its own. She thought of the patients she'd treated, crippled by the strictures, terrified of heat and healthy desire.

192

"I'm sorry," she said. "That was foolish of me."

His face hovered over her like a golden mask. The flame's shifting reflection glimmered on his brow, satined his arms, patterned his chest with scales. Despite herself, she was frightened. "Say you love me," she said.

The golden man put his lips to her ear.

"I do," he whispered.

The sound of his voice reassured her. She put her hands on his back, closed her eyes and tried to relax.

Was it Dorner's warm breath, something he said or the flame had suggested? She imagined the earth's ice had melted. She was far from the dome, on her back, with soil beneath her. The night was starless. Ricks of fire were burning around her. They puffed and popped, ember clouds whirling. And as the fires sensed her arousal, the clouds grew thicker.

Rin felt for Dorner's waist and loins, wanting him near. But she kept her eyes closed, too enchanted to let the imagining go. The embers were whirling like a horde of insects. They were darting, stinging her face and chest. She kept her mouth closed. If one got in, it would burn her insides.

She parted her lids. The flame's magnified shadows flickered on the walls and ceiling like incoming waves. As she closed her eyes, something made her gasp. The ember cloud was suddenly thicker. A thousand hot pins were pricking her skin. Without thinking, she opened her mouth and breathed the broth in. Her throat, her chest— The bright flies were in her head, weaving dizzying patterns. Their glowing flight paths were interlaced loops and molten wires.

Her chest was slick, her thighs so slippery they could no longer clasp. She opened her eyes. The flame's shadows seemed to be mounting, and she was sinking beneath them. Dorner was lifting her, rolling her onto her side. The embers were buzzing and stinging now, calling her back. She closed her eyes and rejoined them. They'd infested her body. They'd filled her head with luminous webs.

Rin began to shudder. Her center convulsed. A sound came from her lips that she'd never heard. Heat, heat on her back— Her body clenched and erupted; and—all at once— the flies were released.

Shock. Fear. The end of time. She was with the flies, her transmuted essence growing larger and larger—glittering, sublime. Ravishing. Beatific. Infinite.

Slowly, the winking swarm dispersed.

Rin lay still for what seemed a long while.

That's what love is. The thought rose without prompting.

I'm a novice, she thought. *What do I know?*

She turned onto her back.

The patterns on the walls and ceiling were gone. The room was dark. Had the candle gone out? She could hear Dorner's breath.

A draft made her shiver. He felt distant.

She edged off the bed, stood and switched on the light.

Dorner was lying on his hip, gazing at her. His hand

gripped the candlestick. In the collar was a crooked stub of wax.

"I wanted you to know," he said.

"Know what?" She knelt on the bed, relieved there was no cause for concern.

"I held the flame to your back," he said.

She smiled, disbelieving. Then her smile froze.

"What have you done?" Rin stood, feeling behind her.

"At the base of your spine."

She ran her fingers down. When they reached the spot, the pain made her gasp.

Dressed for work, Rin stood before the full-length mirror in her bedroom, running the comb through her hair. Her hand halted. She peered into her eyes for a moment, set the comb aside and began stripping off her clothes.

Two days had passed since her experience with Dorner and the candle. She'd been agitated. Confused. Uncertain how to judge his words.

"I proved to myself," he said, "that I could make love to you without thinking I was burning you up."

"Did you think of YoEllis?" she asked.

"No. My fuel is for you."

Rin faced the mirror. Usually her gaze skated over the naked image. She rarely found much to admire. She counted herself attractive, but never more than that. The body, and her cold and judgmental nature, had stood between her and feminine wiles—the mysteries of expression and dress and manner that stir a man's desire. She was a model of Clemency culture: restrained. That was not the woman she had wanted to be when she was a child.

She turned her hip to the mirror, lowering her chin, letting her fingers glide over her thigh. She made a quarter turn, letting her eye drift to its corner, giving the mirror a peek at her breast.

"Rin?" Eudriss called from the kitchen. "You'll be late."

"I'm not eating," Rin called back.

Her eyes were on the elision of her waist and the arc of her midriff. She was seeing a new Rin in the silvered glass. The stiffness was gone. Something had softened and relaxed inside her. This body, that she had so long ignored—had magic. Her curves had a litheness, an irresistible grace. Dorner wanted this body. He wanted it badly.

Could feelings like this be wrong? She doubted the merit of the strictures. They'd caused so much grief for so many. Had she been a victim, without even knowing? Was it Optimal Temp that had brought so much sadness into her life? Before Dorner, she never thought about love. She had given up hope.

Rin shifted, exposing a rear quarter view, summoning the feelings that the night with Dorner released. Wonder, euphoria— The intense sensations. She wanted to feel that way again. Soon.

She turned an inch farther, and the burn came into view. *An emblem of daring*, she thought. Rin laughed. The blister was the size of her pupil, and the flesh was rosy around it. No bandage. No scar.

Dorner was right. It was nothing.

6

MONUMENTS

Rin stooped over an open suitcase on her bed, laying folded blouses inside it. By her vanity was another already packed, a basket of towels and a bulging valise. Eudriss turned from the closet, holding a dress in each hand.

"You'll want these," she said.

"They're tired," Rin told her. "I'm going to buy some new things."

"I'll enjoy seeing them," Eudriss said, "when you visit."

"Oh Mom—" Rin straightened and hugged her. "We'll be here all the time."

A month had passed since her reconciliation with Dorner. The growth of their intimacy exceeded her hopes. Her trust in him wasn't misplaced. He limited his time with Tongue, visiting her once or twice a week from his apartment. Rin didn't pry. They agreed it was better if they didn't discuss it. As for fire, Dorner was in control. He'd faced his obsession and mastered it, for the good of them both. "Fire's our ally," he said. "Fire will inspire us." And it had. Fire had changed her life.

In the market or on the tube train, strangers noticed her. Men turned to look. Leese and Firooka read the change daily. Her outlook was so much brighter. Professional achievement had earned respect for her over the years. But Dorner's devotion brought something new. Word about them had gotten around.

"Look what Leese gave me." Rin dug in the suitcase and handed her mother a teething ring.

"Rinnie—"

"It's a joke, Mom."

"It's nothing to joke about," Eudriss sighed. "It's the crowning joy. What happened to your arm?"

There was a bandage below Rin's elbow. "Accident in the lab," she said, pulling down her sleeve.

The apartment door buzzer sounded. Eudriss left Rin's room. A moment later, she returned with Dorner. He smiled and nodded at the packing, but Rin could see the gravity in his eyes. "Can we go up to the roof deck?" he said.

They were in the lift, on the way to the 40th floor. "What's wrong?" Rin asked.

Dorner shook his head.

Finally, as they ascended the stairway to the roof garden, he spoke.

"I know I promised. I said I'd keep Tongue away from you. You haven't heard a word about her." He met Rin's gaze. "I'm sorry."

He led her past plots of vegetables and around an arbor. A couple was seated at a stone table. Above them, the breeze jittered the blossoms of an old wisteria.

"I'm going to break my promise," Dorner said. "I don't have any choice."

He was headed toward the northeast corner of the building. As they approached the parapet, Patience Palisades flashed through the dome's glass. Dorner halted, set his hand on the guard rail and peered down. He motioned to Rin. She stepped beside him, leaning out, following his gaze.

Forty stories below, a woman stood on the corner, facing the windows of Rin's apartment on the 21st floor. As Rin watched, YoEllis lifted her head and stared at Dorner, putting her hand to her curls as if to arrange them.

He drew back.

"She followed me here from Planning," he said.

"She was waiting outside?"

"Somehow she got through security. She walked into my office. The wrap she's wearing—" He glanced toward the parapet. "She's naked beneath it."

He folded his arm and swung it, as if he was opening a wrap around his own body. "'For you,' she said. Maisy saw the whole thing. They called the guards, but YoEllis ran out."

"Has she ever—"

"No. She didn't want to be seen in public with me, even after her husband left. Tongue's using her." Dorner bowed his head. "Last night was terrible."

"You flew."

"No. She descended in a rage."

"The old Tongue."

Dorner faced her. "She was out of her senses. 'She's crossed the line.' That's what she said. She doesn't want us to live together."

"Jealous."

"There's no appeasing her when she's like that."

Over his shoulder, Rin could see the high-rise across the thruway. Its roof deck was covered with greenery and white umbrellas. Banners fluttered from the balconies, advertising boutiques and salons.

"I want to fly from the lab," he said. "Tonight. I want you with me. Tongue has to understand: she can't make you disappear."

Dorner was a silver projectile, shooting through space. The Soap Bubble appeared, the green scallops of the Mermaid's Wake, the Golden Cabbage— Rin was in the chamber back on earth, watching and listening. *You're here, in my heart*, he told her.

The braid of Tongue's voices was thick beside him. He had prepared himself for their fury, but the choir was pensive. Tongue missed him. She was glad he was returning.

Ahead, the Wormhole flared. *Click*, his sight blurred and refocused. The connection with Rin was cut and he was arrowing through. The fleecy walls flowed. The winds rushing with him were forceful and earnest.

As he shot from the Wormhole, the fires turned on like lights in a theater. The Ovum rumbled, its belly flashed and lightning wired down. There were halos around both of Tongue's moons, great circles of swirling mist.

"My one—"

I love you, he told her. *I can't live without you.*

"Buttering me?"

A fierce wind struck him, and the peaks of Vapos upended, canyons spilling their fires on every side. "Don't waste your breath."

It's the truth. Dorner thrashed his wings to right himself.

"I know why you're here," she sighed.

I have a life on earth, he said. *Rin's at the center of it. You have to accept her.*

"You're in too deep with me. If Rin understood, she'd run for her life."

You don't know her, Dorner replied.

"There are things you must see," Tongue said, lifting and carrying him. "Things you must know. Things I haven't shown you."

The winds hurled him into a cloudbank of churning soot. The haze choked and tumbled him along. Tongue was silent.

Then, through the hazy billows, he saw silhouettes and shadows. A ragged mountain, a narrow valley— Had he been here before?

Where am I? he thought.

"To the north," Tongue said. "About to set down."

Abruptly the air cleared. He was falling out of the cloudbank. Below, a fireless field rushed to meet him. His trunk had already shortened. His legs had reappeared. He flexed them to take the impact, and when his feet struck, his body shook. He bounced on his hip and rolled to a stop.

Dorner gathered himself and stood. The field was puddled with fuel. Embers were falling. They fizzed and spit, and as he watched, spouts of flame rose.

"Follow the path," Tongue said.

Light from the moons struck a path through the spouts.

He remembered how she'd led him to the gorge of Sealacium.

"The path is yours," Tongue told him. "You made it. You and the ones you brought with you. Follow it, Dorner. To the past and the future."

My future's on earth, he said. *With Rin.*

"Rin," she replied, "is here."

Here? Dorner turned in a circle.

"Follow the path."

Dorner edged forward, one eye on Tongue, scouting the way.

It was no random channel. In the soil, he saw prints of naked feet.

Who's been here?

"Follow the path."

The field sank and fed into a cinnamon cleft. As he approached, flames jumped the gap, and showers of sparks rained down. Then the walls of the cleft lay back, and the path angled right, winding through flesh-colored hillocks where flames wriggled like newts on fuel-drenched soil. The hillocks were swollen, and the ravines were seething, leaking oil from a myriad seams.

"You," Tongue said. "Unconsumed you."

A pool on the right was bubbling. But the one on his left was dry. Its floor was cracked and its shores were crumbling.

"There's only so much of it," Tongue said. "This place will be parched and useless one day."

He rounded a bend, heard fire huffing; then a hissing red bramble came rolling down a cobalt stream. The Ovum flashed, and bolts struck the ridges ahead.

It was a region he'd seen from the air. The hills continued to climb, rising toward a ragged mountain, its heights shrouded in smoke. The wind hurried at his back, urging him on. At the foot of the mountain was a narrow valley lit by Tongue's moons. The valley was hung with swollen lobes, gleaming with fuel. The path wound through it.

"You'll see," Tongue whispered.

As he entered the valley, an odor of roasted meat mixed with the resins. Beneath his feet, the path softened. It gave like clay. On either side, the earth looked turned and plowed, massed with clods. Coils of smoke twisted up from the tumbled ground.

"Nothing but dirt now," she said.

They weren't clods, Dorner realized.

They were curled bodies. Burnt and contorted.

Who are they? he thought. *Who did this?*

"We did," she said. "Follow the path."

The lips of the wind were greased with fuel, its breath steeped in the fumes of incinerated flesh. He recoiled, but Tongue herded the fumes around him. Dorner choked, burying his nose in the crook of his arm.

Are these people I know?

"You don't remember?" Tongue's tone was ironic.

At the head of the Charnel Valley, a horizontal slab came into view. The sight was dimly familiar, like something he'd seen in a dream.

"The anointing place," Tongue said.

The slab was twelve foot square, blackened at its center. Rusty stains radiated to the broken edges.

An altar, he thought.

"It's all coming back."

He imagined a woman on the slab, clasping the shadow of a man. She was covered with flames, naked and writhing, smokes twisting up.

"I set them on fire," Tongue said. "That's what you wanted."

Dorner shuddered. His stomach was turning.

"There's no explaining," Tongue said, "the things we've

done." Her irony was gone. Her voice lilted with sorrow.

A chill breeze blew, and the imagining faded. The Altar was empty, but its surface was littered with knobs of char.

No one sees this, he told himself. But the thought did nothing to comfort him. *Please— That's enough.*

"This is our life," Tongue said. "The one you're going to share with Rin."

I don't want to be here.

"I can't force you. Love isn't like that." Her voice was soft, almost meek. "Only desire can keep you here. There is more to see up ahead."

The path led past the Altar. Beyond, the mountain rose, its heights curtained by smoke. Broad benches ascended its flank like a crude stair.

"Follow the path," Tongue said. Her moons lit the way.

What about Rin?

"She's up ahead, with the others. Pondering your future."

That can't be true.

"I'm not going to lie," Tongue said, "to the one I love."

The wind pushed at his back, urging him forward. The moons throbbed and irised. The Ovum churned. "When you reach the Temple," Tongue said, "it will all be clear."

The wind pushed again. Dorner faced the ascending benches. Then he drew a breath and clambered onto the first tread. It was sized for a giant. As he rose, winds raveled the smoke that hid the top of the stair. A rumbling inside the Ovum, and the sky was rent by a jagged bolt. It struck the stair above him, and when the dazzle cleared, an arch of fire rose over the highest bench, scarlet and gold, with flickering pillars and glowing spans. Dorner felt the heat as the vaulting flames crackled over the entrance.

It was a welcome. Tongue was inviting him in. The arch exhausted its fuel and disappeared with a flash.

When he reached the last tread, Dorner paused, trying to see what lay beyond. The slope was dark, swimming in smoke.

There's a temple here?

"A private place. A place of secrets."

The sky went white, the mountain shook, and a bolt tore through the air, exploding before him. When his sight came back, the slope had opened around him.

It was thick with stone uprights. The bolt had lit fires among them.

Dorner stepped forward.

They might have been natural formations, extruded or eroded from the mountain rock. There was no symmetry to their arrangement—some were clustered on bluffs and shelves, others were solitary. Fires torched from their bases or darted like lizards between them.

"Your Temple," Tongue said.

As he approached a group of uprights, the Temple flames brightened and a crosswind stripped away the lingering smoke.

They were human likenesses. Statues. And they all faced Tongue. A low stratus hooded her eyes now. Her voice died back to a whisper.

"The chosen ones."

Who put these here?

"You did," Tongue said.

Their bodies were long, legs close, arms at their sides, and they were striated horizontally as if they'd been bound like mummies or strafed by storms.

"They look pleased, don't they," Tongue said.

He could see the proudness of posture. But there was tension in every one, as if they'd been lifted without warning from the traffic of life. As if they were waiting for something. He recognized one—a girl from his youth. He'd barely known her.

"You brought her to the Altar," Tongue said. "You drenched her with fuel. I lit the fire."

A few yards away, a statue stood taller than the rest. Dorner stepped closer. It was a figure of YoEllis. Her face was unlined. It had the polish of youth. She was perfectly rigid, banded like a snake. "She made you her world," Tongue said.

Flames rose around the statue's ankles, blowing up embers. It was layered with accretions, as if it had grown shell upon shell.

"The harvest of so many years," Tongue said.

Dorner peered at the moons, then crossed the slope, taking slow steps. He passed the statue of a classmate in school. Then the music teacher he'd adored. A few yards farther, a woman he'd never spoken to; but he hadn't forgotten her. At her feet, where fuel had pooled, flames licked and twisted.

"Just wishing," Tongue said.

He continued up the slope, winding through the monuments. All were women. He knew every one. A college classmate. An Archive librarian he'd met on the train. A woman he'd slept with, one he'd known briefly, one he'd only observed from a distance.

"Intimations of Tongue."

The statues stirred feelings, deep feelings. Not sensory jogs. Not words or caresses, or—for those he'd slept with—memories of release. They roused something deeper.

"I saved the moments," Tongue said.

In her wind and her voice were the yearnings of a wild Dorner. For her, he was still alive—the reckless young man whose needy eye lighted so many objects of desire, and who could only find kinship with the malformed YoEllis.

The icons lower down were drawn from his youth. Higher on the slope, the relations were recent. He saw Bez. Maisy. Leese. The waitress, Zuna. Faces and feelings, lost or achieved. Loves, real or imagined—

"No one knows you as I do," Tongue said.

The wind huffed, clearing the smoke from a rugged bluff. On it, a monument of Rin stood alone.

"There's your doctor."

Blazes rose from the statue's feet, branching up her thighs and across her middle. Dorner could feel Rin's vaunt in the breadth of her shoulders. He could see the reverence for Tongue in her face. On her breast was the flame-shaped birthmark he'd noticed the night she'd first stirred his desire. Standing by the door of her apartment—he could barely hear what she was saying.

Unbidden, another memory rose—from that same night,

after he'd returned to his apartment and fallen asleep in his bed. A strange dream, vivid as life. He'd dreamt that he was down in a narrow valley—one like the Charnel Valley—on a path like the one that led past the corpses.

A woman's voice had sounded behind him.

"I know what you want," she said.

Dorner had turned. It was Rin, naked, twenty feet away.

"I know," she had said. "Tongue told me."

Rin's body was slick with sweat, dizzying to look at. A breeze mussed her hair.

"It will be our secret," Tongue had said. "No one is watching."

Rin stepped toward him. Moonlight glinted her teeth and whet her breasts. Her eyes hinted at thoughts Tongue had planted. Dorner took her hand.

He escorted her past the corpses, feeling her warm skin against his. The Altar was hemmed with flames, like glittering brambles. As they approached, he motioned her onto it. Rin left his side, barefooting to the slab's center. The flames waved their branches around her.

Dorner leveled his hand and lowered it. Rin knelt, her gaze hanging on his.

Face the sky, Dorner had thought.

Rin did as he said.

I'm going to anoint you. Dorner spread his arms.

A gurgling mounted, and fuel bubbled around the Altar's edges. Then it was streaming toward her, finding her limbs, soaking her back.

I'll have the wind now, Dorner had said to Tongue.

A breeze whistled to life, shaking the brambles. On the flicking twigs, gold capsules popped, spraying embers like seeds. The seeds landed on Rin and burst into flames. Dorner stepped closer.

She had seemed ungainly at first, jerking as the flares hopped over her body. Then, as they joined, her movements grew fluid. Her arms waved, her legs rubbered. The heat melted her innards and bent her bones. Her spine curled, lifting her head. The blackened creature was huffing and shrilling, singing like Tongue and her flames, joining the chorus. Then her cheeks blistered, and her hair caught fire.

The sweet smoke entered his nostrils, and Rin's song ribboned into the wind.

When he looked again, her trunk was a purple knot. Above him, the Ovum flashed and bulged. A bolt reached down, striking the Altar, and everything went white. Dorner's body shook as the current went through it.

When the judder and dazzle had faded, the slab was empty. In the Charnel Valley, a plume of smoke had risen from a roasted corpse. High on the Temple, a blue flame appeared.

Here, here on this bluff— In his dream, it was a magic moment. Suddenly he was here, standing on the bluff, watching a blue flame jet from porous soil. To the glowing sleeve, the jet added particles, sintering and fusing them together. A knee-high tube, then a chest-high column as the jet fired the particles and piled them higher. Before his eyes, a statue rose, built by yearning, lasting and rare, expressly for him. Feet planted, back straight, the suggestion of arms at her sides. A glorious creation, worthy of the storm of emotion that Dorner had felt. Above the jet's tapered point, Rin's face had emerged, an image to worship, with nothing to concede to her copy on earth.

And with that, the dream ended. The memory sank, falling back into the dark well from which it had risen.

I'm glad you're here, Dorner sighed.

The statue was silent, but he could hear Rin's wind braided among her sisters. Together they paid homage to the furious mingling, sublime and interior, lit by Tongue's lightning and fed by his fuel—the majestic eroticism that inspired them all.

He looked up. Tongue's eyes were sulky, lidded by fog.

"Before she crossed the line," Tongue said.

Her scorn echoed inside him. He felt, all at once, irretrievably forlorn. Something terrible was happening. Rin was gone. And so was the world she came from. The futures he'd imagined for himself were lost and forgotten. There was nothing now but Tongue and her songs.

"The summit lies ahead," Tongue said.

The view forward was hidden by a curtain of smoke, but as Dorner watched, a squalling wind hooked it and swept it aside. Before him, another great trunk appeared, like a tree but translucent, towering into the sky.

"The Temple Trunk," Tongue said.

Its thick roots gripped the mountain's backside, and on the steep slopes, he could see the flames rushing around the tree's roots, eager to be swept up. Through the trunk's pearly bark, bundles of arteries were visible; and inside each, the fiery effluvia flowed in either direction.

Dorner turned. The Sealacium Trunk was visible to the south, and a third farther east, where converging rivers had threaded together.

"The summit," Tongue said.

Her winds nudged him. Dorner faced the incline and continued up.

The statues had vanished, the gravels were steeper, and from them knee-high fumes coiled up. As he moved, the pungent air bit his lungs.

The vista spread out: bloated peaks, sodden plains, fatty spurs and flowing canyons. Lightning fired near and far, igniting fuel wherever it touched.

"Lies, just lies: that a human womb bore you, that an old woman took you when your parents died." Tongue's voice was breathy, close to his ear. "I gave you life. I sustain you. Dorner— Nothing matters to me—nothing—but you."

He gazed at the moons. Slowly he loosened his emotional armor and let it fall. Tongue was speaking to his deepest part.

"Do you understand why," she said, "Rin can't be with us?"

She loves me as no woman on earth ever has.

"Do you think she wants to share you?"

Dorner didn't reply.

"Do you think she wants us together?" Tongue asked.

No, he sighed.

"She doesn't know who I am."

Tongue's voice was rueful, but she spoke the truth.

"Does fire afflict you? Do you hate what I do?"

No, he said.

"Do you want me out of your life?"

No— The purpose of life was to exalt Tongue, to follow her plan.

"Well then," Tongue said. "You have to choose."

He could feel the corrosive fumes in his chest. The wind chafed his back.

"It's time," she said, urging him forward.

Dorner's feet took him over the gravel, onto solid rock. The slope leveled off.

"The future," Tongue said. "Ours, together."

A ring of megaliths, tall as a man, crowned the summit. Scarves of fume were winding among them.

"The circle of fate," Tongue said. "Step inside it."

What happens here?

"A dream comes alive."

My dream or yours?

"They are one and the same."

Dorner approached the circle.

"Human trifles, withering sex— You must let go of things that aren't real."

As he passed between two standing stones, a fierce rumble sounded above him. The Ovum flashed, its belly distending, then the sky shook and lightning broomed down. Fresh fires rose around the mountain. Madder lakes, fountaining peaks, bastions dripping alizarin—

He halted in the center of the circle.

215

"My one—" Tongue was breathless.

Smoke roiled from below, drifted with cinders. The soil of the circle was pitted, and from every hole a fume twisted up.

"You won't be sorry." Tongue spoke like a child trying to please. "On earth I've brought torments. But here—"

The fumes were addling, dizzying, narcotic—

"Here, in this circle, rapture's been waiting. Without interruption, without surge or decay— When our climax starts, it will never end."

Her words razored his heart.

"I'm going to show you what love is," Tongue said.

Deafening thunder. The Ovum inflated as if it would burst, and a hundred bolts fired, all grounding at once. Vapos was caged by platinum bars, and its skies were webbed with electric nets. Ignitions sounded in an unbroken stream.

"We will burn," Tongue whispered, "till there is no fuel left."

Now? Dorner thought. She meant now.

"Is that what you want?"

"Now, now—" The voices of Vapos rose as one.

Dorner shuddered with shame. *Rin*, he thought, *Rin*— Was it this he wanted? Tongue, an endless oblivion. Burning and burning—

He begged Rin, *Forgive me.*

Then he raised his arms to Tongue and groaned his assent.

An invisible hand sealed his mouth. He could breathe, but the air was sour and chemical.

"You're mine," Tongue shrieked.

Keep me, he cried at the swimming moons. *I don't want to leave.*

But his body was fading. His vision blurred. Tongue's eyes were shrinking. And her voice, just a moment before so ardent and keen, was like the echo of a train in an underground tube.

The Trauma Ward was a melee. Leese barked at an orderly and whirled around. A rattled nurse pointed at a lime screen. Severans loomed over Dorner's body, the shock of white hair hidden by his cap. He eyed the oxygen mask and the read-out. "Silence," he demanded. Rin stood beside him. She raised Dorner's hand, tubes trailing, and kissed a spot beside the catheter.

Severans stiffened. Dorner's chest was sinking. An alarm on one of the monitors began to chirp. "His lungs are giving up."

Leese stared at her husband. Rin's lips parted.

Severans grasped a hanging syringe and depressed the plunger, sending purple fluid through one of the tubes. He watched the lime screen. Then he drew a slow breath and raised himself.

Rin looked ravaged. "Please," she whimpered.

"He's gone," Severans said.

"I need you—" Rin hunched over Dorner.

He was perfectly still. A thread of white spittle crawled down his cheek.

Then his trunk spasmed. His jaw twitched and his chest heaved. Rin gripped his hand.

"He's breathing," Severans cried. "Get him on his feet."

Two orderlies raised Dorner. Rin lifted his head, struggling for breath herself. Dorner lifted his hand and pulled off the mask.

"Not so fast," Leese protested.

Two nurses forced the mask back over his mouth. Rin pulled the catheter from Dorner's arm.

Severans straightened and his arms went slack. "Walk him," he said.

The woolly twilight was smeared with orange and red. A face rippled through the smears. What was her name? He'd burnt her on the Altar and erected a monument to her. She was wearing a cap. Her blonde locks fell from beneath it, spilling over her shoulder.

"Dorner. Look at me."

He turned toward the voice. The model for the statue of Rin was beside him. Her words came and went. The rumble of thunder echoed in his ears, drowning her out.

"Where are you?" Rin said.

Clouds of soot shifted. Through the paling haze, he saw a corridor. He was shambling down it. Lights grew brighter and brighter. *The hospital*, he thought. *Clemency. The remnants of humankind.* A bitter memory from a past life.

A wall to the right was transparent. Rows of incubators held organs and body parts in fluid suspension. Hearts, lungs, forearms with hands. Rin was holding him up. So was Leese.

A woman in street clothes was approaching, walking with a limp. She squinted at Dorner and slowed, eyes glassy. And then—the brazen stare.

"You remember me," Rin said gently.

He halted and stared at her. Then he raised his hands, parted her top and lowered her chemise, finding the birthmark.

"You brought me back," Dorner said. His tone was harsh.

"What has Tongue done?" Rin whispered, hurt and confused.

Dorner looked wretched, inconsolable.

"You called my name," Rin said. "Again and again."

He was silent.

Leese waited, eyeing Rin as if her old friend was someone she no longer knew.

The lift descended the shaft. Rin stood beside Dorner, brushing lint from his morning coat. "I'm going to do a scan tonight," she said, combing his hair with her fingers.

Dorner didn't respond.

"If I have time, I'll go see Mom." She sighed. "I need some fresh clothes."

After his release from the hospital, Rin had escorted him back to his apartment. She'd stayed there with him, and they were in the fourth day. His lucidity had returned, but he was still hard to reach, unwilling to reveal the reason for his malaise or to talk about what had happened with Tongue.

On the ground floor, Rin accompanied him to the super's door and knocked.

Minole appeared and held out a sandwich. "Squid," she smiled.

Rin thanked her, took the sandwich, slid it into Dorner's coat pocket and accompanied him through the front door, onto the stoop.

Dorner patted Franklin's shoulder. Franklin saluted him. Then Dorner kissed Rin and descended the stair.

"Fine boy," Franklin said.

Rin nodded, watching Dorner start along the thruway. At the corner, he stopped, reached into his pocket, pulled out the sandwich and dropped it in a trash bin.

She returned through the lobby and stepped into the lift. As the door closed, she slapped the green sensor. Then a storm broke inside her, and she was beating at the walls and door with her fists.

⌢

"The flights have cost you." Rin peered into Dorner's eyes. "Vapos is changing."

They stood in the viewing room of her lab, facing the same large screen on which Dorner had first seen Tongue. Rin was in her lab coat, Dorner in tunic and pants.

The screen blinked on, and a familiar image appeared: Tongue's twin moons, her Ovum and trunks. As Dorner watched, Rin zoomed in on a spot beside one of the trunks. It was rippled and threaded, pink and gold.

"This is how this bit of tissue looked the first time we scanned it," she said.

The screen image changed. It was the same perspective and zoom, but the spot near the trunk was flat and gray.

"And this is what it looked like ten minutes ago. That's necrosis."

Dorner stared at the spot.

"Tongue is spending you like there's no tomorrow," Rin said.

"You're trying to frighten me."

A doctor and two technicians were studying a screen image ten feet away. Firooka stood behind Rin, waiting.

"*I'm* frightened," Rin said.

"I can't help that."

He seemed to look through her.

"What happened?" Rin grabbed his arms. "Why won't you tell me?"

Dorner shook his head.

"Did you talk about us?" she pressed him.

Others in the viewing room had turned to watch.

"Go change," Rin said, pushing him away.

As Dorner retreated, Firooka stepped forward.

"I'm not going to be a part of this," Firooka said.

"Part of what?" Rin glared.

Firooka stood her ground. "You missed surgery yesterday, and two straddles this morning. That's six no-shows in three days."

"Is that all?"

"Maybe it's time we put a spider on *you*," Firooka said.

Rin raised her arm and brought it around, slapping the nurse in the face.

Firooka straightened, palm to her cheek, staring at Rin with disbelief. Vexations, managed for so many years by humor and disregard, boiled to the surface. Firooka nodded to herself, switched the viewing screen off and strode away.

The conflict with her nurse sobered Rin. When Dorner left for Planning, she forced him out of her thoughts, following her schedule for the rest of the day. On the tube train back to his apartment, she talked to herself. Their bond was strong. His desire for her wasn't gone. *He'll find his way back to me*, she thought as she exited the lift on the fourth floor.

But as she stepped down the hall, she feared something was wrong.

The apartment door was open. She could hear a hissing.

She entered, looking around the front room. The shower was running.

That relieved her. But when she stepped into the bedroom, her fear returned. The bathroom doorway was open, and billows of steam were rolling through it.

"Dorner?"

No response.

Rin barged through the steam, waving her arms to clear it. Dorner was crouched in a corner of the stall, naked beneath the scalding spray, his head in his hands. Rin thrust her arm through the boiling drip and turned off the tap. Then she stepped into the stall and lowered herself, huddling beside him. Dorner raised his head. His eyes were closed. He leaned toward her. She put her arms around him.

"I'm sorry," he said. "I thought I could control her."

"You can. I know you can."

"She's too powerful," Dorner said.

Rin kissed his brow. "Tell me. What happened on Vapos?"

In a halting voice, riddled with self-reproach, Dorner told her about the Charnel Valley, the Altar, the mountain Temple and the monuments he'd erected with Tongue.

"Is there a statue of me?"

Dorner nodded.

"That's an honor." She put her hand on his knee. "I suppose."

"On the summit of the mountain, above the statues, there's a circle of stones. Tongue wants to end things there."

Rin held him tightly. The steam was clearing. "She told you that?"

"Lightning, explosions— Flames everywhere. It wasn't going to stop." Dorner's lips moved silently. "She wants to burn with me, until there's nothing left."

He shuddered.

Rin shuddered with him and shut her eyes. The water was

223

soaking through her. The fate Tongue envisioned etched itself in her mind.

Dorner shook in her arms. A sob rose in his throat. "When I called your name, I was saying goodbye."

She held onto him.

"What Tongue wants," he sighed. "I want it too. I've been hers all my life. I'm not going to change."

His words echoed in the shower stall.

No, Rin rocked against him. *Please*—

"You'll find someone better," he said. "Tongue and I will go our own way. Fire is our fate."

/⁊

Rin was in her bedroom, standing before the mirror. A knock sounded at the door.

"Yes, Mom."

Eudriss stepped forward with a cooking mitt on one hand. "It's ready." And then, "I miss our time together."

"I do too."

"Anja's out with Rufus tonight. Will Dorner be joining us?"

"No. He's busy."

Eudriss gazed at Rin's bed. The two suitcases and the bulging valise were where Rin had left them days before. "Are things alright—"

"It's nothing," Rin said. "We've both been distracted."

"Leese called me yesterday. It was a . . . strange conversation."

"You may as well know, Mom. The friendship is fading."

"What's that mark on your thigh?"

Rin didn't respond.

"I noticed it," Eudriss said, "when you put the roast in the niche."

"I had an accident," Rin said.

"Another one."

Rin turned with a snarl, and the bandage at the base of her neck rose above her collar. Eudriss put her hand to her mouth.

"It's not your affair," Rin said.

Pain rose in the old woman's eyes. "Please, Rinnie. Tell me."

Rin glanced at the mirror. What could she say? She was in a different life. The night before, she hadn't gotten any sleep. After the bout of passion, Dorner dropped off. She squirmed against him, trying to feel close, but she could smell Tongue's smoke in his hair. Was he dreaming about her? Had he already flown? Was he with her, at that very moment? *I'm not going to lose you*, she had thought. Then she was talking to Tongue. *You're not going to frighten me or drive me away.*

"It's Dorner," Eudriss said. "Isn't it."

Rin shook her head.

"Love keeps you with a man," Eudriss said.

Rin felt her mother's hand on her shoulder.

"And so does forgiveness," Eudriss went on. "But there have to be limits."

"Stop."

"Sweetheart—"

"I said stop." She pushed her mother's hand away.

"It happens to women," Eudriss said. "They fall for a man and give up everything to hold onto him."

"Stop," Rin screamed.

The old woman's eyes were wide.

"I'm not going to listen to this," Rin said.

Eudriss put her hands to her temples. "What has he done to you."

Rin grabbed a jar from her vanity and hurled it at the glass.

A yelp came from the doorway. Tad stood there, peering from one to the other, waggling his hands.

"We're fine," Rin assured him. "I'm a woman now," she said, facing her mother, speaking in a measured voice. "Try and accept that."

"Take care of my child," Eudriss begged.

Rin saw her mother as she never had before. The accordion throat, her straggling gray locks, the careworn eyes and a roast in the niche.

"Eat by yourself," Rin said. She grabbed one of her suitcases, stepped past Tad and hurried for the door.

The next morning, when Dorner rose, Rin was binding up her hair.

"We're going somewhere," she said.

He showered, but left himself unshaven. When he emerged from the bathroom, Rin was in black. It wasn't mourning attire—the dress was short and form-fitting. She put on a hat, black as well, with a bowler crown.

"Fasten me," she said, turning her back to him.

Dorner found the snap button, regarded it for a moment and pinched it closed.

"Do you think about death?" Rin said.

"Sometimes." Dorner reached for his shirt.

Rin watched him put it on. "I'm fond of that," she said, eyeing the Guardian pin.

It was a strange tableau. They were walking the strandline at Tropica Bay, barefoot. Dorner was holding their shoes. Rin was a few feet ahead with her eyes closed and her arms spread. Air exchangers blew a gentle breeze, and the waves from the automated generator were rolling in.

Dorner watched her, feeling the sand beneath his feet, wondering. She hadn't shared her reasons for coming, but he knew the beach was where the "famous picture" was taken, the one she and Eudriss had shown him the night he first entered their home.

"I'm here," Rin sighed.

Had she come to commune with her father's ghost?

She began to cry. He hurried beside her.

Rin opened her eyes and faced him. "I've done this before," she said, removing her hat. "I always imagined he was expecting me."

He dropped the shoes and circled her with his arms. Their noses touched, and the breeze made a cove of her hair.

"When I met you," Rin said, "I was still a little girl—"

He kissed her tears.

"A worshipful girl," Rin said, "with a perfect father."

He put his hands on her waist, feeling the constriction of the black fabric.

"It was all a fantasy," Rin said. "The Myth of the Perfect Family." Her dark eyes probed his. "I never knew why she desired Dad. Or what kind of man he really was.

"When they had 'private time,' I put my pillow over my head. She cried out. Sometimes she sounded like she was choking. A child is frightened by things like that."

Dorner heard the bewilderment in her voice.

"Secrets," she said. "The ones it takes a straddle to see— They had them too."

"Why are we here?" he said gently, thinking he knew.

"I wanted to be his little girl," Rin said, "one last time."

From the beach, they followed the East Rim trail, ascending the slope overlooking the Bay. Beyond the dome's glass, seals barked and basked on the bergs floating past. The slope was thick with tube flowers, and Chilean firecrowns flashed among them. Two Kiribati families were picnicking beside the trail. They recognized Dorner and waved. He waved back, as if nothing had changed. As the trail turned, a gazebo appeared. A young couple left the view balcony and ambled away.

Rin took Dorner's hand and led him to it.

This was planned, he thought. They were there for a purpose.

She gazed at the view and turned.

"I know who I am," Rin said. "And I know what I want."

Dorner stroked the air an inch from her cheek.

"I'm not going to share you with Tongue," she said. "If things are going to end, they're going to end with me."

"You don't know what you're saying."

Rin's eyes were black and hard. "I know exactly."

Dorner turned away. Her hands gripped his shirt front and wrenched him back.

"I'm going to make you feel," she said, "what you feel with her. And I want what Tongue feels—for myself. I want fire. With you. Not the little flames we've been playing with. Real fire. I want a burn. A real burn. Close to my heart."

"I'm not going to do that." Dorner pulled her hands from him.

"It's what I want."

"Like YoEllis."

Rin struck his face. "How dare you."

"I'm sorry."

"Is that how you feel about me?"

"Of course not," he said. His hand brushed her hip. The other touched a seam on her bust. The tight dress had drawn a red line across it.

On the trail, people passed. A child spotted Dorner, and a group of them chattered and pointed. Their parents silenced them and shooed them ahead.

"You belong here," he said. "I don't."

"I spoke at a seminar yesterday. You know what I thought? 'Why do you bother? You hate living in this test tube. You're just playing along.'"

"We've gone far enough," he implored her.

"We all turn into ash." Rin's lips were trembling. "We all have to say goodbye—"

"Tongue owns me," he said.

"I'm better than Tongue."

Rin seemed to grow as he watched.

"And I love you more," Rin said.

Was that true? he wondered.

"I need your fire, Dorner. And I have—" Rin put her hand over her heart. "A Vapos of my own."

He looked into her eyes. "There's a place we can go."

7
LIZARD SOUL

It was late at night, and a faulty fountain had flooded its catch basin. Dorner led Rin around the spreading pool, down a causeway lit blue-green by algal lamps. Rin gazed down the deserted street, then up at the ranks of darkened windows on either side. Her heels clicked on the paving. As they passed a tree, a gibbon sleeping on a low branch opened one eye. An embankment appeared between two buildings. She remembered the entrance from their visit to the aquaponic farm. That had been a minor infraction. This was serious.

They approached the embankment. Dorner swiped the mole on his wrist past a sensor, and a large hatch slid open. She followed him into the dim passage.

He paused to look and listen. A faint hum echoed between the walls. The air was warm and humid. He continued forward, following the passage till they reached a cylindrical lift. He motioned her in, tapped a glass panel and the lift descended.

Rin watched the sublevel indicator panel, listening to the winch growl, trying to stiffen her resolve, wishing she didn't feel such peril.

The lift stopped, and the door opened to a corridor tube. It was ovoid in the vertical, just tall enough to stand. Dorner took her hand. A reassuring squeeze steadied her, and she stepped out of the lift. Then he let go and started down the corridor. She followed, eyes on his back.

The tube was suspended, and on the left, it was lined with portholes. They were dark. Dorner's steps rusked the metal floor. Mingled with the foot sounds, Rin could hear the *shoof* of combustion. Without warning, Dorner slowed. Was there someone in the tube ahead? She could sense his wariness. Then his pace resumed.

Reflected fire blazed on Dorner's coat. Through the portholes, Rin saw flashes through the dimness. And then the combustion arena and its vertical rivers of flame appeared. It was like a giant pipe organ in the throne room of hell. Cylindrical stoves, forty feet tall, were clustered together. Each stove had many grates, stacked at equal intervals; and on the grates, blocks of frozen methane burned. Rivers of fire snaked up the pipes, connecting with flames above and below. Where the rivers met, roiling together, fireballs detached—blue, purple and topaz—expanding and bursting as they floated free.

Inside, the cylinders were blackened with soot, but their silver exteriors gleamed, as did the igniters at the base of each, with their lush manifolds and arrowhead valves. On every side, cranes moved fresh blocks of methane onto the grates. Between the roar of flames, the grumble of cranes, the snap of igniters and the shrieks from heating and cooling stoves, the noise in the arena matched the violence of the sights.

The air around the pipes was warped by heat. Rin could feel it radiating from the tube walls. She could see the full extent of the level now. Through the sinuous miasma, the hive seemed endless. The gleaming stacks covered more than an acre, and over them all was an enormous hood. Higher, a jungle of tarnished ducts elbowed and angled into the darkness. Robot leak detectors crawled among them like bugs.

Dorner had slowed. The tube was turning, and he was peering around the bend. A connecting tube branched to the right. He clasped her hand and hurried her into it. Twenty feet along, the stub tube ended at a small door. He lifted the lever-latch and pulled her inside.

The maintenance cell was small, fifteen feet square, lit and comfortably warm. One wall was a sheer pane of glass facing the arena. On a side wall, heatsuits hung, wrinkled and grimy. The rear was benched and shelved, crowded with tools, damaged parts and metal subassemblies, scorched and oily.

Rin was breathless, excited but fearful.

"Are you okay?" Dorner said.

She nodded.

He unfastened his coat. "I talked about doing this with YoEllis. But I never had the nerve."

Rin turned her back to him.

Dorner took her arm and brought her around. "I'm sorry."

After a moment of silence, he removed his clothes. Then he removed hers.

Dorner averted his gaze. Rin opened her hand to shield her breast. It was as if they were strangers. *He's seeing a different woman*, she thought. And it seemed there was a different man before her, one who'd been hidden inside the Dorner she knew.

She turned to where the heatsuits hung and ran her fingers down a scorched bib, picking up soot. Then she approached the window wall. Using it as a mirror, she drew black rays around her eyes and scaled her cheeks. Dorner was watching. "I'm going to do this," she told his reflection.

This. A new threshold. A new understanding of fire. And a new connection with Dorner, one she had never felt. Was it crazy to think this bold act would free them? No, that's why they were here.

In the glass wall's reflection, she could see him moving toward the bench at the rear. He retrieved something and came forward again. She followed his movements like a zookeeper in a cage with a dangerous animal. He set the object on the metal table beside her.

It was an eight-inch canister with a burnished handle, and a blackened flash-fork angling from its top.

He stood behind her now, facing the raging furnaces with her.

Rin closed her eyes. She had imagined Tongue's flames in aching detail, made believe they were hers in Dorner's em-

brace. She had aped Tongue's allure, felt Tongue's strength—
She reached for those memories, then she stopped herself.

It's time, she thought, *to summon my own demons.*

She felt Dorner clasp her hand and guide it to the scar on his hip. She could feel alligator skin. Then she heard the organ pipes roaring, and the alligator was gliding down the bank, into the pool.

As their rhythm began, she opened her eyes to the spectacle blazing through the window. A block of methane was burning on a nearby grate, icy on its face and purplish at its base, where ignition made it bubble. As she watched, its top exploded and a snake of flame reared, reaching the next higher grate, touching off a second eruption. That snake rose too, higher in the pipe, to the next grate and the next.

Beneath her feet, the floor shook. Heat flooded her middle and surged through her limbs. In the window, her body seemed caught in the fiery net as it shifted and stretched. The rivers were gleaming and roaring. They flowed with a liberty she'd never felt.

Fury, in her chest. Her breath was rushing and shrill. *Bolder*, she thought. Rin gasped and swore. She turned to face Dorner, mounted him and closed her jaws on his cheek. Could he take her weight? Would she break his back? There was blood in her mouth. The fire was inside her— Once it was loose, you didn't control it. You trusted its greed. Behind her, the net of flames flashed. And then, it seemed, it peeled from the window and fell over them both.

When she bit his face, Dorner recoiled. Rin's head was

jerking as if something had hold of her chin. Her eyes were wide, her lips bloody. Her sucking breaths swelled her chest, and her body shook. Seasoned with dread, his ardor mounted.

He imagined the room was leaking. The ceiling was drizzling, and the floor was pooled. The walls were porous and beaded with fuel, and the air of the cell was choked with resin. Rin's skin was slick, her thighs so oily his hands couldn't grip them. Her hair was drenched and so was his. *We'll burn*, he thought. *That's what she wants.* Rin bucked, and the fire inside her threw sparks from her eyes and lips; and wherever sparks landed, flames flapped up. His chest grew fur, scarlet and gold. The thrills mounted, and along with them—fear.

Fear for himself, and fear for her.

Flames emerged from her shoulders, circling her arms like vines. They pierced her sternum and pushed out of her neck. A crimson tongue wickt at her navel and rose as he watched, unzipping her front. In the gleaming cavity, a knot of flame pulsed like a heart about to burst.

The time had arrived.

Dorner reached for the canister, grabbed its handle and raised it. *I can't do this*, he thought. Rin was holding her breath. Her legs and middle had started to spasm. "I want fire," she had said. "Close to my heart." *I can't*, Dorner thought. *I won't.* But he aimed the flash-fork at her side. A distant scream started from Rin's lips, mounting like an emergency van racing closer. Her lips parted, her eyes sank into pits with red coals at their bottoms—

Dorner depressed the pinch bar.

A split-second hiss of pressurized gas, a *whoosh* of blue flame, and Rin's scream reached its peak. He dropped the canister and held her close.

Rin hung suspended, the scream below her. Every nerve of the body it came from had been dissected. Fire was burning the nerves like hair, melting and twisting them. She was free of that body, free of death and the dome, free of the crisis of love that plagued her. She had joined a discarnate future, where fear had no meaning and everything was fire.

The breath she was holding released, and she descended slowly. Her burnt body welcomed her back with convulsive weeping.

Dorner held her close.

"Brave," he whispered. "So brave."

"You see," she sobbed. "You see—"

"I see," Dorner said.

"You won't leave me."

"Never," he said.

"No matter what she does. Swear. We'll face her together."

"I swear. Tongue will never come between us again." His voice broke.

She kissed the scar on his shoulder. "You're a beast," she said. She put her finger on the webbed flesh of his chest and followed his midline down to his groin. The creature that had so often thrilled and frightened her was soft, like the puddled wax of a candle.

"You didn't climax."

Dorner shook his head.

Rin lifted her shoulders and groaned. "I can feel it now."

The latch clicked and the door of the maintenance cell opened.

A man in a blue uniform and a visor hat stood in the doorway, drawing a weapon from his belt.

Dorner rose, holding his hands in the air. "We're harmless."

The guard's lips parted. There was shock in his eyes. Dorner noticed his cracked incisor.

"Kenton?" he said. "Is it you?"

The blaster Dorner had saved from the Ibarra collapse seemed too shaken to answer. He turned to Rin.

She was on her knees, trying to cover herself with clothing. Dorner wondered what Kenton had seen through the window.

"Please," Dorner said. "Put that away."

Kenton holstered his weapon, eyes still on Rin. Her head was turned down and hair draped her face. She had drawn Dorner's shirt over her side, but Kenton seemed to see through it.

"I'll call an emergency van." He focused on his Joinspace.

Dorner grasped Kenton's arm. "She'll be fine," he said gently.

Kenton peered at him. "Why are you here?"

"That's hard to explain."

Kenton swallowed, looking down at the canister.

Rin stood, hiding her face and her burn.

"It's not as bad as it may have looked," Dorner said.

Kenton didn't reply.

"Let's keep this between us," Dorner said.

Kenton's face was ashen.

"Alright?" Dorner said.

Kenton nodded slowly.

"Let's go," Dorner said to Rin. Then to Kenton, "Will you wait outside?"

Kenton drew a breath, turned and exited the cell.

Dorner helped Rin into her clothes and put on his own. As they emerged, he saw Kenton had posted himself by the entrance. Kenton saluted.

Dorner hurried Rin back down the tube.

When they'd disappeared around the bend, Kenton sighed and removed his hat. He wiped the sweat from his brow and stepped into the cell. The canister was on the floor where Dorner had left it. Two inches away, was a collar pin with the letters "GD." It glittered in the shifting light of the furnace fires.

As they exited the hatch and stepped into the night, Rin groaned again and grabbed Dorner's arm. "I want to go to the hospital."

"I know what to do," he said. "And you're a doctor."

They started down the causeway.

"Fire lives for itself," he said. "Fire has no regrets."

The words sounded pompous and false in his ears.

"I feel sick," Rin told him. "And ashamed."

"I understand." He held her close, avoiding pressure on her burnt side.

A grumble of thunder reached him. The darkness above the dome was lit by a stuttering flash.

A hundred feet ahead, a woman stood in the blue-green pool of a lamp. She wore a long skirt and a sweater hood. She was holding what looked like a large purse at her side. Dorner was instantly wary. Rin stared at the paving, in an awkward shuffle, nursing her pain. As they drew near the woman, she turned to face them and pulled the hood back. Dorner saw the cracked lips and wasp nest of hair. He halted. Rin raised her head.

"What are you doing here?" Dorner said.

"How could you," YoEllis answered. She looked worn, as if she'd gone days without sleep. There was grime on her cheek.

Despite himself, Dorner reached to wipe away the grime.

YoEllis shrank from his touch, turning to Rin, brow waxen, her eye unwavering, like the light on the prow of an icebreaker leagues away.

"You want fire?" YoEllis said, swinging her purse.

But the purse was a bucket, and as she brought it around, liquid flew out, drenching Rin's face.

Dorner grabbed Rin. The bucket *clanged* on the paving, then the odor of stove oil reached his nose. He turned to see YoEllis waving a trigger stick, snapping sparks at Rin, trying to ignite her. The air crackled and popped. Dorner hurled himself, driving her back. The trigger stick fell from her hand.

YoEllis tottered, then she began to sob. Her whole body shook.

Dorner gazed at her, speechless.

YoEllis hid her face, then she wheeled and hurried down the causeway.

When Dorner stepped toward Rin, she was crying too. Softly, to herself.

The surgical floodlights were hot. A masked nurse dabbed the sweat from Rin's face. Rin's gloved hand was on the patient's neck. The other was slicked with blood, and the two first fingers were in the man's head. Rin straightened, trying to take pressure off her side. She'd risen that morning unsure if she could make it to work. A pill and some ointment had dulled the pain. But it wasn't the burn that troubled her most. She was sure she would see YoEllis again.

A nurse handed a scalpel to her. "Tighten that retractor," she ordered another. As the tissues spread before her, Rin lowered the blade.

"Fool," a voice said. The tone was malignant.

Rin looked up. The eyes around the operating table were all intent. Rin sensed no distraction in any of them. She looked down, focused on the patient and made the incision.

"I'm talking to you," the malignant voice said.

Rin recognized the voice.

"You're simple," Tongue hissed. "Artless. Weak. You'll do anything to keep him." She was smoking with envy.

I'm exhausted, Rin thought. *I haven't had enough sleep.*

"Do you think he won't abandon you?" Tongue said. "You've been deceived."

This isn't happening.

"Dorner doesn't have to listen to me," Tongue said. "He can shut me out whenever he likes. But he hasn't, he won't. He loves the sound of my voice."

"Is something wrong?" one of the doctors asked.

"Mind the drainers," Rin snapped.

She raised the scalpel.

"It's Tongue he loves," Tongue whispered. "When Dorner's inside you, he's thinking of me."

Leave me alone, Rin thought. She was losing her grip. Tongue was in Dorner's head. She was part of his psyche.

"You're going to pay," Tongue said.

I hate you. Rin shuddered from head to foot.

Above the masks and beneath the caps, eyes were watching.

"Dorner will forget you," Tongue said. "But I won't. I won't forget."

The scalpel fell to the floor. "I'm not feeling well," Rin said. "Finish this for me."

She backed away from the operating table and peeled off her gloves. Then she hurried through the door and down the hospital corridor.

She turned into a washroom. It was empty. Rin stumbled to a sink and hung over it, trying to recover her breath. Tongue was silent. *A moment*, she thought. *A moment of madness.*

She drew the tube of ointment from her pocket and set it

on the counter. Was Tongue about to return? She could feel her presence. She could hear Tongue's breath. Or was it her own?

Rin stripped off her bloody scrubs and chemise, eyeing the burn in the mirror. It spanned the left side of her ribcage, tapering to her hip. The flesh was red—swollen and raised. She put her fingers to it, feeling the heat. She was applying the ointment when Tongue spoke again.

"You've been looking for fire," she said. "Now you've found it."

Silence.

And then voices seemed to rise at a distance. Rin had heard the singing inside Dorner's head. And now, as she listened, Tongue and her choir began to sing to her.

"Snarls of fire," Tongue chanted, "sun soot rolling." Her voice had a wheedling insinuation. "A lizard soul in there. From scaly lips—"

Rin turned on the tap and splashed cold water in her face. The choir mounted, enlarging their mistress. Rin shivered and scrubbed, trying to wash Tongue away. But Tongue wouldn't go. Her words were enticing and intimate, as if Tongue had reserved some ugly fate especially for her.

"Now you dream, but so unprepared."

On a river of sound, Tongue would carry her away.

"Head on a pyre and growing. Look in my eyes and you're knowing."

In the mirror, Rin saw a ghost, a homeless spirit.

No spider, no straddle, no Joinspace— Tongue was no longer a phantom in Dorner's mind. Somehow she'd crossed over.

Dorner exited Planning headquarters at a run and started around the Hub. Rin had left the hospital and was doing the same. He saw her jostling through strollers, reeling and crying, hands cupped over her ears. She threw herself into his arms, jerking like a bird in a storm, directionless, beating one way, then doubling back. He held her tightly, ignoring the gawkers. Then he circled her waist and led her up the steps of the Academy.

They crossed the lobby and entered a lift. He embraced her again as the lift rose. The floor numbers climbed on the illuminated panel. By the time they reached the 40th floor, her sobs were subsiding.

"Is she gone?" Dorner said, stroking her head.

Rin nodded.

The lift door opened. He took her hand and led her out.

The top floor of the Academy was the Study Deck, a retreat for students. It was massed with alcoves, polycrete cocoons where singles and couples sat quietly, reading, talking, or mingling in Joinspace. Alcoves lining the parapets had views of Clemency and the icefields beyond. With her hand in his, Dorner headed for a spot facing north and west, away from the hospital. The apartment towers sparkled as the sun set.

Rin found her voice as they reached the parapet. "'From scaly lips,'" she shook her head, "'a river of prayer.' Do you know those words? 'Now you dream.' I could hear her, Dorner. 'Look in my eyes.' Tongue's left her hiding place."

Rin gazed over the rooftops. "She's here, in my world."

Dorner didn't interrupt her. Inside he was raging.

"She said you'd abandon me." Rin faced him.

"We can't let her divide us."

Rin drew against him.

"That first night," he said, "she knew. You were the woman I'd been looking for all my life."

She pressed her temple to his chest. "I don't care about Tongue. Or Clemency, or anything else."

Two teenagers were necking in an alcove nearby, violating the strictures. They had tired of reviewing lectures in Joinspace. They were in the black, learning the mysteries of lips and breath.

"She can't hurt us," Dorner said.

"We have each other," Rin whispered.

The breeze whisked her hair. Tongue was wrong, he thought. Rin wasn't naive. Not anymore. She knew how ruthless Tongue was.

"My future," he said, "belongs to you."

As he spoke, he could feel Tongue's grief. Vapos was dark, and her moons were hooded. They were peering at him across the vastness of space while cold winds whistled around her.

"You're saying what I want to hear," Tongue said, "but you're saying it to her."

Rin looked up at him. "Is Tongue listening?"

Dorner nodded. *I'm beyond lies,* he thought.

"You're lying to *me,*" Tongue said. "Everything about you is false."

"She's upset," he said.

Rin didn't reply, but he could see the glint in her eye.

"Marry me," he said.

"You're afraid of real love," Tongue mewled. "You're not man enough for that."

"Take me as your husband," he asked Rin again.

Rin met his gaze. "That's what I want—to be your wife."

As he kissed her, the alcove lights came on. The pink glow from the clustered cocoons was like a vision of a blissful brain.

Rin put her lips to Dorner's left ear. "You've lost him," she said.

Dorner woke in the middle of the night.

He rose on his elbow and saw Rin sleeping beside him. They were in his bedroom. But something was very wrong. His head ached and his ears were ringing. He was hot. His face was sopping. Rin jerked, startling him. She was asleep, but her shoulders were twitching. When he touched her cheek, it felt like his—hot and damp.

He stood and stepped toward the bathroom. It was only a dozen feet away, but as he moved, the door retreated. The floor stretched beneath him. It became a dark street. Dark and long, with algal lamps lighting the way. He passed beneath footbridges, lacy spans and winding catwalks, webbed and crawling with serpentine designs. Finally the door was in reach, but as he put his hand on the knob, he realized it wasn't his bathroom door. It was a different size and a different color. It was the door to the bathroom in Rin's apartment.

He turned the knob and opened it slowly.

Eudriss was standing in her nightgown, regarding herself in the mirror. She seemed not to notice him. She stroked her face, examining it closely. She seemed pleased with what she saw.

Dorner heard a scratching, then a high-pitched squeal. The noises were coming from the bathroom's outside window. Through it, he could see the dim shadow of the building across the street. Eudriss turned toward the window. She seemed unalarmed. Dorner could see her reflection in the mirror. Her look was expectant.

A sooty fist appeared on the other side of the window, floating in the dimness, knuckles toward him. It rapped on the pane.

Impossible, Dorner thought. They were on the 21st floor.

"Come in," Eudriss said. Her tone was inviting.

The sooty fist rapped. It rapped again.

Eudriss watched and waited, knitting her fingers, looking impatient.

The fist rapped harder and the pane cracked. Through the spidered glass, an eye appeared. A man's head, bigger than life, filled the window. He was wearing a black mask. In the mirror, Dorner saw Eudriss smile. Her eyes glittered.

Eudriss cried out, and the window glass fell to fragments on the tile floor. A blast reached through the window frame as the light popped out.

Dorner heard a grunt and a whine. The wind huffed in the

247

darkened bathroom as if trapped and mad to get out. Where was the man? And Eudriss— Dorner couldn't see a thing.

Someone buzzed the apartment's front door. Dorner turned. Over the sound of the wind in the bathroom, he could hear the front door open.

"Mom?" Rin called out.

Steps crossed the front room and started down the hall. Ponderous thuds, like a labored pulse. As Dorner listened, the steps grew louder. In the bathroom, mingled with the wind, came the sound of a choir: the singing of flames, the voices of Vapos. The steps grew louder and louder. The wind mounted and the choir swelled.

An ear-splitting *click*, and a lane of light beamed down the endless hall.

"Mom?"

Rin was approaching.

The hall light lit the bathroom now, and when Dorner looked, what he saw stopped his heart.

Eudriss was on the tile floor, and the man was on top of her. He was naked, black and red from head to foot. His body was charred, and the split flesh leaking. His mask was still on. His ravaged face couldn't be seen, but his blackened jaw hung and waggled beneath.

Beneath the man's threatening grunts, Dorner could hear Eudriss whimpering.

He threw the door wide and lunged, knees banging onto the tiles, grabbing the assailant's shoulders. Pieces of the man's burnt back came away in his hands. The monster, mad with lust, seemed not to notice. He'd torn the old woman's night-gown open and was between her thighs. Dorner circled the charred torso and tugged. He could see Eudriss on the grid of white tile. Her eyes were closed and her head was rocking, pancake breasts jerking from side to side.

"Get off her," Dorner raged, heaving to free Eudriss from the bucking man.

The attacker paid him no heed. But Eudriss opened her eyes.

She glared at Dorner, then she raised her hand, touching the monster's mask, lifting it with her fingers. She gazed at the grisly face with fondness and caressed his blackened cheek.

"What's going on?" Rin's voice sounded through the doorway.

The charred man halted abruptly.

Dorner turned, seeing Rin standing there naked, peering at the three of them embroiled on the bathroom floor.

The charred man faced Rin. He grinned. His dripping cheek twitched, then he turned back to Eudriss, grasped her neck with both hands and began to squeeze.

Rin screamed.

∕∩

The scream echoed in Dorner's head, while he twisted and flailed above the Clemency thruways with the wind rushing around him. He flew through the wall of his apartment and landed, sprawled across his bed.

Dorner gasped and raised himself.

The lamp on the nightstand was on. Rin was hunched beside it, speaking over her signaler. Her voice was clipped. Urgent.

"In five minutes," she said. "I'll call for a van."

Fear tugged at Dorner like the undertow in LaBerge inlet.

"It's Mom," Rin said, disconnecting. "Rawji's with her."

Her eyes shifted with bewilderment. And then, as Dorner watched, they were drowned by some terrifying surmise.

"I had a dream," she said, searching his face.

"You were in your apartment," he guessed.

"It was a dream," she murmured, shaking her head.

"I was in it," Dorner said.

He rose and pulled on his pants.

She sat there motionless, staring at him.

"Rin— One of us better call the hospital for an emergency van."

When they arrived, the van was out front. On the 21st floor, the apartment door was open. Rawji was in the front room, holding Tad. Tad saw Dorner and squalled. Dorner took him into his arms.

The medics were in the dining room. Eudriss was on a stretcher.

Rin hurried to her mother. "What is it?" she asked a medic.

"Her heart," he replied, securing the webbing over the old woman's middle.

"Mom—" Rin knelt.

Eudriss sighed. Her face was slick, her nightgown matted with sweat.

"Are you in pain?" Rin asked.

Eudriss smiled.

"She's had some kind of accident," the medic warned.

Rin stared at him, sensing the shock beneath his words.

"There are heat boils," the medic said, "all over her chest and thighs. Alright—" He motioned and they lifted the stretcher.

Rin rose. "We're coming with you."

In the van, Dorner sat beside Rin. Two medics were opposite, and the stretcher rattled between. One of the medics was attaching a monitor cuff to Eudriss' ankle. The other pushed a hypodermic needle into her arm. Rin clasped her mother's hand.

Through the van's windows, the polycrete towers were beginning to sparkle. The siren sank beneath the gibbons' morning howl.

Eudriss turned to her daughter. "Rinnie—" Her voice was hoarse and wheezy. "Where have you been?"

"I'm here, beside you," Rin said. "That's all that matters."

Eudriss noticed Dorner. "Are those poor people safe?" She worried her eyes.

"You're going to be fine," Rin said.

"Of course we are," Eudriss replied.

Dorner could see the marks on her neck.

Eudriss smiled, recalling something. "He was with me," she sighed.

Rin swallowed. Her lips parted, but nothing emerged. She turned to Dorner.

"Who was?" Dorner asked.

One of the medics leaned over Eudriss. "Are you having trouble breathing?"

"What a nice young man," she said.

"Who was with you?" Dorner asked her again.

Eudriss looked at her daughter. "Dad," she said softly. She patted Rin's knee.

Rin closed her eyes. Her frame shook, as if she was sobbing inside.

Eudriss smiled to herself. "We were having private time."

Dorner was stunned. He turned to Rin. She had clenched her fists and was forcing them between her thighs. He stooped and touched Eudriss' shoulder. "Are you sure?" he said gently.

The old woman regarded him.

"He attacked you," Dorner said.

Eudriss' eyes grew wider. She laughed. "You don't think I know my own husband?"

Dorner struggled for words. "Can you remember—"

"Please—" One of the medics held up his hand. "Let's save our breath," he suggested to Eudriss. "I'm going to give you some oxygen." He adjusted the feeder and placed a glass cup over her nose and mouth.

Dorner exhaled. Rin opened her eyes.

"She's confused," he muttered.

Rin met his gaze. "Not about that."

He frowned, shaking his head at her, puzzled by her words.

"It was Dad." Rin bowed her head. "A terrible shadow of him."

"You recognized him?"

Rin's gaze returned to the body on the stretcher.

The medics exchanged glances. One of Eudriss' arms rose, as if she was grasping for something. Then it settled back down.

"He was kind and gentle." Rin sounded helpless. "Not like that."

"No," Dorner replied. "I'm sure he wasn't."

"It was Tongue," Rin said.

The words echoed inside him.

Dorner nodded slowly. "She brought him back."

The driver of the van turned up the siren.

8

FORGIVE THIS, I WON'T

Rin and Dorner crossed the threshold of her apartment with Tad between them. They stood in the front room together, silent. Dorner's eyes were grainy, and his vision blurred. Tad whimpered and clung to his leg. The gibbon had spent the night with Rawji, but according to her, neither had slept.

Rin faced Dorner. "I had so much I wanted to tell her."

"She heard you," he said.

"I hope so." Rin eyed Tad as if he might know. "The last time her mind was clear, everything was wrong. She was worried. About my burns. I got angry." She looked at Dorner. "How could I explain?"

"You couldn't."

"She was trying to protect me," Rin said.

Her head hung, her back was bent. She looked like

something had scooped her out. "What happened last night?" she muttered.

He shook his head.

"Mom was dreaming. About Dad."

"That wasn't your dad," Dorner told her. "He was a monster sent by Tongue."

"I don't know what to believe," Rin whispered.

"Your Dad was a good man."

"Mom is gone." Rin's eyes were dark with doubt. "And it was Dad who—"

"Eudriss saw what Tongue wanted her to see. And so did we."

"I'll never forget," Rin said. "I'll never get that image out of my head. He was strangling her."

"You know why this happened." Dorner spoke softly.

Rin regarded him. "Because I said, 'yes.'"

Hatred burned in Dorner's heart. "She's not going to—"

He grabbed Rin's shoulders, but the defiance died in his throat. The threat of marriage had brought an end to Eudriss and poisoned a lifetime of memories for Rin. What would Tongue do if they actually went through with it?

Rin looked around her, gazing at the walls and furniture. "What did we bring into my home."

"You shouldn't stay here," Dorner said, lifting Tad. Dorner held him against his chest and stroked his head.

Rin looked worried. "I don't want to move him. I need to take care of Mom's affairs. We'll stay for a while."

"Do you want a bath?" Dorner asked the ape.

Tad chattered his approval.

"I can't understand." Rin's eyes sidled, checking her Joinspace.

"Nothing from Anja?"

Rin shook her head. "I've tried twenty times."

"You'll hear back this morning." Tad shifted in Dorner's arms, pretending to scrub his middle. "Let's get a soak," Dorner said, and he stepped toward the hall.

They filled the tub with hot water, and Tad floated on his back with his arms and legs spread. When he was dry, Dorner put him to bed on his pallet and turned off the light. Rin was in the bedroom. She'd collapsed in her clothing and was already asleep. Dorner left without waking her, heading back to his place to collect their things.

For long hours, he'd managed to keep his balance, but as he strode through his apartment lobby, he dashed his arm to the side, knocking over a potted plant. He reached the lift and hammered the sensor. The super's door opened. Minole stuck out her head as he boarded the lift.

He swung his apartment door open, entering his place in a rage. "Cruel—" He hurled the dining chairs at the wall, knocked over a floor lamp and stomped into the kitchen, opening the utility cupboard. "You're vile." He grabbed a claw hammer from the caddy.

Dorner strode into the bathroom. He faced the mirror, brandishing the hammer's steel at his left eye and earhole, imagining what kind of self-mutilation it would take to destroy her.

"A snap button," Tongue whispered. "Remember?"

Dorner dropped the hammer in the sink and marched to the window. He threw it open and looked down at the street.

Foolproof, he thought.

"Are we going for a ride?" Tongue sounded amused.

He forced his front through the opening, feeling the breeze in his face.

"Only four floors," Tongue said.

Four is enough. He got his waist over the sill.

"You won't die," Tongue told him. "You'll lie there on the thruway, broken and helpless. I'll be watching, enjoying the show."

He lifted one hand from the sill, teetering over the drop.

"'You've lost him,'" Tongue mimicked Rin.

A shriek sounded behind him. Dorner turned to see Minole hurrying forward, hair draggled, arms reaching. "No, no—" Her small hands clutched him, tears starting from her eyes.

Minole pulled him back over the sill. He didn't resist.

They tumbled to the floor beneath the window. The super's wife clasped him. "Dorner," she sobbed, "Dorner—"

He was limp. He began to sob with her.

"Whatever it is—" Minole shook her head.

"The woman I love—" He spoke through his tears.

"The doctor?"

"I've destroyed her mother, her family— And it's not going to end."

"That can't be," she protested. "You wouldn't do that."

He looked in her eyes. "I was going to marry her."

258

"Don't give up," Minole said.

"Giving up is just fine," Tongue whispered.

"She'll forgive you," Minole rocked him. "Whatever you've done—"

Dorner returned with two suitcases of clothing, enough to last them a couple of weeks. Rin's apartment door was ajar. He paused before it, seeing Anja through the doorway in a backless dress.

"Where were you?" Rin asked her cousin.

"With me," a male voice answered.

Dorner set the suitcases down and eased the door open.

Anja and her boyfriend Rufus were standing in the front room. She was airing herself with a satin fan. He was suited in black with a gray top hat. Dorner stepped forward, entering Anja's perfume cloud.

"Too bad," Dorner said, bowing his head.

"Too bad what?" Anja flared. Above her brow, a large curl of hair stood stiffly, the canary rocking beneath it.

"About Eudriss." Dorner glanced at Rin. "Do they know?"

"Don't know, don't care," Rufus said. "I'm hungry." He nodded to Dorner, as if that explained their visit. "Eat, eat, eat," Rufus laughed. He scanned the wall hangings and furnishings, and Rin as well, as if he intended to devour everything there.

Rin glared. "Do you have any idea—"

"He's hungry," Anja protested.

Something's wrong with Rufus, Dorner thought. The toes of his shoes were pointed and curled. The brim of his stovepipe was scorched. As if he'd heard Dorner's thoughts, Rufus unbuttoned his coat.

He was shirtless, and an ugly welt crossed his chest. A fresh burn. Rufus smiled and put his hand on Anja's hip. His eyes glittered like embers.

"I'll fix him something myself." Anja stepped toward the kitchen.

Rin barred the way. "Get out," she said, pointing at the door.

"You'd better leave," Dorner told Rufus.

"I'm never leaving," Rufus replied.

Anja scowled at Rin. "Who do you think you—"

Dorner rushed Rufus, drawing his right arm back and bringing it around.

He struck Rufus square in the chest, but his fist passed through. The black figure cracked like an egg, and Rufus' insides burst into flames.

Dorner was blinded. "Tongue," he gasped as he fell.

"Everywhere," Tongue hissed.

The flames were thick around him, like orange birds, bright and beating, snapping and sizzling, thrashing him with burning wings, their clicking claws and their clashing beaks. His face was scorched, his hands were on fire—

Rin was on her knees beside him. The flames winked out.

Dorner lurched around. Rufus and Anja were gone.

The doorway was vacant, but he could see a trail of smoke in the hall.

The memorial service was held in a theater at the Archive. The tributes were brief, but emotional. Those who spoke— Rawji, Leese and a few family friends—rose from the dais and read from their notes. At Rin's request, Dorner was on the stage beside her, and when the time came, he stood with her and escorted her to the podium.

Rin nodded to him, doing her best to smile. The guilt and despair that had nearly cast him to the street was welling inside him. They were here, grieving the passage of Eudriss, because of him.

Rin had refused to think or talk about their future. She was too upset. And there was too much fear.

She started by calling attention to what she was wearing, an ill-fitting black dress with a magenta shawl which, she explained, Eudriss had made. Her initial remembrances were muted and composed, but when she reached back to her childhood, the anecdotes brought tears to her eyes and she was forced to pause and collect herself.

Dorner's senses were keyed for signs of Tongue. He expected to hear her at any moment, to feel her winds or be scorched by her heat. Anja and Rufus weren't among those seated. In the front row, Severans had Tad on his lap. Rawji's daughter was beside them, nursing her child. Succeeding rows were full of Clemencians Eudriss had befriended or helped or worked beside over the years. Firooka sat alone at the rear of the theater with a scarf over her head. Dorner checked the wings of the stage and the double doors.

They had considered a private ceremony. At one point, Rin thought they should do nothing at all. But in the end, the sense of community, so important to Eudriss, prevailed.

"She was a mother in her soul," Rin said. "Loving and positive. Always finding a way to bind us together." She drew a breath. "Her purpose was kindly, even when she was stern."

Dorner remembered the night of the Zenith party, the moment Eudriss had squeezed his hand to welcome him back. She had been, in her way, a mother to him. The mother he'd never had. He felt regret now, for the many missed chances. He could have been closer to her. He could have— The creak of a chair. Dorner's caution returned. In the wings, a curtain was shifting.

"Mom—" Rin's tremulous voice echoed in the theater. "I know your spirit will find the peace it deserves. Our world will be so different without you."

Rin stood in the quiet with her head bowed.

At the direction of an usher, the speakers filed down from the dais, and a procession formed. It left the theater through the double doors, following a proctor along a gravel walkway by the Archive's north wall. Like all of Clemency's deceased, Eudriss had been cremated on a memorial barge in the Felosia Canal. Her ashes were put in a sealed urn. Rin carried the urn. Dorner walked beside her.

Through a polycrete arch, the steel face of the mortuary vault appeared. There were beds of flowers and butterflies on either side. The proctor approached the flank of the vault, ascended an outdoor stair and stepped along a catwalk. Rin and Dorner followed. The mourners gathered in the gardens below.

The banks of compartments were on their right.

An urgent alert appeared in Dorner's Joinspace. He turned his signaler off.

The proctor called a halt. He nodded at Rin, put his key in the scutcheon of a little door and opened it. She looked at Dorner. Then she raised the urn and slid her mother's ashes into the pigeonhole beside her father's. A moment of silence. Then the proctor closed the door.

Rivelle stood behind his desk, fists in the pockets of his blue morning coat.

"You've made a mockery," he said, "of Planning and of me."

Dorner shook his head. "How?"

"By abusing your power. By violating the strictures. In the worst way."

"What are you talking about?"

Rivelle pulled his fists out of his pockets. He opened one, and the Guardian pin rolled from his palm onto his desk.

Dorner stared at the pin, his fingers moving to his shirt collar.

"You didn't even notice it was gone," Rivelle said. "What in blazes were you and your doctor—"

"Can we keep her out of it?"

Rivelle sighed. "You're on leave, as of now."

"For how long?"

"You're not coming back."

At Rivelle's request, Dorner went directly to his office on the 29th floor to remove his things. Drawers were open, and personal items were on his desk. Maisy appeared in the doorway with a box and an armful of packing material. She stepped over to the Invincible Sun.

"Let's wrap this up," she said.

Her voice warbled. There were tears on her cheeks. Over her shoulder, Dorner could see members of his team—Nidlers and a half dozen others, watching, looking glum and confused.

"Maybe you can find a home for it," Dorner said.

"Seven hearings today," Maisy reported dully, eyeing her Joinspace. "Five appeals. All of the appeals are floor additions."

Dorner laughed.

She opened her mouth as if to speak, and then turned away.

He stepped closer and embraced her. "I'm a happy man," he said grimly. "I'm in love."

She searched his face. "You deserve to be happy."

Rin was seated at the dining room table. "I've asked the hospital for a leave of absence," she said as Dorner entered.

He set his box down on the front room floor. "I'm through at Planning."

She gazed at the box, then returned to his face, seeing the calamity in his eyes.

Dorner looked around. The wall hangings had been removed and were piled beside the door. It looked like the apartment was being cleared for a new tenant.

"I don't want all this history around me," Rin said.

"What are you doing?" Dorner approached her. A copper baking pan was on the table, and the collared candlestick stood at its center, with a white stub burning. On either side were stacks of photos. The pan and table were covered with ashes and charred scraps.

"I gave Mom's things to Rawji," Rin said.

Dorner watched her turn a photo over the flame. It curled to escape. On the pan, blackened corners were raised like hands, waving goodbye.

"What is this?" he said.

"I don't need them," she murmured. "I don't want them to see me. And I don't want to see them."

Among the burnt scraps on the pan, he spotted the little girl sailing over the waves. "The famous picture." He picked up the fragment.

"The ones with Dad—" She gazed at him. "They're the worst."

"He loved you," Dorner said, pulling her up. The idea that

Rin was erasing her memories was more than he could bear. "This is just what Tongue wants."

"She's taken everything."

"We're still here." He looked into her eyes.

Rin sighed. "I haven't given up."

"You said you'd marry me." Dorner spoke softly.

Her brow creased, as if she was trying to remember.

"You're everything now," she said. "But it's a frightening thought."

Dorner was silent.

"There's no telling what she would do." Rin looked down at the ashes.

"I know," Dorner said.

Dorner reached a liturgist, and the man agreed to marry them at the end of the day. As the hour approached, Rin made herself ready. After a shower, she returned to the bedroom to find Dorner holding a white gown and an antique veil.

"Rawji found this," he said.

Rin noticed the bronze tiara on the bed.

"From your mother's trousseau—"

"I gave them away for a reason." Rin stepped toward the closet. "I'll be fine with this." She drew out the black dress she'd worn to Tropica Bay. As she put it on, Dorner knotted his tie in the mirror. Tad stood beside him, posturing and making faces.

"Fasten me," she said.

Dorner did as she asked. "We need a ring."

"I have something we can use," Rin said.

She returned to the closet and pulled out her linen coat. She draped it over her arm and touched the bloodstains. Then she reached in the pocket, removed the cat's neckband and held it toward him.

Dorner was appalled.

"We know what's coming," Rin said.

He didn't reply. Her jaw was set. Her eyes were as black as her dress.

"I'm through with fantasies," she said.

He retrieved the bronze tiara. "We can have a little hope." He set it on her head.

The ceremony was performed in the rooftop garden, between the fishpond and the lemon grove. The liturgist brought a folding table on which he set his testament and a little wax apple. Rin and Dorner stood with Tad between them, chittering and holding their hands, and when the liturgist prompted them, they recited the vows that they had penned two hours before.

"Without shame or regret," he told Rin, "you'll be my fire, and I'll be yours."

Rin repeated his words.

"You'll be my strength," Dorner said, "and I'll be yours."

Rin repeated the vow. Then they joined hands and spoke together.

"No one and nothing will ever come between us."

Rin's delivery was dogged, knowing the marriage included Tongue.

When the liturgist called for the ring, Dorner took the cat's neckband from his pocket and slid it onto Rin's wrist. The silver bell tinkled.

"You may kiss the bride," the liturgist said.

They sealed the bond with their lips.

Dorner thanked him, Rin took Tad's hand, and the three of them headed for the stairwell.

Tad squawked.

"What's up?" Dorner asked him.

"Look who's here," Rin said.

A dozen feet from the stairwell, beneath a tree, Dorner saw YoEllis. She was standing with her feet spread, hands on her hips, glowering like an angry governess. He started toward her. YoEllis lifted her chin, turned on her heel and ducked into the stairwell. Rin hurried behind him. By the time they reached the stairwell, YoEllis was gone.

"Get ready," he said.

Rin grabbed Dorner's arm. "I'll be your strength."

They had a light meal. Dorner toasted Rin and their future together. After they ate, Rin escorted Tad to the pantry. When she entered the bedroom, Dorner was already naked. He came up behind her, embraced her and kissed her ear. In the distance, a vagrant wind whistled, huffing and shrilling as he listened, drawing closer.

Rin removed the tiara and stripped off her dress. Then she pulled back the sheets and lay down. He turned off the light.

"I don't want you inside her," Tongue hissed.

I can't hear you, he thought.

Dorner put his knee on the mattress and lowered himself. Rin's chest was pricked with gooseflesh. She reached for him and closed her eyes.

Listening, wary, he touched her thigh. He put his palm on her belly, feeling her heat. He turned his head, feeling her breath on his cheek. Then slowly, quietly, he violated Tongue's ban.

"My husband," Rin sighed.

She felt Dorner above her. He was cradling her with his arms. He was kissing her neck. She squirmed against him. Were they in her bedroom, or was it his? The space around them seemed larger than either. She could hear a whistling, and she was chilled by a breeze. Dorner seemed to be holding his breath. And his rhythm, so steady at first, was skipping beats. She could barely sense the weight of his body, and when she felt with her hands, it wasn't there.

Rin opened her eyes. The ceiling was dissolving, and as she watched, the walls fell away, revealing a night full of stars. Where was Dorner? Had Tongue taken him from her? All at once, the stars detached from the sky. They were falling like sequins through the cavernous night. One landed on her hip and silvered her flesh.

Is this Tongue? she thought.

Dorner, she called. But no sound left her lips.

Sequins, more sequins—on her leg and her belly, on her neck and brow. A fierce wind was blowing. She could hear it moaning and howling in the distance. The stars fell more thickly and the blow came closer. It was mobbed with voices—Tongue's voices—so loud now they were shaking the sky.

Rin shuddered as they reached her, circling, gathering around her. They panted and whooped, drubbing her sides, diving beneath her.

Dorner, Rin cried. Her body looked like his when he was silvered for flight—long and sleek, arms flattened like blades. Tongue's winds were lifting her, bearing her away.

Speed stung her eyes. Her brow sloped, and her legs stretched back. She was streaking through space, with Tongue's rushing song thick in her ears. Would there be a return? Would she ever see Dorner or Clemency again?

What were the voices saying?

They didn't sound wounded or vengeful. They were longing, wistful—as if they meant to recall all the things Tongue and Dorner had felt together.

"You don't know him," Tongue said.

Yes I do, Rin thought.

"Secrets," Tongue said, reluctant, wounded, accepting.

What was her game?

"The truth then," Tongue said. "If that's what you want—"

The Soap Bubble appeared—a rainbow orb. And the looping tide of the Mermaid's Wake. Vivid and cosmic, so much sharper than the images Rin had seen in the straddles. There— The glowing ruffles of the Golden Cabbage. And then the mouth of the Wormhole flared through the darkness.

Tongue's choir mounted. It was almost a welcome.

The opening throbbed as Rin arrowed into it. The stars winked out, and the fleeced walls were streaming around her. The choir was with her, singing beside her. The braid of voices twisted and shrilled, running like a rope through the rushing tube. The far end was clenched, screening the view. The flowing walls writhed, as if the Wormhole could feel her inside it. Then its egress belled, and the bolus of fire appeared.

The pulsing mass was as Dorner described—scarlet and gold, blurred and misshapen by scuds of smoke. Where was he? she wondered. On the bed, returning to sleep; aroused, holding her close; or panicked, trying to revive her? A rumble, a flash— A bolt tore across the portal, electric white. Then the winds of Tongue grabbed her and hurled her through.

Vapos opened below, webbed with fire. The great bladdered Ovum floated before her, lit by interior flashes. Low in the sky, like an aircraft approaching, were two giant lights— the moons of Tongue. Watching her.

What was Tongue thinking? The winds carried Rin down. Her arms were like wings, but she couldn't move them. The chanting throng was ardent and frenzied, but not a hint did they give of Tongue's intent. Rin could see the three venous trunks now. They throbbed, sucking flames from the asteroid's surface.

Flames, flames—

271

Depleted, they rose in the trunks. Through the Ovum's translucent skin, Rin saw Tongue's churning essence, thick and viscous, and as the flames arrived, the churn swept them up, soaking them, tumbling them, infusing them with Tongue's pure emotion.

"My children," Tongue told her. "Dorner's and mine."

The restored flames sang with fresh heart.

"Look at me," Tongue said.

Still plunging, Rin looked.

Tongue's eyes were growing. Clouds whorled around them like captive typhoons. Inhuman. Fierce and unblinking. Reptilian.

"This world is Dorner's," Tongue said. "Where he came from, where he's going."

"Going," the flames chorused, "going, going—"

He belongs to me, Rin told them all.

A mountain was rising beneath her. On every side, Vapos stretched out—an island of tissue in Dorner's brain, a flammable world with bursting torches and twisting smokes. And Tongue looming over it, giant, commanding— Rin was headed toward a sheer cliff. Fire rippled across it. Flaming serpents stretched their necks and twitched their tongues, as if eager to consume her. At the last moment, she was lifted by the wind and cleared the cliff's top. Then a blast sideswiped her.

Rin buckled as she struck the ground and went tumbling down a burning knoll. Her body's gleam faded. She came to rest in a wallow and rose, silver no more, fuel-soaked and on fire, swatting the flames while the wind whipped her hair.

She was high on the mountain. Uprights rose from the slope before her, branchless, like trees in a burnt forest. She took a step forward. A resinous odor rose from the soil. It was damp and gave beneath her feet. The Ovum rumbled, a bolt tore down. Dazzled, Rin halted. The mountain shook beneath her.

"You will know him here," Tongue said. Her voice was husky, transfused by the crackling of flames. As Rin's sight returned, wind shifted the smoke. Before her, a giant statue of YoEllis rose into the night. Newly lit flames sang at the statue's feet.

The Temple, Rin thought.

"Examine them carefully." Tongue's voice was soft and close, as if there was a cabal between them.

The moonlight wavered. A flaw was crossing one of Tongue's eyes. It glinted as it passed—a silver sliver—then it plunged through the vapors, erased and reappearing.

Dorner, Rin thought.

He was in a steep dive, headed for the slope below her, seamed with ravines and lit by ember-crowned fountains. He leveled as she watched, coming in low, returning to human form as he burst through the spouts, sheathed in fire, trailing flames from his arms. His legs swung down, and he crumpled as he landed, barreling across the slope.

She hurried toward him, threading the fuel sumps.

Dorner rose to his feet, tacking through the fires to meet her.

She was joyful, relieved. He was rattled and fearful. His

head dipped, as if he was struggling for breath. Instead of facing her, he was looking away.

Rin reached out her hand. He took it and they embraced.

She brought me here, Rin told him. *Alone.*

Dorner nodded.

Above them, the Ovum's belly rumbled. Charges flashed within, and a bolt reached out, striking the air above and around them, blinding them both.

"The Temple," Tongue said.

Geysers of fire were lifting on either side. Overhead, a giant umbrella opened, filling the air with molten rain and twirling smokes.

Rin could see the distress in Dorner's face.

Talk to me, she said.

Dorner avoided her gaze. She put her hands to his cheeks and shifted his head, peering into his eyes. They narrowed. His lips parted to speak, then he stopped himself and bowed his head.

"Memories," Tongue sighed. "His monuments—"

What does she want me to see? Rin asked him.

Dorner was silent.

Rin turned, facing upslope. Through a curtain of drifting ash, the twin moons cast a pallid light on the stony uprights.

"All the innocent creatures he offered," Tongue said, "as tribute to me."

Rin fixed on the moons, trying to hold her hatred and fear in check. Tongue's eyes were convex, concave, and convex again as the fumes billowed past. With what courage she could muster, Rin plumbed their depths, feeling Tongue's power, steeling herself for whatever lay ahead.

Then she started forward, fuel sloshing around her feet, spot fires dashing gold spittle on the incline ahead. The winds died. The singing stopped. Through a veil of haze, the silhouettes of the monuments rose, solemn and still, larger than life.

Rin approached the statue of YoEllis, seeing the detail in the elongated body, the horizontal banding of her trunk, the stone cowl around her head. A nearby torch flared, rouging the scarred woman's face.

You look better here, Rin thought.

Dorner had followed. He was standing, watching, twenty feet away.

Rin continued up the slope. She could hear his footsteps behind her. Statues appeared through the shifting smoke. "Tributes" Tongue called them. *So many*, Rin thought. The memorials here were all strangers to her. But farther up, she spotted Maisy. And Rivelle's wife.

Rin turned to regard him.

Dorner looked away. His pride, his shame— The web of secrets that had hung between them— It was between them again. Above, fog rolled and curled around the two moons, glittering and iridescent. Tongue had the advantage, Rin thought. She knew him better.

As Rin made her way up the broken slope, the breezes mounted. What were they saying? Their voices were high and wheedling, the voices of children. "I'm Tongue, I'm Tongue," they flurried and preened, pushing each other.

Statues were gathered on a knoll, with trickling fuel netted around them. Rin paused before one. It was Leese, her smile bountiful, arms fused to her sides, front bulging with the fetus she carried. Nearby, a monument to Firooka was planted. Her bosom jutted and her expression was salty. Fuel was pooled around her feet.

You've been feeding Tongue all your life, Rin murmured. *It's no wonder she's strong.* She scanned the slope. *Where's my cousin?*

Without replying, Dorner moved past her. He skirted a bluff and halted before Anja's memorial. Nearby, a torch sizzled like roasting fat. Rin approached slowly, raising her eyes with trepidation, bracing herself for the pain she would feel.

The statue was indifferent. Anja's head was high, raised to the heavens. She wasn't thinking about the family bond, ruptured beyond repair. She belonged to Tongue, to Rufus and Dorner. The statue exaggerated her curves, and her hair was stern, bound behind. A stone canary looked down from its perch atop her coiled chignon.

She looks pleased with herself, Rin said. *Proud to be here.*

Enjoying Tongue's power, Dorner said weakly.

Hissing, crackling— When Rin turned, she saw a scarlet flame thirty feet away, switching like a serpent's tail. Above, on a shelf, a lone statue stood—

Eudriss, in her youth.

Rin approached. Tongue's moons watched.

Her mother's back was straight, shoulders rounded, one arm by her side, the other raised. She had the same charm and vivacity Rin had admired and cherished. But she carried none of the burden.

Rin heard Dorner's steps halt behind her. The silence was deathly.

Without looking, Rin knew: Tongue was gloating.

You felt that way about my mother, Rin said.

Dorner was speechless. When he'd asked Rin to marry him, he thought shame was behind him. They'd lived through so much together. But the truths hidden here, that only he and Tongue knew— They couldn't be shared.

Didn't you, Rin pressed him.

I did, he replied.

He watched Rin circle the statue. There was no explaining, he thought. The pose Eudriss had assumed was defiant. Her raised arm touched her necklace, and she was biting her lip, looking randy and keen. Like the others. Without scruple or pang. Had this Eudriss walked the earth? Or did she exist only here, hidden inside him, with the winding red snakes and glittering fountains?

Dorner saw Rin shudder. He felt the wind lift and twist around them. They were a long way from Clemency, he thought. There were no schools or hospitals near, no tube-side eatery with a warm cup and a smile.

He stepped beside her. *Can you forgive me?*

Rin peered through the darkness, toward the summit and the circle of stones. *I don't know you*, she said.

The wind whistled in her ear, shaking the flames around

her mother's feet. A puff of embers sprayed into a puddle beside her, and a flare ignited. As she watched, it boiled and cephalated, the wind feeding it from beneath; then, as Rin leapt aside, the flare exploded, hurling fiery snake heads in every direction. The burst lit a monument on the shelf above Eudriss. Above its windings, a stark face appeared, lips parted, eyes staring.

Rin froze. The face was hers.

Don't. Dorner tried to restrain her, but she pulled away.

An image of her was in his Temple—she knew that. But she was still unprepared.

Rin climbed the incline toward it.

Please—

She halted before it and lifted her gaze, examining the motionless replica.

Dorner caught up, embracing her from behind while Tongue's spite beat around them.

In the statue, Rin saw herself as Tongue saw her. And Dorner too. Envious, worshipful. Hopelessly naive. An artless disciple.

"Silly girl," Tongue sneered.

"Tongue," the winds tittered. "I'm Tongue, I'm Tongue."

Rin's eyes glazed. Tension bled from her frame. She reached her hand back. It touched Dorner's thigh. She turned to face him.

Is that what I am?

It's an old statue, he said. *It was built the night—*

"Silly," Tongue chanted, "silly, silly—"

278

Dorner raised his arm to fend Tongue off.

Rin bent over, hugging her middle, feeling as if something sharp had run her through. Dorner held her against him. But that pained her more. *Pity*, she thought. From him—the man she'd married.

No woman on earth is your equal, he said.

Rin raised herself, stiffening, pushing him away. She scanned the monuments, then she turned and faced upslope. *I'm glad I know.*

Tongue's wind blasted, goading the flames at the base of Rin's statue. An orange taper hooked her, scorching Rin's cheek, singeing her hair.

I'm going to stand on top, she said.

The moons dilated. The Ovum rumbled.

You've seen the worst, Dorner said.

Rin seemed not to hear. She was eyeing the Ovum, bloated and flashing, with what looked like a dare. Then she threw herself forward. Dorner scrambled after her.

The winds shrieked and lightning struck. The explosion blinded Dorner, and the mountain shook beneath him.

"The games are over," Tongue boomed.

The slope returned, torches blooming around him. Rin had spotted the standing stones and was headed toward them. Flames speared from the soil inside the circle.

"Stay clear," Tongue threatened.

The rumbling Ovum was brewing a monster charge. Rin passed between two megaliths, and as she entered the circle, the spears became fountains, the throats of choked nozzles spewing bright phlegm as they cleared. Rin raised her arms and shook her fists at Tongue, while the blazes painted her with jagged patterns, coppering her face and crisping her hair.

Dorner charged into the circle and grabbed her.

Do you love me? she whirled. *Do you?*

I do, he replied.

She caught his hand, put it on her breast and pressed against him. Her mouth sought his, and her tongue went deep. In an instant, Dorner knew. Here on the summit, in the Temple's sanctum, Rin was going to throw herself in Tongue's face.

Tongue was shrieking. Her moons had red haloes, their centers white-hot.

Can't you see? he said. *Don't you hear?*

Rin wasn't listening. She was clawing his loins. Tongue's gall webbed the air, prickling his skin, sparking the stones—

Rin's softness, Rin's spirit—

I don't care, Rin raved. *I don't care, I don't care—*

She parted her legs. With Tongue watching, with Tongue staring down—

I don't either, he said. Desire poured out of his heart.

And when it did, Tongue went to pieces.

A glowing sword sprang from the Ovum and drove at the summit, then a fork with three tines and another with two. Tongue's egg was a pulsing goliath. Lightning broomed from its belly, striking the mountain again and again. One of the megaliths cracked. The falling halves shook the ground. High and low, from the Temple's slopes, flames gyred up.

Fuel welled from the soil around them, oily and bubbling. A falling ember landed in a pool beside them, and a nest of bronze vipers appeared, hissing and wriggling through the gelatinous blue.

Rin was heedless. She was pulling him down. Her lips urged, her hands gripped, her thighs invited— She was frantic, panting in his ear, hissing with a heat of her own. Dorner went with her. They were joined now, moving as one, sealing their marriage under Tongue's nose.

The singing flames choked. Smoke blotted the moons, and the heavens turned green. Then the moons bulged back, brighter than ever, and Tongue's injured pride swept the sky, her full-throated rage like a sonic boom.

Dorner was deep with Rin, his center melted to hers.

Tongue was roaring, and the roar drew out without break or breath. It rasped and roiled from the dregs of her nature, grisly, hateful. Near and far, the flames wailed betrayal. The Ovum stuttered and jerked, as if its walls were about to crack. A ripping sound, and the air turned white. The summit quaked, caustic fumes swamped them—

Dorner turned his head. From a smoking crater on the Temple's slope, a serpent of gold was coiling into the night. It looped and tensed, scales flashing. Wind glossed its nose and raised a ridge on its back. Down the incline, flickering and red, monsters were rising between the statues. Limping lizards, glistering crocs, thrashing birds and starved snakes. Strangled desires, hunted and shunned. Infernal beasts— And the beasts were advancing.

Rin heaved beneath him, ardent, senseless.

Tongue's doleful choir and the monster horde were roaring as one—roaring and burning their way up the slope, approaching the circle of stones. Rin clawed Dorner's ribs and champed his chest. *Listen*, she hissed, as if the din came from her.

The fiery beasts rose above the megaliths now, glowing and flowing together, hemming them in, merging into one hellish creature with a hundred heads. Tongue held the giant snake back. Dorner could see it coiling and twisting outside the ring.

Rin was oblivious. *Release them*, she whispered. *Maisy, Leese, Anja— The souls you've burned— Set them on me.*

The beast Tongue held back was fighting for freedom. A golden boa, saddled with flame, dripping fire from its jaws.

"Set them on me," Rin urged Dorner.

And Tongue unleashed it. The boa came slithering toward them.

Rin— Dorner froze. *Stop.* He withdrew.

Her eyes opened and peered into his.

We can't stay. He embraced her, lifting.

His chest silvered, his middle drew out. The boa behemoth was inside the circle now, onyx eyes fixed, long head ticcing.

Dorner tried to take flight, but the boa was coiling around their legs. Ulcers bloomed red on Rin's calves.

I'm burning, she said.

The boa was melting his thighs. A terrible heat rose into Dorner's chest. The demon snake's coils rode over their hips, glided around their middles, and began to squeeze.

Dorner reached through the smoke and grabbed the snake's neck. The seeking head shook, dashing flames from its crown. The glossy lips parted, the scarlet mouth gaped—

An awful sound filled Dorner's ears: Tongue was screaming an oracle of woe. "Won't, I won't— Forgive this, I won't."

She would never forgive him, and she would never let go.

How old was Tongue? How many lives had she taken? How many worlds had Tongue consumed? The boa winched tighter, crushing Rin's chest and Dorner's with it. Blindly, his fingers dug at the glowing coil.

"Never," Tongue screamed. "I'll never let go."

Fire in his mouth, fire in his throat— He was drowning in fire, and pain—a pain he had never felt. Not the ravishing pain of heat and desire. This pain was deeper. It hollowed and disemboweled. He was dying, and Rin was dying with him. He would never feel her love again.

"Die," Tongue raged. "Die, die—"

The boa's jaws spasmed, its forked tongue snapping, black eyes bulging as it tightened its coils. Rin's eyes closed. Her breath was gone, her chest twitched. Over her heart, the birthmark flickered. That flame, so frail and human— They were weak, man and woman, creatures of earth. With his eyes on the flicker, he aimed his mind, trying to fly.

This isn't our home, Dorner cried.

His love welled. He focused, focused and rose.

Rin, Rin— Ten feet in the air. Holding her close. Tongue's demon rose with him, clenching and shrieking.

Rin's back burst into flames, then her front and face. She

was still in his arms, but he could feel her melting. The flames rose up his neck, cooking his head.

His mind skipped. Then it found its track. His body thinned and his legs went long. In a flash, he silvered completely, cleaving the air and the swirling smoke. He was streaking skyward with Rin in his arms.

She was burnt and limp, head lolling, chest caved.

Tongue was still screaming. The winds were fierce. Bolts from the Ovum exploded around him. But he was a missile now, and the Wormhole was straight ahead.

9

NOBODY WILL ESCAPE

Rin's room was dark and silent. Two stiff shapes lay on the bed, a foot apart. While they bore traces of humanity, they were unlike humans. Their parts were thick, their frames oversized, and the heads were enlarged, hairless and glossy. The eye orbits were funnels, as if they'd been drained. Where arms might have been, scaly appendages were melted into their sides. And from the hips, the bodies narrowed, vestigial legs fused together. Tapering tails hung over the mattress.

The shapes were motionless, gleaming like objects of clay fired in a kiln—the embalmed remains, perhaps, of creatures that had preceded man.

One quivered. Then the other. A crackling filled the room, and splits appeared in the fronts of both. Steam rose from cracks, and the halves spread like opening pupae. From one, a hand emerged.

Dorner raised himself, naked and slick. Rin rose beside him. They clambered out of their annealed exteriors like reptiles casting their molts.

He dragged himself toward the door, struggled to open it and pawed the light switch. The overhead came on. When he turned, their eyes met. Rin looked at the bed. The sheets around the broken molts were soaked. She stepped to the mirror and gazed at her reflection. Dorner moved behind her. Their flesh was rosy and glistening, but they were whole and unharmed. When he touched Rin's shoulder, she flinched. Her skin was hot, tender and oily.

Dorner tried to speak. A rasping filled the space between them.

Water, he thought.

Rin clutched her throat and lurched past him. He followed her through the doorway, wheezing.

They stood in the shower, leaning together beneath the cold spray, drinking and cooling their bodies. As their temps subsided, the confusion cleared. Rin examined her arms and middle.

Her thought reached him: *We're alive.*

I can hear you, he replied.

Rin nodded, her eyes wide.

He circled her with both arms. The Temple's secrets, their nuptial on the summit, Tongue's monstrous attack— Something had changed them.

I felt strong, Rin thought. *And then— Helpless.*

I loved your strength.

Fury had transformed her in the circle of stones. What she'd seen in the Temple had fed her power instead of depleting it.

Rin touched his back and thigh, slinking against him. *Please*, she implored, remembering the boa's embrace. *Dorner, please— I can't breathe.* Her eyes fathomed his, as if she could see Tongue's snake.

A buzz came from the living room. Someone knocked on the front door.

Rin's gaze narrowed.

"It's the middle of the night," Dorner said, turning off the tap.

A moment of shared suspicion. Rin stepped out of the shower, grabbed a towel and wrapped it around herself. Dorner did the same, following her down the hall and through the dining room, stopping behind her as she unlatched the door.

Rin took a breath and opened it slowly.

Rawji stood before her in a silk gown, eyes bulging behind her thick glasses. An antique egg timer hung on a chain around her neck.

"We're all waiting, dear," Rawji creaked.

"Waiting— For what?"

"To celebrate the marriage."

Rin heard Dorner: *How does she know?*

"What are you talking about?" Rin said.

"Word gets around," Rawji purred, patting her hand. "Everyone's here. On the roof." She smiled at Dorner. "We've gone to a lot of trouble."

Dorner didn't reply.

"Hurry up now," Rawji urged Rin. She clucked and returned down the hall.

Rin closed the door.

"'Word gets around?'" he said.

She checked her Joinspace. "It's 4 a.m."

"That wasn't Rawji," Dorner said.

"If there are really people up there—" Rin shook her head. "Maybe Tongue's with them."

"What should we do?" she wondered.

"Ignore it."

"We can't just hide down here," Rin said.

Dorner was doubtful. "It's some kind of trap."

"You think if we lock ourselves up, she'll leave us alone?"

Rin stepped toward the bedroom. Dorner followed.

She found a dinner robe in her closet. When she'd fastened the buttons, she handed him his shirt and pants, and he put them on. Rin brushed her hair, then turned and ran the brush through his. The cat's neckband was on her wrist, and its bell and tag tinkled.

As they were leaving, Rin took the tiara from the dresser's top and placed it on her head. In the hall, they heard Tad's chitter. Rin fetched him from the pantry, and the three of them took the lift to the top floor. From there, they climbed the stair to the roof garden.

The garden was packed. As they stepped forward, a hundred heads turned and a clamor rose. "Surprise, surprise—" The partyers welcomed them and shared a laugh.

Rin waved at the gathering.

Is this real? she wondered.

We're still asleep, Dorner thought, scanning the crowd, recognizing faces, greeting them with a smile or a nod. Tad whimpered, hugging his leg.

Maisy stepped forward with a basket on her arm. She kissed Dorner's cheek. Her eyes were moist, as if the tears she had shed when he cleaned out his office hadn't yet dried. "Especially for you," she said, glancing at the guests.

Rivelle and Severans were behind a table, serving drinks. Firooka circulated with a tray, talking loudly, offering hors d'oeuvres. Dorner spotted Nidlers and the tall waitress from Soledad's—what was her name? And Franklin, the old Planner—he was there too, waving from his wheelchair.

Leese approached.

"Congratulations," she reached for Dorner's hand. "It all worked out." She made a victory clasp and shook it to show how strongly she felt.

"I'm glad you're here," Rin said.

"Our loss, his gain." Leese spoke to Rin, but her eyes were on Dorner.

Bez stepped toward them.

"My true love," she sighed, halting before him. "I was hurt when I heard. But I understand." Bez was wearing the Guardian pin on her shirt collar. Rivelle must have returned it to her. Bez smiled at Rin.

Rin smiled back. *Who is she?* Rin asked.

An old flame, Dorner said.

And the bald man by the bay tree? He looks familiar.

You met him at the Zenith party, he said. *My chief engineer.*

"May I?" Bez leaned closer and kissed Dorner's cheek. When she drew away, her eyes were closed. "Excuse me," Bez said. She had stepped on Rin's foot. "So sad," she gave Rin a sisterly look.

A man in uniform stepped forward. "Kenton," he introduced himself.

Dorner nodded slowly. "Yes, I remember." He shook Kenton's hand.

Kenton craned toward him. "You're always a step ahead," he said softly.

A sound like a gunshot. Rivelle raised a foaming bottle and began to pour. Scarlet party streamers festooned the potted plants. Rawji was knotting one around Tad's neck. Finger food came from a grill, and the super and his wife, Minole, stood beside it, feeding each other. Two hearing judges and a clerk handed flutes of gold liquid around.

"There are people from the hospital here," Dorner muttered. "People you know."

"Some of them. But they're *all* people you know," Rin guessed.

Dorner examined the crowd. "They're all people I know."

"A toast," Rivelle shouted. The crowd grew quiet. "He labored on our behalf for so many years. Now— A higher purpose calls." He raised his flute to Dorner. "Here's to a blazing future for you and your bride."

Glasses were lifted.

"You'll be missed," Anja called through the crowd. Beside her, Rufus raised his top hat and smiled. YoEllis stepped from behind a planter. "He knows how to light up a woman," she said.

Rin grabbed Dorner's arm.

Leese set her hand on his shoulder. "We hate to lose him," she boomed, addressing the crowd. "But we all know: he went to the best."

Their affirmation sounded as one, and the flutes were sampled. A group of Kiribati in traditional dress raised their instruments to Dorner. Then they were strumming and swaying, and a wispy woman closed her eyes and began to sing.

Your human connections, Rin thought.

She has strings to them, Dorner guessed.

Rin eyed him gravely. *They're Tongue puppets now.*

Maisy approached Rin, basket in hand. "You look lovely."

"She's done so much for him," Leese explained.

Rin stared at Leese. "Will Tongue be joining us?" She asked the question loudly enough that all could hear.

The chatter ceased, and the faces turned—curious, startled, puzzled or disturbed.

"Of course," Anja laughed.

"What a question," Bez said. "Tongue invited us."

Laughter spread through the crowd.

"She's Dorner's prize," Rawji cooed.

"The blushing bride." Leese winked at him.

"It's time," Maisy said, and she opened her basket and handed flowers around.

"That's crazy." Dorner raised his hands to the crowd. "I'm not marrying Tongue."

More laughter and sapient looks. "Cold feet," Firooka quipped.

Dorner looked at Rin. She was rigid and pale.

"I have a wife," he said, putting his arm around her.

Leese plucked the tiara from Rin's head. It passed from hand to hand until it reached Anja, who sailed it off the roof. Dorner glared at the impeaching faces. He turned back to Rin and kissed her. A jeer rose.

"The first kiss belongs to the bride," Leese said.

"That's her perfume," Rivelle's wife shouted.

The guests wheeled and sniffed, scouting the garden. "It's her," one agreed.

Firooka dropped her hors d'oeuvres, pointing.

Smoke was rising through the roof gravel. Was something burning on the floor beneath?

The party raised a welcoming cheer, and the tempo of the music increased.

"Tongue," Severans shouted, and the crowd chanted "Tongue, Tongue—"

Dorner peered at Rin. He could feel the heat through his soles.

A *whoosh* rose around them. Points of flame pierced the roof deck. As they watched, the blue jets grew to copper lances. Bez convulsed, speared from beneath. Leese shrieked and twisted. A jet rose up her backside and torched her hair.

"Dorner," Rin cried. She threw herself at Leese, batting the flames.

He tore off his shirt and lunged, covering Leese's head. But Kenton grabbed him from behind and held him. "Let her enjoy it," Kenton said.

She seemed to be doing just that. Leese writhed her hips, and her eyes pooled with desire. Rin drew back, appalled.

Dorner saw Severans hurry through the crowd, but when he reached his wife, instead of trying to save her, he touched his cuff to her flaming cleavage, lighting himself.

Bez was down on her knees, blades of flame jerking inside her. "Goodbye," she gasped. Her eyes sought Dorner's.

"Bez, no—" He knelt, circling her with his arms.

You're too close, Rin cried.

But the flames curled away from Dorner, focusing their heat on Bez. Her eyes shrank in their sockets. Seared and limp, she slipped from his hands.

Dorner rose, speechless. Minole was facing him, darkened, blistering— Her hair kinked into ringlets. Her chest burst, flames piping out of the holes. He watched her burning frame buckle and fall in a heap. Her smiling head shifted atop it.

They're possessed, he said numbly.

"It's been a pleasure," a deep voice groaned.

Dorner turned as Severans opened his arms. The doctor's front was on fire. He sank onto what remained of Leese, charred and smoking on the deck at his feet. Dorner's stomach heaved. He whirled, holding his middle.

Can't you see what she's doing? Rin said.

Rawji was limping toward them, fists clenched, chest ablaze. She reached for Rin, lifting her chin. "To feel what Tongue feels," she said. "To see what she sees." *Foof*—her ashen hair glowed.

Rin extended her arms, as if to embrace Rawji and smother the flames. But Rin's steps took her backward, and there was terror in her face.

Dorner grabbed Rawji, and the old woman laughed. Her face bubbled and slumped and slid from her skull. Her body sagged through his arms like hot molasses and lobed around his feet.

He could hear Rin sobbing. *Can't you see?*

The music was frenzied now. The Kiribati were in flames, and they sang while they burned. Nidlers danced through the crowd, his back ablaze.

She's destroying your bonds, Rin said.

Yes. He could see. With each incineration, his link to humanity was weaker.

"Dorner," a woman called out. He scanned the fray.

A crowd had formed around a blazing guest.

"Dorner," the cry came again. Rivelle's wife waved him toward her.

The crowd parted to admit him. He saw Maisy lying on the gravel with fire leaping on her belly and thighs. "How does it feel?" someone asked.

"Glorious," Maisy replied. "Where is Dorner?"

"I'm here." Dorner knelt and clasped her hand. "Stay with me," he begged.

"Sweet man," Maisy touched his lips.

"Please—" Dorner broke down, the word caught in his chest. "Stay, stay—"

"You belong to Tongue now," Maisy said.

The fire flared up her front, swallowing her face.

"Amen," Rivelle's wife said. The guests bowed their heads.

Dorner stood, dizzy with dread. Anja was lurching toward him, her head on fire, eyeholes white-hot. It was Tongue, peering through a human mask. Between two trees, Rivelle stood on a planter, gesturing at the fallen bodies. "This is her way," he said, preaching acceptance, venting smoke from his lips.

I'm losing them, Dorner thought. His world, these people— Losing them all. They were going up in smoke, like the photos Rin burned in the baking pan.

Anja, Rin cried.

Her cousin halted ten feet away from her. Anja opened her jaws and fire pushed out like a rocket's nose. Then her legs folded, and she fell to the deck.

"There's nothing left for you here," Tongue said.

Dorner gazed around him, her words like a verdict with no appeal.

"In some other time," Rivelle's wife said, "some other place." She raised her arms to him, fire dripping from her elbows and wrists. "Here I go."

"You have a home, Dorner." Tongue's voice was kindly.

Stop, Rin shrieked, grabbing hold of his arm.

His chest had chromed. His legs were spindling, lengthening beneath him.

"You're finished here," Tongue spoke in his head.

I won't let you, Rin cried.

The tall waitress, Zuna, was hobbling toward them, moaning and drooling brassy mucus. She made a trumpet mouth and shot fire at Rin. Then she flailed her hands and fell to the gravel.

"Fly," Tongue commanded. "One last time."

Dorner's arms flattened and his brow leaned back.

Rin flung her arms around him.

"Fly—" Tongue's chorus swelled in his ears, and her winds descended, sweeping the roof deck to bear him aloft. "It's over," they chanted.

He rose from the gravel.

"I'm coming with him," Rin raged.

The winds dropped. They fell to the deck together, and the sky was filled with a woeful howl. Dorner looked up. His silver was gone. His skin prickled, his hair stood on end. Eyes wide, Rin scanned the rooftops around them. The howl was mounting. The apartment block shook. A deathly moan, then a rumble and rushing—

Above, through the glass of the dome, a tunnel of daylight hollowed the darkness. The sky was lit by a comet—head gold, orange tail tapering, with knotted blue ropes trailing behind. Dorner faced Rin, disbelieving.

"Nothing comes between her need," Rin said, "and what

it takes to fulfill it." She grabbed his arm and pulled him up.

The rushing redoubled: a squadron of meteors, some far, some near. One hit the dome, and its glowing head burst. Another struck, and the convex glass cracked.

With a yowl, Tad appeared from behind a potted tree. He mounted the pot and shook the tree's trunk, calling as he might to warn his troop. Dorner opened his arms, and Tad looped toward him.

More comets striped the night. Some roared past, leaving smoking gray trails. Some shattered the glass, landing on buildings, exploding like bombs. The high-alert sirens went off. Clemency rocked on its raft.

Dorner gazed at the holes in the dome, and the tornados of steam twisting toward them. "They're going to freeze." Tad leaped into his arms. "Or burn," he said, seeing the fires rising from burst buildings.

Rin faced him as another meteor struck.

I was a fool to think I could ever control her, Dorner said. *There's only one chance left.*

Tad looked from one to the other.

You've got to cut her out, Dorner said.

A reflexive tic, then Rin shook her head.

He looked in her eyes. "There's no other way."

Dorner let Tad down and took Rin's hand, hastening her across the roof deck toward the stair. Tad raced after them.

The smoking remains were scattered around them. Beside a small pyre, Dorner saw the crown of Nidlers' head. To one side, Franklin's charred body slumped in his wheelchair.

White light, a bone-jarring crash. Then a furious hiss, like rain pouring down.

A crack opened directly above them. Gouts of steam billowed as Clemency's air met the freezing cold. Through the steam, the bright shrapnel of a comet descended. Where fragments landed, blazes roared up. With a *yip*, Tad bounded ahead.

"Hurry," Dorner urged Rin.

As they approached the stair, the last guest stepped out of the shadows: a woman in a lace dress, seen in silhouette. She strode through the smoke and halted before them, legs spread, barring the way. Dorner shuddered as the light from a burning corpse splashed over her.

"Don't," YoEllis said.

In the amber flicker, her creased face was grim.

"You need Tongue," she said.

Dorner halted by the corpse. "Please. Get out of our way."

"She loves you," YoEllis said. "As much as I do."

The grief in her voice made him ache. Dorner reached and grabbed the charred arm of the corpse by the wrist. "Get out of our way." He pulled, and the black arm came loose. The shoulder joint flamed.

"We're nothing without her," YoEllis said.

Dorner charged, swinging the torch like a club.

YoEllis just stood there and watched him come. She did nothing to protect herself. Her expression was knowing, sure he wouldn't harm her. Dorner choked his heart, met her gaze and brought the torch around. It struck her head, and the wasp nest of hair blazed up. YoEllis lunged, grappling his shirt. He swung again, bashing her front, and the moth-eaten dress ignited.

He lit her sleeves and the ragged hem.

"Remember," she cried.

He staggered back.

YoEllis grabbed her dress and tore it open. Her dugs were scarred. Tufts of fresh fire sprouted below them like angry weeds. She lurched toward him, arms wide, as if she meant to embrace him.

Dorner struck her again, square in the face.

The love of his youth stumbled back, cheeks blistered, eyes cracking like glass. Smoke poured from her mouth. Her hips banged against the parapet.

He followed with a scooping swing that caught her chin and sent her over the barricade.

A dwindling cry sounded as YoEllis fell forty floors to the street.

Above, the comets were roaring.

Dorner dropped the torch.

Rin grabbed his arm.

They faced the stair and hurried down it, Tad bounding beside them. The lift was gutted with flames.

Dorner was shaking from head to foot.

He looked into her eyes. She combed his hair with her fingers, pulling him close. The kiss was long and deep.

It's over, Rin said, as they continued down the stairs.

"Over for who?" Tongue whispered.

For YoEllis, Dorner told Tongue. *And you.*

When they reached the ground floor and opened the door, a blast of cold air met them. Dorner hurried forward, leading the way through the lobby and out of the building.

The walkway was icy and the air was freezing. Beyond the dome's shattered glass, a fresh pack of comets streaked. They raced down the block, and as they turned the corner, one struck the building opposite. Its top exploded. Orange clouds rose, pierced by debris and flying bodies. From the upper floor windows, flames spouted. Lower down, fearful faces appeared behind panes. In the street, a mob was gathering, half dressed, panicked. The mob grew as people poured out of the buildings.

"Fly to me, Dorner," Tongue said.

A meteor slipped through the gap between two high-rises, tore through a third and exploded in the street ahead of them, leaving a smoking pit and a web of charred bodies.

"Stay close to me," Dorner told Rin. "I'm your shield."

He skirted the carnage. Some in the blast pit were still alive, broken and twisted, hair smoking, rolling to quench clothing or flesh. The guests on the rooftop had embraced their incineration. But these here did not.

"Vapos," Tongue said, "and the fate I promised. That's all we have now."

Dorner didn't reply.

"Our dream," she said softly. "Yours and mine. To burn till there is no fuel left."

300

The promise of death, Rin said.

"What do you know of dreams?" Tongue shot back.

This way, Dorner motioned.

He turned at an intersection and jogged down the street, Tad at his hip, Rin a half step behind. On either side, people were shouting, jumping from windows and balconies. Before him, a comet was coming in low, head glowing, sizzling the air, striking the ground floor of a hotel complex. The explosion gutted the lobby. A gale of debris flew through the billows, then a horde of flames swarmed into the street, a human inside each.

Dorner kicked into a run, avoiding the swarm. Panic ruled Clemency now. A crowd had gathered at the corner, and as Dorner forced his way through, he smelled the tart odor of a transformer leak. There was a power annex beside the hotel. "Clear out," he shouted, waving his arm.

Amid the jostle, a little boy peered up at him. His expression was dire, and his cheeks were wet. Dorner swept him up as the automated sirens began to scream. He put the boy on his shoulders, grabbed hold of Rin and swerved into an alley. They were twenty feet down it when the annex exploded behind them. Ahead, between the buildings, Dorner could see the thoroughfare and the depot. A train was pulling in.

"It's still running," he nodded to Rin.

Dorner raced for the depot. The little boy clung to his hair.

The buildings they passed were burning, and the trees were torches. Sap popped while birds careened through the crowns. Beneath a large beech, a group was huddled. Dorner saw the white bandannas. The men rose as he approached, hailing him. Dorner didn't stop.

People had gathered around the depot. A woman sat alone on a bench, weeping.

"Mommy," the little boy cried.

The woman stood. Dorner hurried to her and delivered the boy into her arms. "Forgive me," he said. "This is all my doing."

The train was intact and the car doors were open, but none at the depot would risk taking a seat. Dorner led Rin and Tad across the platform. Heads turned, eyes followed. A man stepped forward. "It's not safe," he warned. Dorner ignored him. Tad bared his teeth.

A comet landed behind them, blowing the last car off the track.

"Fly," Tongue said. "Fly, fly—"

Dorner boarded. Rin followed, with Tad alongside. The doors slammed shut. Then the train pulled away from the station.

"Let go of the earth," Tongue told Dorner. "What are you here?" Her voice was condoling. "A bony thicket for the flames to wind through. Nothing but tinder."

Through the car windows, the nightmare slid past. Frantic gibbons raced through the trees, moving hand over hand. Fire dammed the streets. The apartment blocks had flaming crowns and bodies draped over their balconies. A red wave topped a shopping center. A crowd fled before a gale of sparks. Another was trapped in a cul-de-sac with a mass of flames closing in. The train shook, comets landing on either side.

"I won't be denied," Tongue said.

A meteor scored the sky, striking the track ahead.

The car bucked, and Dorner was thrown to the floor. Rin tumbled with him. The train groaned off its rails. A terrible grinding, the car rocked and shimmied, raised an ear-splitting screech and skidded to a halt.

Dorner rose and beat at the doors. He took off his shoe, smashed the glass and reached through, throwing the lever and forcing the panels apart. Tad vaulted past him. He and Rin stumbled out.

"Fly, Dorner. Now!" Tongue demanded.

The pilot car lay on its side, flames spiraling through the broken windows. Dorner headed across the smoking ground.

"Your own flesh and blood," Tongue wailed. "Minion," she seethed at Rin. "You peeper. You pitiful thing."

She's my wife, Dorner snarled.

"She mates like an ape."

I love her, he said.

"I'll decide who you love."

A fresh spate of comets descended, golden heads boiling. One landed on the boulevard before them, leaving the road and buildings choked with fire.

"The next one hits you," Tongue promised.

Go right ahead.

"You can't let her cut your head open."

I've taken enough from you. Dorner grabbed Rin's hand.

303

The downtown causeway was a black ravine now, fenced by flames and crawling with bodies. A woman sprang from a doorway, hair on fire and streaming behind her. A man sank where he stood as if grabbed from below. A dog hurtled past, back blazing, while above, from the dome's shattered shell, gibbons were falling like dying stars. Where were the high-alert squads, Dorner wondered. Here, at the heart of Clemency— Why wasn't anyone trying to put out the fires?

What remained of the Hub lay ahead. Meteors had struck half the buildings, and the ash was hot underfoot. Bodies lay twisted and torn, mixed with the wreckage. The sight made him sick.

"Don't lie to yourself," Tongue said.

I care, he thought.

"No you don't. You've never cared."

He wanted to revile her, but the dig rattled him. There was no denying: his loyalty had been divided.

"Grand speeches," Tongue jibed, "theatrical deeds—"

How authentic, he wondered, was his devotion to the colony? Had it all been a pose, an intentional deceit? A façade to hide the flames and the feasting?

"You were laughing at them all," Tongue said.

A mounting roar. Dorner raised his head. A giant ball of fire was hurtling toward them. Rin stopped, but Tad kept on. The comet grew larger and larger, filling the sky. Then it landed, jolting the ground, swallowing Dorner's senses.

The blast threw him into a pit. A blazing aureole rose over him like an alien sun. His hair smoked, his clothing burst into flames. He beat them down, then he huddled, fevered and shaking until the din died.

When he climbed out, Rin was rising from behind a rubble heap twenty feet away. Forward, the stumps of buildings appeared through the smoke. They were black, like the trees and the street. At the end of the block, a small figure was dancing, arms on fire.

"Tad—" Dorner raced toward him.

Tad squealed. His arms fell, his thin body collapsed.

Dorner sank beside him, using his hands to smother the flames. Tad's eyes were dim. He touched Dorner's cheek.

Rin stifled a sob.

Dorner scooped his arms beneath Tad.

"There's no time," she said.

As she spoke, the light in Tad's eyes went out.

Dorner groaned. Another comet roared over them.

"Leave him," Rin said, standing.

Dorner felt her hand on his shoulder. He folded Tad's arms over his middle. The wrinkled face looked ancient. If the little man had some wisdom for him, the time to share it had passed.

Dorner removed his charred coat and covered Tad's body.

Rin led the way toward a blackened skyway.

"Think about *us*," Tongue said.

Dorner was silent.

"She'll destroy your mind."

I trust her.

"What does she know? She's not here inside it."

305

She's given up everything. To be with me.

Rin stopped and faced him. Over her head, the battered silhouette of the hospital loomed. *I can do it,* she said.

I know you can, Dorner replied.

The drum-shaped hospital buildings had all been struck. The higher floors were blasted away. Some floors looked vacant, lifeless; others had windows still lit. Before the once-elegant entrance, a rooftop angel lay, wings shattered, torso cracked in two. The giant glass doors were sooty and cracked. Flames thronged the entrance, but a water main had burst, and the torrent cleared a tunnel through them. Rin hurried toward the gushing main. Dorner followed.

Tongue was quiet. Was her anger spent?

They strode through the water tunnel, beside the torrent, flames on either side. Soaked and shivering, they reached the hospital steps, and as they mounted them, Tongue returned, her voice low and grave.

"She's going to butcher us both," Tongue said.

Dorner listened for more. But there was nothing.

Before the glass doors, guards struggled with an unruly crowd. One dragged a burnt man down the steps. Another held off a gang, waving a weapon, threatening to fire. A third tried to talk reason to a man who'd fallen on his knees. "It's worse than out here," he said.

Dorner could see fires in the windows. Flaming shrapnel fell from a high floor.

"No admittance," a burly guard barked at Rin.

"I work here," she said.

The guard raised his firearm, aiming the muzzle at her chest. "Sure you do."

"I'm a doctor," Rin insisted. She caught the eye of a guard she knew. He recognized her and motioned her forward, and the burly guard turned to stop three women with blackened faces.

Rin opened one of the giant doors, and she and Dorner stepped through.

10
TOO LATE

Smoke drifted through the hospital lobby. The blue light was still rippling, but the walls were cracked around the holographic whale, and a girder had impaled its flank. Bodies were everywhere, beneath the collapsed partitions, twisted among the overturned furniture.

They passed the upended reception desk and Rin halted.

The lift bays were black. An attendant sat at her post, body charred, glasses melted over her nose. Rin opened the stairway door, and they started up.

When they reached the 19th floor, Dorner got a look at the colony from the landing window. The Hub was in ruins. Planning headquarters had taken a direct hit. The edifice in which so many schemes had been hatched was nothing but rubble. There were blazes in every sector now, and comets were still coming down.

He could see why no one was fighting the fires. The emergency squads were swarming at the southern rim. Comets had struck Patience Palisades, and the collapsing ice had landed on the dome. Tropica Bay and the area south were flooding. If they couldn't remove the load, Clemency would sink beneath the sea.

He felt Rin's hand on his shoulder.

He turned and nodded.

She led the way through the mangled corridors. As they approached the neurology wing, the floor shook beneath them. The building groaned, and the lights flickered. Bedridden patients appeared over broken walls and through burst doorways.

An orderly emerged from a jungle of gurneys. His weary face brightened. "Doctor Rin—"

She waved him away.

"Wait—" The man hurried after her. He caught up, grabbing her arm.

"Let go."

Dorner tugged the man loose.

Rin jogged down the corridor to a crossing. As Dorner reached her, she swore. The ward was dark. "There's an operating room on twenty," she said, heading for the stairwell.

On the next floor, the walls were undamaged and the lights were on. Robot sleds appeared in the doorways, disinfecting the empty exam rooms. Rin led the way down a narrow passage. At the end were double doors. She barged through and tried the overheads. They flashed on. Aside from a toppled stool, the room was intact.

She threw open cabinets and drawers, then she faced him and began stripping off his wet clothing. A comet roared over them. The building was jolted.

He caught Rin in his arms. *Can you operate, with it shaking like this?*

Rin didn't reply. She continued undressing him. When he was naked, she straightened and led him to the operating table. *Lie down*, she said.

She faced the monitors and powered them up. Then she returned to the drawers and cabinets, and loaded a container with instruments and ampules.

Dorner climbed onto the operating table and stretched out on his back. He could hear the comets landing nearby and the roar of collapsing buildings. He listened for the sound of Tongue in his head. But she was perfectly still.

Rin approached with a bulky foam object in her arms. *Turn onto your right side*, she said. He did as she directed. She lifted his head and slid the foam beneath it. *To brace you.* The foam cradled his neck and the right side of his skull.

He could see her removing her scorched robe. Then she stepped out of view, and he heard water running. When she reappeared, she was wearing a tunic and gloves, and a surgeon's cap. She emptied the container, arranging its contents on two silver trays. At her side, a half-dozen electronic devices were lit. She drew beside him, felt his chest and arms, and began inserting catheters.

Dorner closed his eyes. *Put me under quickly.*

I need you awake, she replied. *To guide me.*

Again the room shook. Rin drew her hands back.

Everything's moving—

Don't worry, she said.

Between her cap and the mask covering her nose and mouth, her eyes were visible. They were as dark and impenetrable as the day they'd met.

Another explosion rocked the hospital, clattering Rin's equipment and the instruments on her trays.

If your hand slips—

She knows what we're doing, Rin said. *If you die, so does she.*

A buzzing sound. Rin rotated his head. Dorner felt a tingling by his left ear. She was shaving his temple. As she'd done, he thought, to hundreds of other patients. His love for Rin seemed suddenly like a fairy story. A kindly lie you'd spin to a child.

"I'm applying an anesthetic to your scalp," she said.

They were fooling each other, he thought. Tongue had the power. Nothing made of flesh and blood could vie with her.

Rin peered into his eyes. *Ready?*

Somewhere above them, a meteor exploded. The operating table shook.

Are you sure you can do this? he said.

Is it surgery that frightens you?

Dorner regarded her.

Or the thought of losing her. Rin set the anesthetic swab aside.

She's been with me since I was a child, he said.

"After everything that's happened—" Rin sighed.

I don't know what life would be like without her, he said.

Rin placed her palms together beneath her chin and bent, as if she was praying for them both. *You'll be my fire, and I'll be yours.*

Rin had given up everything, Dorner knew. He had to leave Tongue behind.

A comet landed close by. The equipment rattled and the table shook.

Dorner barely noticed. He was held by the daring he saw in Rin's eyes.

Take her out, he said.

Rin straightened herself, tightening the straps around his torso. She switched on the spotlights, and within moments, the heat from the large silver bowls drew sweat from his face. She had her back to him now. An astringent odor filled the air. He heard the *clink* of instruments, the *blip* of a monitor. When she turned back, there was a headlamp on her brow. She stooped over him.

I'll remove a piece of your scalp, she said. *Then you'll hear the saw.* Rin shifted some hoses and drew her hand into the circle of light. It held a scalpel. *Once I'm inside, I'll be asking you questions. Your answers will direct what I do. You need to speak clearly.*

She clicked on her headlamp. The beam shifted this way and that. A lock of black hair swung beneath her cap. Then the beam froze.

I'm starting, she said.

Rin raised the scalpel, lined its blade with her target and lowered it.

Dorner took a breath. The tinkle of the bell on her wrist sounded by his ear. He felt a stinging, as if someone with a sharp pen was drawing on his head. *Clink.* Rin set down the scalpel. She was lifting a small rotary saw. The sound of it whirring to life startled him. Without warning, a grinding roar mounted in his brain. He felt thrust. *Like a rocket,* he thought, *blasting off. Headed into space.*

He was bound, strapped to the table. And then, all at once, his bonds were removed.

Dorner was naked, floating in a frameless night. Alert but drifting, far from the earth. He rolled and turned, peering into the depths of space. In every quarter there were stars behind stars, as far as the cosmos would admit his vision.

"Dorner."

A voice reached him.

Beyond his right knee, a green flash pierced the darkness. As he watched, it grew larger. *A signal, a beacon,* he thought. And then he could see it clearly— The nose light of a starship. Headed toward him.

He rocked himself forward, legs down, front facing. The craft was long and thin, silver from stem to stern. Its nose light winked like the point of a blade. The ship wasn't soundless, but its thrusters were soothing—an unbroken murmur, like water from a tap.

As the ship slid beside him, a hopper unfolded from its flank. A telescoping arm pushed the hopper toward him, then its metal mouth opened, scooped him from the sky and rolled him inside. "Dorner. Can you hear me?"

The arm retracted, and the ship swallowed him whole.

Bright lights and the hum of the thrusters. He was in a transit chamber, floating inside the craft. An airlock door opened, and Rin stood before him. She was naked, except for her hands which were covered with skintight gloves. She took hold of him, steadied him so he could plant his feet. Her lips were straight, her face expressionless. He had never seen such intensity in her eyes.

I need your help, Rin said.

She led him into the cockpit. There was barely room to stand. Rin gestured at a wraparound array of windows and portholes patterned with night and stars. Below the panes, a large console was crowded with video screens, some with moving images, some with graphs or lines scrolling across them. Rin's words came more quickly. Dorner stood beside her, trying to understand. A small ship thrusting through space, a silver ship with intricate controls.

She backed him against one of the cabin struts. *For your safety*, she said.

Thick straps hung from the strut. She drew them around him, securing the latches and tightening the straps. *You're alright?*

I'm alright, he answered.

She turned and lowered herself into the pilot's seat.

He was behind her, secured, watching her tinker with switches and dials.

Name a day of the week, Rin said.

Wednesday, he thought.

What color is my hair?

Black, he answered.

Do you love me?

With every ounce of my being.

Can you feel this? Rin asked.

A cold sensation mounted beneath his left ear. Then it descended, like a steel rod passing through his neck. *Yes,* he thought.

Rin spoke again, but she wasn't speaking to him. She was giving voice commands to the console, and the ship was obeying, adjusting its thrusters, steadying its course. The cabin felt warm, but he was shivering.

We're approaching Vapos, Rin told him.

Are you sure?

There was not a sound from Tongue or her choir. Did she know where they were and what they were doing? The question filled him with dread.

Keep your eye on this window. Rin pointed. *And this one here.* Her finger shifted and the bell on her wristband tinkled. *What do you see?*

Sky, he answered, *and a lot of stars.*

We're headed straight for her. Rin turned and nodded, her

gloved hands on the controls. *Watch for the signs. You should see them soon.*

Signs— He fixed his attention on the way ahead. Was Tongue listening? Watching?

"There," Dorner said, motioning at a pane on his right. The rainbow orb grew as he watched. From inside the ship, the Soap Bubble seemed larger than ever. "Keep your distance. The winds can be fierce."

As if to confirm his words, the ship was jolted. A blast pummeled their front and chucked their tail. "Manual," Rin ordered the console, grabbing a T-shaped fader on her right and easing it forward. The thrusters struggled for traction while Rin jockeyed the nose. A carpet of cometoids skimmed beneath them. The ship pitched and steadied.

Dorner stared at her hand. Her grip on the fader was firm, her movements smooth and precise. Her delicacy, her command of the ship— He had never seen her like this.

To port, the Mermaid's Wake appeared.

We're nearing the Wormhole, Dorner said.

He felt a new confidence.

Once we've passed that cluster of stars, he said.

Where is she? he wondered. Still no sound but the thrusters.

"There." He pointed at the object dead ahead. The Golden Cabbage glittered as they approached, wrinkling and rolling around its natal sun. Beyond it, the entrance to the Wormhole gaped. Its lips were throbbing.

This we do slowly, Rin said, keying in new settings with her

317

left hand while she rode the T-fader down with her right. The thrusters' hum deepened. Their advance toward the Cabbage in the center window slackened to a crawl.

Beneath her mask, Rin's jaw shifted as she studied her work. The operating room echoed with *blips* and sucking sounds. She exhaled and straightened. Dorner heard the *clink* of the scalpel as she set it down. Her wrists were covered with blood.

"The auto-drainers are clearing the incision," she said, turning to the panels, reading bar graphs and blue serrations.

"You'll see her," he said, "at the end of the Wormhole."

"One thing at a time."

The operating room shook. A *boom-boom* of buildings falling close by, and the shaking mounted.

"She knows what we're doing," he said.

Rin turned back to him, head cocked. "I've got some surprises for her. Now—" She raised a gloved hand and inserted her finger into the opening in his head. "We're going to get through this passage." She raised her other hand and brought the scalpel forward, approaching the tissues with reverence, like a lapidist about to cut a rare gem.

Dorner closed his eyes. He was like a passenger standing on the platform, and Rin's arm was a tube train approaching from behind. It slid into the station and stopped.

The Wormhole walls were pillowed and veined with gassy filaments. The craft took the bends cautiously, backing and thrusting every few moments. Except for the engine noises, the cockpit was silent. Rin piloted with a concentration that seemed unbreachable. But Dorner kept his mind quiet, fearful about what it might mean to distract her.

At its end, the Wormhole kinked. When the ship made the last turn and the way forward was clear, he reached out his hand and touched Rin's shoulder.

The moons slid into view, blurred, watching behind a veil of mist. Tongue seemed alone with her thoughts. The Ovum was quiet, as were the three trunks. The surface of Vapos was dark and unlit.

"Has she done this before?" Rin asked.

Dorner peered through the starship's glass, listening. The voices that always swelled at his arrival, dulcet with longing and feverish desire, were mute.

"Never," he said.

Had she spent all her power bombarding the dome? Knowing he belonged to Rin, had she quenched the flames here for good? Tongue's eyes followed the ship. They were small, winched down and dotted with clouds, like bird-pecked fruit.

Rin hunched over the console. "Hang on." She moved the T-fader forward, dropping the ship's nose. "Here we go," she said, spiking the thrusters.

The acceleration threw Dorner back. They shot from the bell of the Wormhole and plunged through the sky. The ship was aimed at the asteroid's surface, and with the thrusters near max, they were approaching fast. Dorner hugged the strut. Rin's fist turned white on the fader. The ship pierced a drifting stratus and the windows fogged. Still, the only sound was the hum of the thrusters.

Then all at once, Dorner felt Tongue wake.

She's with us, he said.

The ship burst through the stratus, and the windows cleared. The moons reappeared in the panes on the right. The twin moons were growing and their edges were sharper.

Her trunks, Rin said.

He gazed into Tongue's luminous eyes, seeing a mottled guile in their depths.

Dorner, Rin said.

He swallowed. Tongue had some cruel design. But what it was—

Which is closest? Rin insisted.

He scanned the forward windows. *The Sealacium Trunk.* He pointed at a plain of hillocks crossed by a river. *Follow the river. It flows into the gorge.*

Can you see the trunk? Rin asked.

Not yet.

The ship was still diving. The asteroid's surface rose to meet it.

Don't get too low, Dorner said.

They were over the river now, diving, still diving—

320

The sky brightened. The Ovum flashed.

What are you doing?

Cut her away, Rin growled. *Every bit of her.*

Two hundred feet from the ground, one hundred— The Ovum rumbled.

We're too close, he cried.

Rin drew the T-fader back. The ship leveled as the Ovum fired.

A horrendous ripping— The windows turned white. The air erupted, the ship battered and hurled— Dorner clung to the strut. Through the center pane, glowing swords plunged into the river. Along its course, a wall of fire was rising. Rin was thrown back against her seat, fader arm shaking.

Where's the trunk? she asked.

A shrill chorus filled his ears.

There, he pointed. *Past those spurs.*

She jerked the fader. They veered from the river as fresh bolts struck. Great amber flames rose around them, hissing and lashing, beating the hull like dinosaur tails.

The ship careened through the lunging tapers and drapes of ash. Jolts. More jolts— Flashing windows and showers of sparks. Blowups, orange and vermilion; gasps of ignition and roiling smoke. Turps of fuel, oily and heady—the resinous odor invaded the cabin. The fuselage creaked. He felt heat in the soles of his feet.

"You're under her spell," Tongue lamented.

She's going to save me.

"She doesn't give a damn about you," Tongue replied.

He glanced at Rin. She was intent on the course, but she'd heard every word.

"She wants power," Tongue said. "My power."

Another jolt— Lightning forked on either side of the nose. Explosions below, flares towering on either side, and as the starship passed through, the two flares united. The ship rattled and chugged, drowning in fire.

"Death, little miss," Tongue hissed at Rin, and the choir joined in.

The ship was sinking, plunging into the blaze. It rolled full over. Then the alizarin shredded and the thrusters dug in. Through the windows, Dorner could see the flames spreading. Orange spouts, crimson towers, copper cascades—

A little farther, he said.

Below, fire rippled like watered silk. Through the starboard windows, the river was burning. Ahead, the gorge of Sealacium appeared, its rim clenching and loosening, a great pall of smoke drifting aside.

There—

The opaline mass of the Sealacium Trunk towered into the sky. Its roots were deep in the gorge, sucking and pulsing, while worms of fire wriggled around them. Flames rushed into the trunk, rising inside the glassy arteries, bound for the Ovum.

"Our sacred bond," Tongue said to Dorner.

Kiss it goodbye, Rin told her.

She depressed a rocker switch with her left hand and

wrapped it around a pistol grip on the console. Through the center window, Dorner saw a hatch in the nose open. A black nozzle emerged. Its bulbed tip had a sapphire gleam.

"Resection pending," Rin said to the guidance system. "This will hurt."

"Stop her," Tongue hissed.

She's my future, Dorner said. He put his hand on Rin's shoulder.

A lightning bolt struck the gorge of Sealacium. Through the ship's windows, Dorner saw a giant blue wave rise up, a great gusher of fuel, crested with flame. All at once it ignited. The ship's walls gonged and shook. The air in the cabin was searing. Through the portholes, hordes of flames kinked and twisted, striking the ship like lunging snakes. Rin bellowed at the console and wrenched the fader, and the ship swung aside.

In the operating room, Dorner bucked on the table. The hospital was shaking and the spotlights flickered. Rin stood frozen, dread in her eyes. Her mask had fallen around her neck. Hair dangled beneath her cap. She was pouring sweat, head cocked, as if she was listening to Sealacium roar.

Then the overhead lights blinked out. The silver bowls went black. There was only the blue-green glow of the monitors, and the *blips* and sucking sounds.

Don't panic, he thought.

Rin was silent.

The juice will come back. Dorner took a deep breath. His heart was racing and his brow ached. His left cheek tingled, his left ear was numb. What was Tongue thinking? What was she doing—

Rin wheeled the monitors closer, crowding them around him. In the eerie glow, she scanned the readout panels. Then she faced him. Her lips were trembling and so was her hand. It held a device with a pistol grip and a black nozzle. The bulbed tip was sapphire and streaked with blood.

"You can do it," he said.

She raised the device and nodded. Then she reinserted it into the opening in his head.

"No tributes." Tongue's voice rose with a chorus of flames. "No mourning."

The starship had turned and was pointed back down. The Sealacium eruption had settled. A few fires still wandered the rim, but the fuel in the gorge was exhausted.

"When I die," Tongue told him, "you'll be quiet as a corpse."

The Sealacium Trunk was swollen with flames, its translucent arteries quivering and red. The starship was headed straight for it. Rin gunned the thrusters, her hand clasping the pistol grip. Dorner clung to the strut.

Ready, she muttered.

Cut her away, he said.

Rin squeezed the trigger.

Bursts of light shot from the black nozzle's tip. Through the windows, they beaded through space like a string of pearls. As the nozzle continued to fire, the beads connected, striping the night. Closer, closer—

An alarm buzzer sounded. The beam turned white hot and met Tongue's trunk. The flames screamed, the sky shook, and the white stripe passed through.

The corded base of the Sealacium Trunk was lurching, the cut spewing bright fluid. The hanging crown was doing the same. All the flames of Vapos were moaning, and as Dorner watched, the Ovum dimmed. Tongue's eyes turned red, veiled by a wave of expelled effluvia.

Rin stepped back from the operating table, smiling, relieved. She held the black nozzled cutter point-up and twitched it toward herself, as if inviting a response. Dorner saw steam swirling by the side of his head. Was it wishful thinking, or had Tongue's hold on him dwindled? An onus was lifted, a crushing imperative—

It was as if all the floors of the hospital above him had dissolved. The unbroken glass of the dome was like the lens of a giant eye. Day was dawning—a new day with a bright sun and blue sky, and a myriad Tads, acrobatic with joy, swinging across it.

The hospital shook, the monitors flickered and his illusion faded. Tongue was still raining hell on Clemency, bent on removing him from the family of man.

The Sealacium Trunk's severed crown hung limp from the Ovum's underside. Clouds of scarlet effluvia filled the sky.

"That's your blood," Tongue whispered. "Your life."

"Am I alright?" Dorner looked at Rin.

"The Delta Trunk," she said.

"Strangle her," Tongue ordered. "Take the controls."

You're finished, Rin said to Tongue. She turned to Dorner.

"You're in danger," Tongue warned him. "Grave danger."

Dorner met Rin's stare. "Tail to the moons," he said. "The trunk's at the mouth of the interlocked rivers."

Rin commanded the guidance system, eased back the T-fader and turned the ship on its heel.

"You fool," Tongue said.

"Past the canyon," Dorner pointed. "Beyond that ridge—"

"You pitiful fool."

The Ovum was rumbling, brewing a charge.

"Here it comes," Rin warned.

A blinding flash, a deafening crash— A cavernous stutter rocked the ship, and a lake exploded beneath them. Rin struggled with the controls. Through the windows, the sky was a tempest of embers. Below, the upended lake boiled with flames.

"Land your contraption," Tongue ordered Rin, "and give him up."

Rin didn't reply.

"Dorner and I can't be divided," Tongue declared.

"Sheer ten west," Rin directed the ship.

"His fate was mine," Tongue said, "before the earth froze."

They were over a canyon now, low, slowing— Flames snaked from within, heads swollen like cobras. They flew at the ship, fangs flashing.

"Take the controls," Tongue raved at Dorner. "Take the controls—"

"There it is," he said.

The Delta Trunk rose from a broad valley, where descending rivers came together. Lines of fire burned on the valley's slopes, one behind the other. Beneath the ship, banks and bars slid by, the giant roots planted among them.

The trunk hove before them, translucent and corded, the scarlet essence chugging within.

"Resection pending." Rin said, clasping the grip.

"Don't let her," Tongue shrieked.

The Ovum rumbled, and a bolt of lightning reached out, rocking the ship. Missing it.

"You won't—" Tongue's voice crackled with anguish.

"I will." Rin triggered the grip, and beads shot from the nozzle.

Dorner saw the gaps close, beads connecting. The alarm buzzer sounded, and the stripe glowed white, slashing through the bundled arteries.

Tonguc's scream was joined by a myriad flames.

"No, Dorner. Don't—"

Every blaze on Vapos was singing her pain.

"Don't let Rin destroy her," the choir sang.

His source, his rapture— Mother of all the strange things he had felt so deeply—

Above, the Ovum convulsed. From the trunk's severed vessels, effluvia gushed, filling the air between the thrashing stump and the detached crown.

The choir choked, a swamp of warbles and mumbling, shocked and distraught.

"He betrayed me," Tongue groaned to the heavens. "Whatever I said went straight into her ear."

Through the forward windows, the gushing effluvia twisted and whorled.

What's happening? Rin said.

Dorner shook his head. The flood seemed endless. The loose flames were binding and turning, combining in a way he'd never seen. From the rotating mass came a woeful moan, a dirge of loss, and the ship was in the middle of it. Churning, churning, a great vortex of bitterness, foaming around them—

Dorner saw Rin's face reflected in the forward window.

Her eyes were wide.

The moan was deafening. In all the ship's portholes, the gyres of the whirling flood rose—a cyclone of fire, a blazing barrel, its flames bound together like twisting staves. The bloody edge curled and mouthed the ship. And then the cyclone engulfed it, spinning it, shaking it, warping the hull, melting the nozzle that jutted from its nose.

Rin was thrown forward, arms splayed across the lit panels.

Dorner watched Rin, holding his breath. She was motionless, arms spread, hanging over the glowing screens. The dim room quaked. Instruments *clinked* in the metal trays and the cables sparked. Slowly Rin raised herself.

Dorner exhaled.

Her gloved hand clutched the smoking cutter. Its black nozzle sputtered. He noticed the gash in her hip. Her tunic was torn, and blood covered her thigh.

Rin stared at the cutter, pressing its trigger, trying to arm it. Then she glanced at the equipment. It was ribboned with smoke. She swore, dropped the cutter and turned to the trays.

"See how you like this," she said, raising a scalpel with a long blade.

An unearthly roar filled Dorner's ears. The room seemed to explode—the table bucked wildly beneath him. He felt a blast of heat, then freezing cold.

A comet had taken away the room's walls and the building above him. From where he lay, Dorner could see what remained of Clemency. The dome's glass was nothing but a shattered skirt, and the raft was listing badly. Where fires weren't raging, the flames had burned low and the ground was black. Those who'd survived the blasts were out of sight, huddled and freezing no doubt, dreaming of help that would never arrive. And the comets continued to fall.

As he watched, one struck the methane fuel bunkers.

That's it, he thought.

A flare blossomed, crimson and gold. The explosion that followed shook the hospital to its roots. The *boom* deafened him, and a storm of ash hid the view.

Then the din faded and the arctic wind swept the ash away.

Down a thruway that led to the Hub, a canyon opened. The Clemency raft was cracking—

Before him, half of the colony rose like a bristling wall. People appeared, hanging from the giant polycrete spikes, swinging and falling. As the section shifted, its edge appeared, along with the sublevels. He could see the igniters flashing and hear the ducts shrieking as they tore loose. The pipes roared and belched smoke as the section of raft slid into the sea.

The operating room was intact. Rin was picking herself off the floor.

She stepped beside him, shivering, scalpel in hand, her breath fogging the air.

We're out of time, Rin said.

/𝒏

"The Temple Trunk—" Rin shook her head.

She stood by the pilot's console with the windows behind

her. Half the readout panels were dark. The banks around the pistol grip were smoking.

"Our guidance is dead," she said, "and the cutter is useless. We have only the ship. Our exhaust could do damage—our thrusters, our burn tail. We'll have to get very close."

"Two of her moorings are cut," Dorner said. "She's weak."

Rin touched his chin. *I've hurt her.*

Dorner raised his hand. *Listen.*

"Heartsick," Tongue whimpered. "Wounded, bleeding—"

"She's still attached," Rin said, "still drawing strength from you."

A light was flickering inside the Ovum, but the charges were no longer crackling or firing.

"What have you done?" Tongue grieved.

Was she lost in self-pity, in terrible pain? Or was Tongue acting?

All at once, every light on the pilot's console went dark, and the ship keeled onto its side. Unearthly silence. The air of the cabin turned blue-green.

Rin? Dorner thought.

She didn't respond. Her body leaned, her arms floated over her head. A string of bubbles rose from her lips. Then a string was rising from his.

The lights flared back. The console was lit. Slowly the ship righted.

Dorner gazed at Rin. He opened his arms and looked at himself.

"A wretched end," Tongue whispered. "They all went down."

Was Clemency gone?

"Peace," Tongue sighed. "Peace, Dorner. Peace."

At that, all the voices of Vapos rose as one. "Peace. And mercy. Not to the death," the choir sang. "The one who nurses us— Spare her, Dorner."

"She's surrendering," Rin said.

Dorner stared at her. "Take the ship north."

Rin stared back.

He turned her and sat her in the pilot's seat. "To the Temple Trunk."

"No," the choir swelled, "no, no—"

Rin grasped the T-fader and primed the thrusters.

"Heartless, unfeeling," the flames arraigned him. "Cold-blooded and cruel—"

The starship raced above the asteroid's surface. Rin steered, taking Dorner's directions. He watched through the windows, spotting landmarks and adjusting the course. Tongue sank into the silence, and the choir joined her. The moons shrank, the Ovum was barely lit.

In the center window, the rugged profile of the mountain appeared. The Temple Trunk was obscured by smoke. There was the Charnel Valley, the Altar and the giant steps. On the mountain's heights, the monuments stood.

The starship wheeled over the peak. Through the billows, flames swarmed on the mountain's backside, fattening on the fuel streaming down it. Then the billows parted and the great trunk appeared, its clawed foot grappling the cliff, roots sucking up fire. Tongue was still feeding, he thought. Was her weakness real?

"I'll have to dive right at it," Rin said, "and pivot as we pass. I'll jet as much exhaust as I can. We'll be exposed," she said. "Close to the ground."

"You can do it."

"No she can't," Tongue murmured.

He put his hands on Rin's shoulders. "I'm right here."

"And I'm right here," Tongue reminded him.

Dorner felt a pain, like a nail driving into the side of his head.

Rin aimed the nose down. He checked his straps and hugged the strut. Then they were in a steep dive, thrusters roaring. The trunk's flames roared back. The cliff was all fire, a bedlam of wailing and shrieking. Scarlet fountains crowned and crashed. Rin took the ship tacking between them.

Flawless, he thought.

The blazes were thrashed by their passing like weeds in a current. The trunk's girth appeared in the forward window, and Rin straightened the course. Her purpose was fixed, her line unerring. The Ovum rumbled. In the starboard windows, Tongue's eyes funneled with murderous intent.

A blinding flash—lightning struck the cliff, raising clouds of pulverized rubies. Another bolt, and a third, whiting the windows and tossing the ship. Rin hunched over the console, staring at the trunk. It loomed giantly now, arteries throbbing.

She's yours, Dorner said.

At the last moment, Rin jerked the craft onto its side, and as they shot past, she wrenched the fader, pivoting their tail. The ship swept around, bellowing as the thrusters cleared. Dorner pitched and clung.

The windows and portholes were suddenly red. Gouts of fiery blood billowed around them.

You've done it, he thought.

Rin fought the fader, choking the thrusters and banking around. The ship burst out of the discharge. Rin looked back.

We clipped her bark, she sighed. *That's all.*

Through the portholes, Dorner saw: the Temple Trunk was still intact.

Rin met his gaze, then she stiffened. Her lips flattened, and she opened the thrusters, wheeling the ship to return to the attack.

A fierce clout shook the sky. A jagged crack divided the Ovum's belly, and a rending filled Dorner's ears. Tongue was shrieking, her eyes enormous. The Ovum halves split, and a torrent poured through the gap, white and electric.

The cabin jumped, flooded with light.

The pilot's seat burst, and Rin flew from it.

A hole gaped in the cockpit wall, and the night winds were sucking, pulling Rin toward it.

Her arm shot out, circling an overhead duct. Dorner lunged, grabbing the other.

The thrusters died, and the voices mounted. "Dorner, Dorner— Look what you've done."

Both of Rin's legs were through the hole, and her calves were banging against the ragged metal.

I've got you, he said, both hands on her wrist.

But the winds were fierce, pulling, pulling—

Rin whimpered. Her arm was slipping from around the duct. It came loose and her only mooring was him.

His straps held him. *You've saved me*, he said.

His eyes found hers. They were gleaming black shells—he could feel her terror. Then the shells dissolved and he could see into them.

I tried, Rin said.

Dorner's arms shook.

Her face creased with age. Her arms beaded, her neck creped—

Rin, Dorner sobbed. The howling winds rose and tore her from him, pulling her through the ragged hole.

Through the port windows, he saw her float away from the ship. The effluvia loosed by the trunks' severed arteries covered her quickly, congealing around her. In moments, the scarlet flux he and Tongue had shared—that fiery essence—obscured Rin completely. The woman he loved and had entrusted his life to—

All that remained was a rotating glow, a crimson eddy that rose through the darkness and passed out of view.

The ship was idling, drifting on the dying wind.

"Dorner—" The choir reached him.

The voices swelled in his ear.

"Try," they pleaded. "Try to forgive."

He loosened the straps, eyeing Tongue's moons through the spattered windows. Their centers sunk and screwed like titanic siphons. *Never*, he thought.

"If it's time for Tongue," she said, "it's time for you."

He clambered into the pilot's seat and grabbed the controls.

From one end of Vapos to the other, a great lamentation rose. "Too late," the flames sang, and they weren't mourning Rin.

Over the throng, Tongue's *sotto voce* soared. "He's gone," she said.

"Too late for Tongue," the flames chanted. "Too late for you."

Dorner grabbed the T-fader. The console was blinking and sparking.

"What can a man feel?" Tongue said.

"His mind so weak," the voices returned. "His frame so small."

"Life without us," Tongue led the chorus, "is no life at all."

Eyes damp, throat choked, Dorner revved the thrusters and turned the craft, circling toward the mountain and the Temple Trunk.

Tongue sighed, "We belonged to each other."

He wasn't listening. With tears marbling his sight, he peered through the center window, aimed the starship, rode the T-fader all the way forward and opened the throttle. The thrusters roared, and the silver nose plunged.

Before him, the great trunk rose with its pumping arteries and pulsing roots. All the voices on Vapos were grieving as one.

It's over, he said, shutting them out.

Crosswinds batted and swooped. The light from the moons dimmed, but his target was clear, and the ship kept its course. The Temple Trunk loomed, larger and larger. Dorner budged the fader, picking a spot. The furrowed bark shone. The enflamed blood was chugging. He could feel its throb through the cabin floor—in his feet, up his legs, in his chest and head. *Rin*, his heart cried. The windows blazed red—

Then everything merged: the cry, the blood, an anguished Tongue's sob, and the crash of the ship as it met its target.

11

SILENCE

Dorner returned to consciousness slowly. He was on his hip on a hard surface, and he was shivering. He felt his chest, his thigh. He was naked. The left side of his head was throbbing. He tried to raise himself, but his shoulder bumped against something. He remembered Clemency. The comets. Racing to the hospital. Being strapped to the operating table.

Colored lights flickered in the darkness. He narrowed his gaze. Slowly the image resolved. It wasn't the operating room he saw. He was looking at the buckled panels of the starship's console.

Rin, he thought. He swallowed, nauseous. He had watched her burning in a blood-soaked sky.

Through the dimness, he could see the crumpled floor of the cockpit. He tried to rise. Again, his shoulder met an obstruction.

339

Dorner felt with his hand. A metal girder. It had nearly crushed him. He crawled from beneath it, rising slowly, reaching for the charred back of the pilot's seat. He drew a breath and the surroundings grew sharper, along with his memory of the moments preceding the crash.

The cabin was mangled. And there was the hole that Rin had passed through.

Dorner tested his legs and groped his way toward it.

Beyond the hole, the night was scarlet. He felt with his hands, then he boosted himself, pushing his head through the ragged aperture. He squirmed, angling his chest, forcing his hips. Then his legs passed through, and he fell to the ground.

Dorner stood and raised his head.

The twin moons had vanished. The sky was swarming with bright effluvia, crimson and bronze, whorled like iron filings in a magnetic field. The Ovum was gone. All that remained were pale curls, like fragments of shell, in the empty space where Tongue's power had brewed. And the Temple Trunk— There was no sign of its crown or its giant column. He could see the ship's damage, but what the crash had done to the last of Tongue's moorings was hard to tell.

He turned full around. The mountain's backside hemmed his view. The eastern ridges and valleys were hidden, and so were the rivers and lakes to the south. To the north, nothing blocked the view, but there was only darkness. The asteroid was quiet. Not a flame in sight.

Vapos. Island in the night. Somehow he'd survived.

And Tongue—

Had the crash uprooted her? Had she floated away? She was nothing but spirit now. Feelings without a voice. Homeless, disembodied. Or— Less than that.

Maybe Tongue no longer existed. If that was true— He was alone here. Naked as Adam.

The terrible tension he'd felt on earth— It seemed to have left him. He was calm now. Emptied of need. Quiet in his heart.

Dorner faced the cliffs, gazing toward the mountain's summit. From that height, he could see what had happened to Vapos. He remembered the circle of stones. For Tongue, it had been a sacred place. Maybe he would find something there.

The ground was charred and warm to his feet. As he approached the steeps, he spotted a shadowed ravine. Dorner entered the declivity and started up it, climbing, pausing at intervals to listen. Not a whisper of fire or wind. Nothing but the trickle of fuel. All he could see, on either side, were the dark ravine walls.

For so long, he'd struggled to find a center, indifferent to feeble affection, dreading the fires inside him. There had only been one who understood.

Her energy was still with him, and her honesty. She refused to bow to Tongue. She matched Tongue at every turn. Did the brave woman succumb to despair as she drifted away from the ship, knowing the battle was lost? *Not Rin*, he thought. She was part of the cosmos now, Tongue's equal at last. Floating in a fever dream amid kaleidoscope nebulae and glittering stars.

His view of the sky opened as he ascended. The crimson

effluvia glittered and swirled, lighting seeps in the rock—trickles of fuel that would wind their way down to streams and lakes. Would it all go unused? Was Tongue really gone?

Tongue had brought them grief. And Tongue had brought them together. The hours with Rin blazed in his memory. Hours he would have bartered his life for. As pitiless as Tongue was, as deranged and inhuman— What power in heaven could ever replace her?

The last flickers from the wrecked starship had died. He could see the deflated remains of the Temple Trunk now. The crash had destroyed it. Dorner imagined Tongue's last moment. The fiery blood—the last of it—flooding the sky. The cracked Ovum falling to pieces. The winds orphaned, the voices fade— Tongue's grasp dwindles and her moons blink out.

The ravine walls shrank, the incline leveled off. As Dorner mounted the summit, the circle of stones rose from the broken ground. In the sky to the west, a strange sight appeared.

A scarlet sphere was pulsing and turning. As it turned, it gathered the fiery effluvia from every direction. The bloody rills and tatters stretched and fined, winding like strands around a ball of yarn.

As he watched, the sphere's force field expanded. The captive shreds fused at the turning center, and those loose in the night curled toward it.

A beautiful sight, Dorner thought. A galaxy of fire. And its glowing center had been seeded by Rin.

The galaxy sped up, the windings joining more quickly. It was moving, crossing the heavens, sweeping the fiery essence, however far flung, into its orbit. Larger and larger— All the blood that Tongue's severed trunks had released was collecting around it.

A sign, he thought. Or the blind effusion of an ardor that has lost its object.

Dorner stepped toward the circle of stones. The ground glittered red, reflecting the sky. His skin glowed too. As he passed between two megaliths, the fiery galaxy passed overhead. When he reached the circle's center, the galaxy halted.

The sphere's pulse quickened. As if it knew the magic of the place and sensed his presence. It was growing larger, tensing and expanding, throbbing like a heart too full. What did it mean? Dorner could feel the expansion inside him, as if his own heart was growing, throbbing to free itself from the prison of his chest.

What are you? he said.

The galaxy's heart had reached its limit, and at the sound of his voice, it burst.

The mountain shook, and Dorner was thrown to the ground. From where he lay, he could see distant ridges and valleys quaking. And then, as he watched, the red tint of the land faded, and the asteroid's surface turned pearly. Dorner looked at his hands. The red was gone. They were pearly too, lustrous as the soil beneath them.

He knelt and peered up. A great white egg hovered over

Vapos, and the scarlet galaxy was turning inside it. Through the Ovum's translucent walls, amid the fiery churn, white webs appeared. Rumbles, crackling— The Ovum flashed, brewing charges.

Dorner raised himself, breathless, dizzy with dread.

A bass grating filled the sky, like a throat clearing. Someone half-asleep. Or undead, returning to life—

Dorner, he heard. The sound fooled his ear. It was like a voice, mumbling his name at a distance.

Dorner, again.

Is it you? he thought.

The stutter of thunder, a flicker, a flash— His heart rose in his chest.

A white bolt drove from the Ovum's belly, striking a valley below. A golden explosion with a blue core, then scarlet flames rose, snaking skyward.

Beyond the Ovum, the sky was brighter. The twin moons appeared behind stratums of leaden cloud, like eyes behind sealed lids.

The stratums parted. The eyes grew larger, focusing.

Tongue's eyes— Were they Tongue's?

Dorner watched and listened— The timbre of the flames singing in the valley. The rhythm of her breath. The warmth in her eyes, and her ineffable scent. Rin was with him.

It's you, he thought.

"Dorner," she said.

Joy choked him. He began to sob.

"My only," Rin said.

Her voice—deeper and clearer than it had ever been. And her eyes—more lucid, more open than he'd known them on earth. He could see a starving soul in their depths. And she could see him, without omission or qualm, as Tongue always had.

"She can't harm us now," Rin said.

The sky echoed with rumbling, and the Ovum flashed.

"We're free to burn," Rin whispered.

Dorner reached his hand up, as if he could touch her.

The sky shook, and a lightning bolt fired—a great sword that plunged into a lake on the western horizon. From the lake, a sun rose, a crimson bow shooting arrows of gold. More rumbling, a flash and a stroke, and in an eastern valley, an amber grove grew, crowns flickering like turning crystals.

Dorner wiped his eyes. The Ovum's bloody interior roiled and churned. Flashes, thunder— Lightning and quaking, more and more. Everywhere Rin struck, fires leapt up. From the folded ridges and gleaming spurs, from pools and streams, from sagging buttresses and leaking cliffs—

"You and I," fresh voices sang.

Winds were mounting, whirling around him. Dorner drew a deep breath, filling his chest with heated air.

Flashes and bolts, towering flares, cascades and fountains, orchards and thickets, coral and marigold, ginger and peach, whirling in canyons, racing through valleys, glowing on hillocks and flowing up slopes; snapping flags and snaking

345

banners, hooking, coiling, twisting like rope; drumming, hissing, bulbing and tattering, wriggling and twitching and rolling in smoke.

From the Ovum's underside, a translucent column descended. Dorner watched it swell, lengthening rapidly, empty arteries visible within. The trunk met the rocky cliffs below. In the light of ripening fires, he could see the hull of the starship and the withered roots of Tongue's holdfast. Below that, the new trunk was planting. When he looked up, he saw two more descending, seeking moorage in distant quarters.

I'm not—

"No," Rin said. "You're not dreaming. This is real."

A bolt struck the mountain's backside. As the dazzle cleared, Dorner saw flames covering the cliffs. The roots of the trunk Rin had planted were reaching to suck them up. The moons swelled, the Ovum churned, and the ignited flames flowed up the arteries to meet their new mistress.

Rumble and flash, and the bolts drove down, hordes of them jagging and brooming, touching off fuel in every direction. A hundred lakes, a thousand blue streams, untold sumps and wallows and bloated slopes. Flames, flames wherever he looked.

The second trunk touched down leagues away. Dorner could see its roots planting. The trunk swelled as the flames rose inside it. In the east, the third trunk did the same. The winds were rising, and with them her voices—frenzied, urgent, demanding.

"You'll be faithful," Rin said. "Constant."

Dorner looked in her eyes. *You know all my secrets.*

"This blazing," the moons swelled giantly, "is for no one but me."

The Ovum flashed. The sky turned white. Rin's rebuke tore through the air, a blinding bolt, storming his ears, shaking his frame, striking the mountain behind him. The wrath that had choked her was finally free.

No one but you, he agreed.

At his rear, thumps sounded. Dorner turned.

The lightning stroke had blasted the Temple. Embers were flying like spindrift in a squall, while a host of flames—scarlet serpents—swarmed the plowed slopes and the broken statues. As he watched, the last of them toppled. Not a one stood.

"No one, no one—" The fires chanted, damning the icons destroyed by Rin's stroke. "No one but you."

Embers were settling around the circle of stones. Where they landed, flares shot up. Above, the Ovum stuttered and flashed without a pause. The sky was livid now, broomed and skeined and wired with bolts. Fire fountained and torched, fire beaded and heaved, fire gushed and fanned and cascaded. On every side, Vapos was a sea of flame.

You're lighting everything.

"Everything," Rin said.

The blazes were balling and joining, hotter and hotter. The reds turned gold, and the golds turned white. Flames mounted each other, reaching into the sky, vaulting and arcing like coronal ejections.

"Burn," the choir chanted. "Burn, burn—"

How long, Dorner thought. *How long will we burn?*

"Till every drop's gone," Rin said. "Till there's no fuel left."

The supernal finish. The end Tongue had foretold. He imagined Vapos ravaged, reservoirs empty, flames burning low. And in the circle of stones: a statue, half man, half snake, facing the darkness.

They were raging now— Every lake and stream, every sink and valley, every ridge and peak and every plain between. The three trunks glowed white, and the Ovum's furnace was glowing as well. The fires weren't charring Vapos. They were melting it. Cliffs slid, hills flattened, valleys bubbled and closed— Peaks and bottoms flowed into each other. The flames were senseless and white as ghosts. The sound of their raving filled Dorner's heart. The crack of her bolts, the demon jolts, the infernal flowing— It was time to let go.

"I don't care," Rin shrieked.

This is love, he gasped, the climax impending.

The heat crowned. Rin began to scream.

Dorner raised his arms and opened his nerves.

Rich Shapero's stories blaze paths into unseen worlds. His previous titles, *Arms from the Sea, The Hope We Seek, Too Far* and *Wild Animus*, combine book, music and visual art and are also available as multimedia tablet apps and ebooks. *The Village Voice* hailed his story experiences as "A delirious fusion of fiction, music and art," and Howard Frank Mosher called him a "spellbinding storyteller." He is the winner of a Digital Book World award for best adult fiction app. He lives with his wife and daughters in the Santa Cruz Mountains.